———————————— ★ ————————————

I leaned forward and got a good look at the man who now lay spread eagle on his back, his rigid grayish-blue eyes regarding the ceiling through a veil that would never be lifted. Above the nicely pressed chinos he wore a short-sleeved, striped shirt that had probably also been neat appearing before something black had stained the entire front of it—blood, I realized. Where had it all come from? A dark crusted trail, like a cooled lava flow, led from his chest around his neck toward the back of his head. Did it originate from his chest or the back of his head or both, I wondered, feeling oddly removed from the situation. From the back of his head, I decided, noting the pool on the floor that fanned out around his head like a black halo.

———————————— ★ ————————————

"Tempa Pagel serves up a clever, twisty story that brings a 200-year-old mystery careening into the present time in an authentic old New England seaport town. It's all pitch-perfect—the town's culture, the characters' voices, the heroine's reluctant courage, the historical details...a terrific novel."

—William G. Tapply, author of
Nervous Water: A Brady Coyne Mystery

Here's the Church, Here's the Steeple

Tempa Pagel

WORLDWIDE.

TORONTO • NEW YORK • LONDON
AMSTERDAM • PARIS • SYDNEY • HAMBURG
STOCKHOLM • ATHENS • TOKYO • MILAN
MADRID • WARSAW • BUDAPEST • AUCKLAND

In memory of
Anne Bresnahan,
And of her mother, Bunny.
Their love of Newburyport
and its rich history planted the seed.

HERE'S THE CHURCH, HERE'S THE STEEPLE

A Worldwide Mystery/April 2007

First published by Five Star.

ISBN-13: 978-0-373-26598-5
ISBN-10:   0-373-26598-0

Printed in U.S.A.

Acknowledgments

Thank you to the Wednesday night group in its various incarnations for support throughout the past eighteen years, especially to Jan Soupcoff and Mary McDonald, who were there at the beginning, to Margaret Ouzts, and to Susan Oleksiw, my longtime teacher and mentor.

Here's the church, and here's the steeple,
Open the door and see all the people.
Here's the parson going upstairs,
And here he is saying his prayers.

—*Children's Nursery Rhyme*
and Finger Play

PROLOGUE

Newburyport, Massachusetts
May 31, 1811
9:10 p.m.

HE LAY AS IF LIFELESS. Numbed to the hard rough floor beneath and the hay that covered him and poked at his bare legs and arms. Numbed to the chaff that stuck in the sweat on his upper lip and closed eyelids. Numbed to everything but one thought: this time the fire would take.

It would take and the colonel would be pleased and would reward him with enough money to get far away from Newburyport and old Stockwell. He allowed that thought to spark inside him and race down his arms and legs like flame along a rope. He allowed, also, a trace of a smile to pluck at the corners of his mouth before stilling it. It was almost time, but he must be patient.

"Pe-tah! Pe-tah! Where are you, Pe-tah?"

The whiny, singsong call skittered off the wood buildings and the cobblestone alley, channeled through the cracks in the walls, and targeted him in his hiding place. But almost as soon as he stiffened, Peter relaxed. It was just Hitty-the-orphan-girl, come to fetch him for the evening baking.

He always thought of her that way, as if "the orphan girl" was part of Hitty's name, for she had no family, no station in life, no future. Unlike himself, son of David Chambers—

however little he respected his father—and a baker's apprentice—however much he detested being one. And soon to be, he reminded himself, his own person, bound to no one, beginning a new life in a new place.

"Pe-tah!"

He guessed from the direction of Hitty's voice that she'd been first to the wharves and Market Square. He held his breath, waiting for her to pass by. Through the thin wallboards of the stable he heard the shhh-shhh of her shoes, big and decrepit so that she had to shuffle to keep them on her feet. Old Stockwell would probably beat her when she returned without him. For an instant he felt sorry for her, but then he chased the feeling away. Just because they were bound to the same family didn't mean he was responsible for her.

The unhurried plodding clop of a horse and rider drowned out the sound of Hitty's shuffling. The rider dismounted and primed the pump just outside. Water splashed into the bushel measure and the horse slurped steady and long. Suddenly impatient, Peter itched to begin. What if he got stuck here past curfew? What if he botched the job for the third time? There would be no money, no getting away. Sweat sprouted anew on his face and palms, and his heart quickened in his chest until it felt like a panicky animal thrashing around in a cage.

He forced the thoughts away, and made himself breathe slower, narrowing his focus until he was back inside himself, centered on the thing that mattered: the fire would take. The clopping had commenced as horse and rider continued on their way. Then the nine o'clock curfew bell began to ring at Mr. Andrews' meeting house, a warning to law-abiding citizens to proceed to the safety of their homes, out of the dangers and temptations of the dark. It was later than he had thought. He checked an impulse to panic; his work would not take long, he reassured himself, and it was probably better this way. There would be fewer people on the streets.

At last all was quiet. Peter waited a few minutes more to ensure that Hitty had gone, that there was no watch outside, that there was nobody next door at the smithy's. Then he jumped up. Spitting dust and straw he scrambled over to the back corner and dropped to his knees. He congratulated himself on his choice this time: a deserted stable, old hay littering its dry wooden floor. Spreading his arms wide he scraped together chaff and hay, which he shoved deep into the corner, and then mounded with more hay. When he determined the pile to be high enough, he flattened the top. He lifted out a small tin box from the barrel behind him, unlatched its lid, and peered in anxiously; coals still glowed in the bottom. Relieved, he upended the box onto the flattened top of the pile, and then flung the box aside.

He rubbed his sticky palms on his pants and began crossing straws of hay above the bed of coals. A tiny flame caught and he fed it more straws. Then a blaze surged up and he jerked back on his heels, surprised but pleased it was taking so quickly. He backed away slowly, judging his handiwork the way old Stockwell had taught him to do with the bake ovens. Was there enough tinder to get it going strong? Dry wood to catch it? Bigger fuel to feed it and keep it burning steadily? When a flame licked hungrily up the splintery wallboards, he knew it had taken.

Quietly rejoicing, Peter closed his eyes and imagined the fire coming into his body, igniting his blood as if it were oil, coursing through his veins. He wanted to savor the exhilaration, to stay until the last safe moment, but he forced himself to turn away. Hand on the door latch, he listened once more before slipping outside. The moon had come up and, while he cursed its brightness on this clear night, the light allowed him to see with a quick glance that the alley was empty. There would be nobody happening by to douse the fire this time.

He ran lightly away from Market Square, keeping to the shadows of buildings. When he reached Mr. Andrews' meeting house, he sidled along beneath the windows towards the front of the building. He paused to check Pleasant Street, then stole around the corner and stopped at the first of the church's three massive wooden doors. The big iron latch made a loud echoing clack inside the meeting house as he swung the door open. He closed it quickly behind him, muffling the latch with his fingers, then groped his way across the dark vestibule to the gallery stairs where he sat down, breathing heavily. He hardly had time to compliment himself on his escape when the door opened again, a shaft of moonlight backlighting a figure.

"Peter—?"

The whine pierced the quiet. The silhouette in the doorway shifted into a familiar form. Hip stuck out on one side, opposite leg bent so that her heel came off the floor, Hitty stood in her annoying lopsided manner. Peter leaped for her, grabbed her skinny arm, and yanked her inside. "You stupid ass!" he hissed, kicking the door closed behind them. "What're you doing here?"

"I was—"

"You'll ruin everything! Damn you!" He flung her arm away from him.

"I was looking for you, Peter," she whimpered, rubbing where his nails had dug into flesh.

"What will I do with you?" His hands flew to his head and he tore at hair which already stood out in thatches on the sides. "Why do you always follow me?"

Hitty sobbed, wiping her nose alternately with the backs of both hands.

"Oh, good gawd, Hitty!" Peter took hold of her arm again and pulled her into the sanctuary where the side windows allowed in light from the moon and the gas street lamps. Halfway up the middle aisle he opened the door to one of the box pews and pushed her inside onto a bench. "Stay there. And stop your bawling!"

While she snuffled and hiccupped, Peter dashed up the aisle and entered another pew. He dropped to his knees, opened the top to the box on the floor, and felt around inside. Nothing. He ran his hand over the rough boards again, but encountered only dried bits of chewed tobacco surrounding the spittoon in the corner. Damnation! Where was his payment? It had never been late before and now, when he needed it the most, it wasn't there. Maybe the colonel was going to pay him in person. If so, that presented another problem: the colonel might find Hitty and, thinking that Peter had told her about the fire, get angry and refuse payment.

Peter went back to the pew and regarded Hitty with contempt. Looking younger than her thirteen years, she slumped on the bench, her narrow shoulders rounded under the old homespun gown she wore year-round, whatever the weather, never outgrowing it. She raised her face, a strip of white between two tangled hanks of hair. "Wipe your face," he commanded.

Obediently, she swiped across it with the sleeve of her dress, her baleful eyes watching him. "I'm sorry, Peter, truly I am," she sniffled. "I was sent to get you and I was scared to go back without you—you know how angry Mr. Stockwell gets—so I sat down at the pump and when I saw you come out of that stable I followed you. I didn't mean any harm, Peter, I didn't."

"I wasn't in a stable. I was running an errand uptown for the colonel—" Peter stopped himself. Damn the girl! She'd gotten him so upset he'd gone and mentioned the colonel. "An errand for somebody you don't know," he amended. "Somebody who doesn't like people knowing his business and might beat you with his cane if he finds you spying on me. So you better get home quick and not tell anybody you saw me, you understand?"

Hitty pulled her mouth to a bunch on one side of her face, and it occurred to Peter that everything about Hitty was lopsided. "You wasn't uptown, Peter," she said, making no movement to leave. "I saw you in that stable."

"You didn't see me in any stable!" Anger congealed in the center of his chest.

"What was you doing there?" she said stubbornly. "It's after curfew."

"Damnation, Hitty!" Peter slammed his fists so hard on the pew rail that he felt vibrations in the floor. Hitty yelped and shrank into the corner of the pew.

He took a shaky breath and tried to order his thoughts. Hitty wasn't smart, but she was stubborn, and if she insisted she'd seen him, he wouldn't be able to change her mind. That meant she knew—or would soon know—he'd set the fire. Peter rubbed the sides of his clenched hands against the rough texture of his pants and looked at her sideways. For all her annoying ways, Hitty had never told on him for leaving the bake ovens unattended, or for stealing a loaf of bread, or for any of the other small infractions he'd committed against Stockwell.

"Peter," Hitty ventured timidly, "what was you doing in that stable?"

"If you stop your sniveling," he said after a moment, "and promise you won't tell, I'll show you. If you ever say anything about it, though, I'll beat you worse than old Stockwell ever did."

She jutted her pointy little chin upward, cocked her head and looked at him over the side of her nose. "I won't never tell," she repeated. "I keep my promises."

Peter turned and strode back down the aisle to the vestibule, with Hitty half-running behind him. He loped up a side staircase to the gallery, where he passed the paneled wall of the organ, and continued down an aisle overlooking the sanctuary. At the back wall he stopped in front of a window. He waited for Hitty to catch up, then held out his arm, palm up, as if the view were his to present. "There!"

At first, Hitty's eyes went to the wharves where ships' masts swayed slightly above Market Square, their bowsprits hovering over wharves cluttered with coiled lines, casks, and carts deserted by their horses. Then a bright flash brought her attention to the forefront where, only a few rods away, a stable was enveloped in flames.

"Oh," Hitty said, forgetting for the moment that this was the stable Peter had just left. "We have to get help, Peter!"

But Peter didn't hear her. He saw that the fire was strong, and that it already threatened the smithy's stable next door. A sudden thrill rushed through him and a thundering began in his ears, accompanied by a high-pitched hum.

Hitty's mouth fell open. "Oh, Peter," she whispered, "what did you do?" She touched his arm but he slapped her hand away.

"I did a job for someone important. That's what I did."

"You started a fire? Why?" Her eyes, big and dark, reminded him of the coals in the tin box.

"You can go on being a slave to the Stockwells, but I'm not putting up with it anymore! I'm leaving as soon as I get my pay." He made his body straight and rigid, his head held high to show that he was proud of what he had done.

Hitty shook her head. The flames outside surged upward, washing her pale face with the orange light. "No, I meant why would anybody want you to do that?"

"He doesn't like the stable owner, I guess." Peter flicked a hand as if shooing a fly. "I don't know." Then, so she would understand that what he had done was all right, he repeated, "I did it for someone important."

"The colonel."

Peter whirled on her. "Don't you ever talk about him. You hear?"

Hitty backed away, flinching. "It's all right, Peter. I don't know who the colonel is and I wouldn't tell, anyway."

"Well, don't talk about him. I don't even know who he is. I just know he's important because of the way he dresses and because his pew is right up front."

"How do you know where his pew is? You don't go to this meeting house."

"That's where he leaves my instructions and my payment," Peter said. "Except tonight he didn't leave my payment so I'm going to have to wait."

Hitty pressed her face close to the window pane. "Peter," she said quietly, "what if—what if the whole town catches fire?"

"Oh pshaw! That can't happen! They're ringing the bells already. Hear 'em?"

They watched without speaking. The warden had arrived at the scene and, using his long pole, was directing a line of volunteers who had come running with their buckets to pass water. A small knot of men began working a hand engine while several others held the long hose.

Then Peter exclaimed, "Look! The next building has caught!" The hum in his ears grew like cicadas in summer and the thrill inside him swelled so that it felt as if his chest itself would burst into flames. For the first time in his life he, Peter Chambers, had caused something significant to happen. It may have been the colonel's orders to set the fire, but it was Peter's skill that had assured its success. The colonel ought to be pleased; in fact, the colonel should reward him with extra money for doing such a fine job. And if he didn't, Peter decided he'd ask for it.

Hitty's renewed sniffling reminded him of her presence. He pinched her elbow and said tersely, "You get home now, and don't tell anyone you saw me, you hear?" Hitty's head jerked up and down, her shoulders shaking. "And don't start crying again! This fire has done you a favor. With all the excitement over it, old Stockwell probably won't give you a beating for being late."

"But what will you do, Peter?"

"I'll wait for a little while—just until I get my money, then I'll be gone from here. Gone far away." He pushed her ahead of him. "Now, get!"

Hitty had barely started down the aisle, floppy shoes slapping the floor, when Peter caught hold of her shoulder and pulled her back. "Shhh!" He clapped a hand over her mouth as the resounding clank of the iron door latch died away into silence below. Shoving her to the floor, he put a finger to his mouth as a warning. "Stay!" he hissed. "Don't make a sound." Then he was gone.

Hitty crouched down between the bench and the low wall that overlooked the sanctuary. She heard a quick murmur of voices downstairs, then it was quiet. She waited for a long time before finally looking over the wall. There was nobody below.

The commotion outside had steadily grown. Hitty picked out the individual sounds: the fire bells, the trumpets, people shouting, water as it splashed onto wood and cobblestones. Then her ears blended it all together and she heard it as a roar. She stood up, took off her shoes, and tiptoed downstairs. In the vestibule, she froze. Straining her eyes in the shadowy darkness she sensed, more than saw or heard, someone on the floor in front of her. She advanced cautiously until a soft moan summoned her to a crumpled form.

"Peter?" Her fingers touched his rough woven jacket and gingerly explored upwards, making contact with something warm and sticky in the spiky tufts of hair on the side of his head. Blood! She recoiled and wiped her hand on her skirt. "Oh, Peter, what happened?" she cried.

"Take me…" he mumbled, struggling to sit up. "Take…"

"I can't see properly," Hitty whimpered. "I'll go open the door so's I can—"

"No!" Peter fell back on his side, and gripped his head with his hands.

"What shall I do? Are you hurt awful bad?"

"Get me…" he whispered as Hitty leaned closer, "away from here." He moaned and drew up his knees.

"Oh!" Hitty wailed, her fingers clutching her skirt. "I better find somebody—"

"No! Just…get me upstairs. He'll come back."

"Who, Peter? Who did this to you?" She fingered the ragged hem of her underskirt. Finding a tear, she ripped off a piece, and touched it gingerly to his head.

Peter struggled to sit up, then fell back, groaning. "Upstairs," he insisted.

"All right." Hitty helped him first to his knees and then to his feet. Once upright, Peter clapped both hands to his head and steadied himself against Hitty's frail body. They staggered to the stairs, rested a moment, then began a slow torturous climb with Peter sagging against Hitty who held him and, leaning against the wall, slid their combined weight upward along it.

At the top of the stairs Peter collapsed on top of her. Hitty pushed him off and half-dragged him into the first pew, where he rolled onto his side and immediately lost consciousness. She found a small cushion and put it under his head, then sat beside him and dabbed lightly at the wound that still bled. Should she go get help? Would anyone come at a time like this? Did the police know Peter set the fire and were they looking for him right now? Still gripping the bloody rag, Hitty put her hands over her face. "Oooh!" she moaned. "What should I do?"

Hitty's father had died at sea before she was born, and her mother had died giving birth to her. Miss Vail and the girls at the orphan home had been her family until two years ago, when she'd been bound out to the bakery. Even though Mr. and Mrs.

Stockwell provided for her now, they had never showed her kindness, and therefore, she had never considered them family. But Peter talked to her and let her stay around, and although he never said so, Hitty knew he was grateful that she often kept him out of trouble with the Stockwells: feeding wood to the bake ovens when he took off; going to find him when the curfew hour was near. Despite his superior ways, Peter needed her as much as she needed him. And he needed her now to care for him.

Hitty raised her face from her hands. Satisfied that Peter was resting peacefully, she crept downstairs and slipped outside where she was brought up quick by the sight that met her. The fire had grown tenfold in the last half hour or so. It now engulfed the whole area where the stables and the pump stood, and was roaring down Mechanics Row to Market Square, where the docked ships moved restlessly in the water like frightened horses pulling on tethers.

Hordes of people ran in all directions, arms laden with belongings or carrying buckets or ladders. Hitty moved unnoticed through the crowds down Pleasant Street to Corn Hill, taking in the awful thing that was happening.

"Here! Go stand in line!" Someone thrust a green leathern bucket with "Daniels" inscribed in gilt scroll at her. Hitty awakened from her daze, took the bucket, and ran across the street to a crowded pump as if she meant to join the fire brigade. She elbowed her way to the front and shoved the bucket under the gushing spout, but when it was filled, hurried away in the opposite direction.

Passing by the apothecary, she saw that the door was open and ducked inside. An orangey glow stained the white paneling of the walls. Hitty felt her way to the end of the long marble-topped counter. Ignoring the various glass containers that were aligned there, including a large round stoppered one that held a dark slimy mass of leeches, she went around back to where she knew the medicines were kept. On a shelf was a collection of small bottles labeled with a name she knew: laudanum. Miss Vail used to take laudanum to relieve the pain of toothaches. She grabbed the bottle, fetched up her bucket, and slipped out onto the street again.

Heading back toward Mr. Andrews' meeting house with its beautiful airy steeple illuminated in the fiery light, her eyes opened wide with a horrible new understanding. Only a miracle had thus far kept the building from catching fire. No, not a miracle, she realized, pushing away strands of hair blowing into her face, but a brisk wind from the west that hurried the fire on its course in the opposite direction: into the heart of the town. Hitty shuffled faster; she must get Peter out before a change in the wind's direction put them in danger. The bucket banged against her legs and water slopped over, drenching her skirt and shoes.

Peter was in the same position as when she'd left. Hitty ripped off another scrap from her undergarment and dipped it in the water. He stirred when she touched it to his head, but didn't awaken. With relief, she noted that the bleeding had stopped. Carefully, she raised his head and poured a little of the medicine into his mouth. He sputtered but swallowed, still not waking. She found a lap blanket in a pew and covered him, then went to look out the back window.

The fire roared like a terrible sea as it swelled and surged forward on its dreadful path of destruction. Flames ascended high into the smoke-shrouded sky. The whole neighborhood was aglow: the tavern, Mr. Jackman's grocery, the houses between, the buildings on Market Square. Bucket brigades and fire wagons and hand engines were having little effect. Long lines of people frantically passed buckets that sprinkled drops of water onto the inferno.

Hitty hurried back to the pew and shook Peter. "Peter, wake up! We have to go!" But he merely groaned. A sudden explosion from the direction of the wharves shook the building. With a cry, Hitty sank to the floor, covered her head with her arms, and waited for the whole world to fall down upon her.

ONE

"ANDY GAMMON, you've got to get a life," I told myself as I lay in wait behind the indoor window shutter, its louvered slats angled for the best view of the front porch. "Being at home with the kids is well and good, but there comes a time when you become as stale as the dried out SpaghettiOs encrusted on the baseboards in the kitchen. Case in point: here you are ready to pounce on a poor newspaper deliverer for his bad aim, probably a kid who never got the chance to play Little League because he was out trying to make money for the family—"

There it was: a beat-up Jeep Wrangler cruising by the house. It didn't stop, barely even slowed down while an arm was thrust out the side window and an unwrapped, untied newspaper was slung in the general direction of my porch.

"Aw, crap!" I watched as my *Boston Globe,* fluttering like a crippled bird, failed to attain airborne status and landed in a shallow puddle on the sidewalk, five feet short of the porch. I hotfooted it over a floor mined with Matchbox cars and LEGOS, and flung open the door. Too late. The Jeep was out of sight. Half-opened, its edges already soaking up the gray water, the newspaper resembled a sinking pup tent. As I carried the dripping mess through the house to the trash I vowed that this time, with a make on the car and a partial description of the suspect—an arm and the back of a head—I'd lodge a formal complaint.

For the time being, though, I settled for Mayta Gammon, my mother-in-law. Not only could she match anyone tale for tale in the injustice department, she was the only other person I knew who would be up at five in the morning.

"God, I hate March! I especially hate March in Newburyport. There is no place more gloomy or bone-chilling than March in Newburyport."

"Yep," she squawked over the receiver. "Wind's blowing horizontal out here, shooting sand through every crack in the house. Went to drink my tea and I swear there was as much sand in the cup as sugar."

"That's what you get for living in a cottage on the island," I said, picturing her wrapped in a quilt, watching out her window for the sun to rise over the ocean.

"Gus should take us all to Florida."

"February vacation is past," I reminded her.

"April, then. Let's go in April."

"Naw, by then there'll be sunshine and flowers and we won't want to go." Then I told her about the newspaper, how it was the third day in a row I didn't have a *Boston Globe* to read with my coffee.

"I'll go with you to complain," she said. "I got a bone to pick with them myself. My last bill was too high. We'll go down to their office in Lynn and complain in person. How's Thursday?"

"I can't go on Thursday."

"Friday, then. We go in right at nine before they get busy. It's better to talk to people face to face. They can't put you on hold, listening to dentist office music."

The thought of Mayta stumping into the *Boston Globe* office to do battle over a bill that was probably over by forty cents brought a smile to my face. "No," I said, "I'm just blowing off steam. Besides, that's not my style."

"It's not about style, Andy," she said. I could hear pots banging in the background. "It's about standing up for your rights—the Yankee way."

"Ha! But I'm not a Yankee, remember? That's what you keep telling me."

"Oh, well, it's not your fault. I'll go another time, then."

"Listen," I said to change the subject, "Gus is staying late at school tonight. Want to have dinner together?"

"Sure, honey. Why don't you and the kids come out to the island?"

"You're always cooking for us," I protested. "I'll treat you to McDonald's—some treat, I know, but the kids aren't eating much else these days."

"Nah! You guys come out and I'll fix up something they'll eat."

"Well, if you insist," I said after the slightest of hesitations. The protest had been a token so I'd feel a little less guilty about inviting myself to dinner. "Can we come early? Right after school? I have a project I think you can help me with."

"Sure, come out anytime. What's your project?"

"I don't exactly know yet. Historical stuff. Dig out your Newburyport books and I'll tell you all about it when I see you. Right now I have to get the kids up and out the door. I've got a meeting with Susan at the church first thing this morning."

"Reverend Tenney? What're you meeting with her for?"

"The research project. Tell you about it this afternoon, Mayta. I've got to scoot." And I hung up. Let her chew on that for a while, I thought, grinning to myself. The First Parish Church of Newburyport has been the Gammon family's church for generations, although Mayta and Gus—her son and my husband—hadn't attended for more than a decade. Gus quit going after eighth grade and Mayta dropped out when Gus's father died. It was me, a non-local, a Midwesterner, who had brought the Gammons "back into the fold" so to speak, and it was ironic that I often knew more about what was going on at "their" church than they did.

My involvement in the First Parish began as a simple desire to find a place for myself in my husband's world—Newburyport, Massachusetts. For the first few years of our relationship Gus and I lived in *my* world. It was only much later that I appreciated what it had taken him to resist family and local tradition to attend college outside New England. As it was, his wild and crazy departure from the norm lasted only a few years, during which he and I met (in a psych class at the University of Michigan), got married, and landed teaching jobs in Detroit, my hometown.

When I became pregnant, a side of Gus I had never seen emerged, a staunch traditional side that insisted the best place to bring up children was where your family had roots. And since Gus's ancestors had practically tripped on their hems as they scrambled out of the ship's hold to get a look at the New World, and then planted themselves ten feet away from their landing spot for the ensuing four hundred years, Newburyport was that place. Besides, he pointed out diplomatically, my parents had retired to Florida and my siblings were scattered throughout the states.

Being an outsider in a small New England city can be a daunting experience. Neighbors hail and farewell you but rarely take the time to get to know you. After my first lonely six months, during which my only daytime companions were an infant and his sixty-odd year-old—albeit feisty and entertaining—grandmother (Mayta), I began joining organizations. Over the years, at different times, I've been a member of the Friends of the Library, the Maritime Museum, the PTO, the

Waterfront Beautification Club, and the Plum Island Lighthouse Association. When I joined the church and became a Sunday school teacher, Gus and Mayta were shamed into attending occasional services. I think they're privately amused that this Motown babe has bought the small town scene hook, line, and sinker.

As for me, some of the organizations have stuck. The First Parish stuck because within the walls of this quaint, historic little white church with its New England spire, I found something I hadn't found in my ultra-modern Midwestern religious training: license to question everything, including God herself if I feel like it.

"PRETTY DRESS," I complimented Nancy Freeman, secretary of the First Parish, as she exited the minister's office. Rumor had it that Nancy, who was in her early thirties, had recently separated from her husband. If true, she appeared to be handling it well. Besides being her usual friendly self, she looked very stylish in a gauzy abstract-patterned skirt and matching blouse, her blond hair cut short and full, and makeup enhancing her wide blue eyes. As nice and pretty as Nancy was, I figured her estranged husband had to be a creep.

"Thanks, Andy. I got it on sale at Marshall's." Nancy smiled and cocked her head at the door she held open. "You can go on in. They're waiting for you."

Reverend Susan Tenney waved me into her modest office. Three sides of the room are lined with tall oak bookshelves, jam-packed vertically, horizontally, and haphazardly with books of all sizes. Decades-old linoleum has yellowed and worn through in spots to the wood flooring underneath. In the corner adjacent to Susan's desk sits an old Olivetti typewriter on a metal cart. The church has a computer and there are members who regularly use it for finances, the weekly newsletter, and other things, but Susan pecks out her sermons on the Olivetti. Modern thinking in all other respects, Susan has yet to enter the computer age.

A tiny woman in her mid-sixties, her brown hair worn in a severe Joan of Arc style, Susan was seated at her desk, barely a head taller than the towering columns of papers and books stacked on it. The appearance of her desk is misleading; the few times I've asked her for information, Susan has found it promptly in one of these piles. Besides her desk, the bookcases, and a battered file cabinet, the only other furnishings are a small table that holds a coffee maker and mugs, and some worn Windsor chairs, two of which now held the Van Amburgs.

"Andy, you know Ginger and Frank, don't you?" Susan said. I acknowledged that I did and we exchanged greetings as I took a chair beside the elderly couple.

Frank Van Amburg, a retired private school teacher and well-respected local historian, is a veritable walking book on Newburyport lore. Ginger, his wife, has for years single-handedly organized the church fair, the Historical Society's house tour, and the YMCA's bean supper. Her name is in the permanent memory bank of the *Daily News* but she's oblivious to the press her endeavors earn. Her motives stem purely from good-heartedness and excess energy.

"I'm so glad you could come, dear." She smiled, her face crinkling up around eyes that were bright and young looking. Despite her gray hair, freckles scattered across her nose and cheeks made it easy to picture Ginger Van Amburg as the redhead that had inspired her name. Her distinguished looking husband nodded in agreement and adjusted his silver rimmed glasses.

"And this is Mark Levenson, chairperson of the new Historical Committee." Susan's voice bubbled with enthusiasm as she gestured to the other side of the room. I pivoted to find the person I hadn't noticed when I entered.

I'd seen Mark Levenson in church and in his antique store on State Street, but we'd never formally met. From the strands of gray in his long ponytail I judged him to be around forty. He wore a small gold stud in his right ear, black jeans and a loose white shirt, the top three buttons open, revealing a thick gold chain. Sitting up straight, his legs crossed at the knees, Mark flicked his eyes my way, stretched his mouth horizontally across his face—an effort I took to be a smile—and nodded curtly.

"Nice to meet you." I returned the smile but he had already averted his gaze.

"Andy," Susan started right in, "as we discussed earlier, I'd like you to be on the Tricentennial Bicentennial Committee which will act as a subcommittee to the Historical Committee. Frank has a wonderful idea and needs help with research. I thought of you because you taught history and you mentioned that you enjoy doing research."

I nodded. It was true that, as a graduate student, I'd spend whole days in library basements with the whir of microfiche tape fast forwarding or rewinding through machines, breathing in the perfume of musty old documents, searching for a few more details to flesh out a historical event or figure for a paper.

"The Historical Committee wants to update the church history for its Tricentennial," Frank explained, leaning forward and peering over the top of his glasses. "We only have a few months if we want to publish it in the Tricentennial year."

"You're probably acquainted with Etta Mae Frisch's history of the church," put in Ginger. I wasn't, but she went on, "It's very good, but as it was written back in the thirties, it needs updating."

"And since we're going to the bother and expense of publishing a new edition," Frank said, "we thought we'd add a section on the early history. The time period between 1801, when the meeting house was built, and roughly 1850 didn't get covered thoroughly in Frisch's book."

"And you want me…" I let the question dangle.

"To research from 1801 to 1850, if you will," said Frank. "My concentration will be from 1930 to the present."

"Merrimack River Press has agreed to print two thousand copies at a good price," said Susan. "They think it will do well because of the local historical interest." She and the Van Amburgs watched me expectantly while Mark inspected his fingernails.

"Well," I said, stalling as I weighed the pros and cons of giving up those precious few kindergarten hours. "Okay. When do you need the research?"

"By the beginning of April," said Frank. "That will give me a couple of months to compile your work with mine and write it up. Merrimack River Press can have it printed in time for our celebration in September."

I hadn't thought to bring a notebook. I rummaged in my purse, came up with a purple crayon and a gum wrapper, on which I wrote, "1801-1850 meeting house."

"The old church records are kept in a chest," said Susan. "I'll have the sexton take it over to the choir room. There'll be more room to spread everything out." She bent her head over an open drawer in her desk for a moment and came up with a key. "This opens both the Parish Hall and the church. Feel free to come and go as you please. I'm usually in my office mornings if you need me."

I took the key and a proffered book from Frank. "Etta Mae Frisch's history," he said. "You'll probably want to start with it."

"Frank and I are going to begin sorting through the old records tomorrow night, if you want to come," said Ginger smiling, her face pleating into dozens of crinkles around her mouth and eyes. "About seven."

Quickly, I ran down an itinerary on the ever-present slate inside my head: Max and Molly to school, pick up Molly after kindergarten at noon, pick up Max at three, Molly to ballet at four, Max to Y at four-thirty. Did Gus have a school board meeting tomorrow night? No, that was Thursday. "Sure!" I said.

Mark Levenson looked up from his thumbnail and spoke for the first time. "Because you are acting as a subcommittee of the Historical Committee, I will need to see your work as you proceed," he said, addressing Frank.

"Well, of course we will want the approval of the Historical Committee before we submit the manuscript," Frank said, carefully choosing his words.

"If you don't mind, I'd like to see the research, as well," Mark said mildly.

"You'll be on the Tricentennial Committee?" Frank's voice rose.

"No, of course not." Mark's chin tilted up. "As chairperson of the Historical Committee, I just feel it's my responsibility to supervise this undertaking."

I could feel the electricity in the air. When Frank, whose face was turning pink, opened his mouth to retort Susan spoke up quickly.

"Well, this is certainly going to be an exciting project," she said with exuberance. She rose and we followed suit. If the men wanted to engage in a power struggle it wasn't going to be in her office. "I can't wait to see the published book!"

Outside, hammering from overhead echoed off the old buildings which closely lined the narrow street, an empty and ominous sound in the gloom. I craned my neck and looked up at our beautiful three-tiered church steeple. A board attached at the ends by ropes like an old fashioned swing hung from it, and a man in white overalls sat in the middle of it, working on the shingled side of the spire. The wind had picked up and the steeplejack's tenuous perch began to sway.

The mother in me came out, and just as I was about to yell, "Get down from there!" the steeplejack came to his senses and pulled himself back onto the sheltered portion of the steeple. I brought my eyes earthward, overcome by a sudden dizziness brought on partly by a realization that had finally seeped into my dense head: the beginning of April, when Frank Van Amburg wanted research on everything there was to know about this church during a fifty year span, was only three weeks away.

TWO

MAYTA LIKES TO SAY that she lives at the end of the world. And it really does feel that way despite a mere ten minute drive through the marshes from town. After you pass over the low bridge that connects Plum Island to the mainland and follow the sandy lane that narrows into her drive, Mayta's cottage is all that's left before the sparse beach grass turns to open beach sloping down to the Atlantic Ocean.

"Come on in!" Mayta greeted us on the screened porch, her backside holding open the door. "Get in here out of that wind!" She hugged each of us vigorously to her plump body and then shepherded us into her warm, spicy-smelling kitchen.

When Gus's father died, Mayta closed up the family home in town and moved away for several years, first traveling in Europe with her sister, and then living in California with a friend. She decided to come back to the area about the time we decided to move East. She offered us a great deal on the family home, which we jumped at, and then bought herself a small cottage out on the island.

I sniffed. Cookies and something else—Mayta's baked beans! Oh, joy!

Settled in captain's chairs around her nicked-up maple table, glasses of apple juice and big soft hermit cookies in hand, Max and Molly slurped and munched and swung their feet happily while Mayta started right in on her favorite subject: local politics. "Ben Barrett's running for mayor again. Did you hear?" The name meant nothing to me. I shook my head and reached for a hermit. "He was mayor for just about the whole decade back in the '80s," she continued. "Gus would remember. And now, after all these years, he's looking to run again!" She waved the coffee pot at me. "Coffee? It's decaf."

"Mmmm, please."

"More juice, Maxy?" Mayta squeezed his arm with affection. "When are you two coming out here to spend the night with your Grandma?"

"Can we, Mama?" Molly wiggled in her chair.

"Sure, anytime Grandma wants you. Not tonight," I added quickly, anticipating the next question.

"How about Friday night?" Mayta suggested.

"Okay by me."

"Oh, goody!" squealed Molly as Max exclaimed, "Yes" and punched a fist into the air. Grinning, Mayta poured more juice for the kids and then wiped the table.

"Mayta!" I pretended exasperation. "Stop waiting on us and sit!" She waved aside my words, but dropped the dishcloth in the sink and plunked herself down.

"So, tell me about this guy who's running for mayor— Barrett," I said, knowing I'd get a generous dose of town history interspersed with her opinions.

Mayta scooched back and forth in her chair like one of the kids, then leaned forward, resting her arms on the table. "Ben's one of the good old boys; he was a high school football star, went into his daddy's law firm after college, lives in one of those High Street mansions. But during his last term of office, all was not on the up and up," she said, one eyebrow rising above her glasses. "There were questions about the use of funds."

"What funds?" I asked.

Meaningfully, she inclined her head toward the children,

stretching her mouth downwards and eyebrows upwards at the same time. "I'll tell you later."

I sipped from the ironstone mug, wondering what juicy bit of history Mayta had with Barrett. "You're about the same age. Did you go to school with this guy?"

"Yep. Ben was a bit of a hellion then. Still is, I'll bet—just more refined about it." She drummed arthritis-gnarled fingers on the table. "But newcomers don't know that. They'll vote for him 'cuz the old coot looks good in the newspapers." She fixed me with a challenging look that I ignored. A newcomer is anyone whose parents weren't born in Newburyport. Since I'd only been here six years, I was still technically a tourist in Mayta's book.

Outside, the wind was tossing around a light snow as it howled off the ocean and around the little cottage hunkered down cozily between the grassy dunes. From where we sat we could see through the living room, which was just an extension of the kitchen, out the big window to the surf crashing down on the beach.

"Will winter never end?" Mayta groaned. "Molly, hand me that dish towel." She got up and poked the towel in the crack between the window frame and the sill.

"Don't you ever get lonely out here?" I asked.

"Heck no. I spent years in the thick of the commotion in town and it suits me just fine to live outside of it now." She sat down again, pulling Molly onto her lap.

Max grabbed for another cookie. "Last one," I said. "Save room for dinner."

I told Mayta about the Tricentennial Committee and what I'd been asked to do. Immediately excited, she went to her bookcase and began hauling out local history books for me to look at. While the kids dragged out their father's old Tinker-toys and little metal trucks from a low trunk that does double duty as coffee table, we looked over the books, deciding which would be of use to me.

Then Gus arrived, bringing in with him the smell of cold salty air as he stamped his feet in the doorway. Flecks of snow melted in his wavy blond hair and on the broad shoulders of his navy jacket. He gave me a quick hug, then gathered up both kids who were squealing, "Daddy! Daddy!"

"Hi, Ma." He kissed the top of Mayta's head. "I'm starved. What's for eats?"

We put aside the books and, while Gus plunked down on the floor and played with the kids, I helped Mayta set out dinner: deli hot dogs, homemade baked beans, fresh fruit salad, and Mayta's creamy cheese noodles. Watching Max and Molly chow down on food they barely touch at home, I marveled at how a good cook can make the simplest meal a feast. The talk turned to my project, which I explained again for Gus's sake.

"You know about the Great Fire of 1811, don't you?" he asked. "It happened during the time you're researching so you'll want to read about it."

"What Great Fire?" I said and they both gave me incredulous looks.

"It was the most devastating event in Newburyport's history," Mayta said. "It destroyed the entire business section of the city."

Later, as we packed up to leave, Mayta went back to her bookcase. "Where is it?" she muttered, running a crooked finger along the spines of the books.

"Where is what?" I asked, zipping up Max's jacket.

"I got a booklet on the Great Fire at the Historical Society some years ago. Gus is right; you might find something on the church." Mayta straightened up. "Well, when I find it, I'll save it for you."

"How did the fire start?"

"It was some kind of accident, I think," said Gus. "That's why downtown is in the Federal style. Everything was rebuilt at the same time."

"Yep," said Mayta. "They didn't want anything like that to ever happen again so they rebuilt in brick with fire walls on the roofs between each building. Our forefathers paid a heavy price for those quaint row buildings with their trendy stores all the tourists flock here to shop in."

"Wait a minute," I said. "The church is downtown and it's made of wood. Didn't it catch fire?"

"Nope," said Mayta. "Miraculously the First Parish survived the Great Fire."

"FOUR," GINGER VAN AMBURG corrected.

"What?" I raised my head from the musty book that lay in the x of my crossed legs. "What did you say?"

"The church has only four silver tankards."

We were in the choir room off the gallery, which was located above the vestibule, and just below the tower that holds the belfry and steeple. Each of us had staked out an area with enough space to spread out books and papers. I was seated on a nearly threadbare Oriental rug in front of a defunct pump organ while, at the opposite end of the room, Frank sat at a long folding table between stacks of scrapbooks. Ginger was stationed at an old battered sea chest with dovetailing and hemp handles which had been donated back in the eighteenth century by one of the many sea captains of the congregation who undoubtedly thought it a practical way to store records. She was going through its contents, the written records kept since the first meeting house was built in 1647—there had been three meeting houses in all—and divvying them up according to which of us she thought should look at them.

The wind shook the windows and a couple of times the

lights flickered. The storm system that had come in the day before had stalled over coastal New England and was alternately pelting us with rain and snow. Despite the weather and in the interest of getting on with the project, we had decided to keep our evening meeting.

"It's written here in the records," I told Ginger, poking a finger at the faded brown script in the book. "For 1776, 'two silver tankards were received of Merriman Tibbits in honor of our country's birth, bringing the total to six silver tankards.'"

Ginger bobbed her head up and down impatiently, her gray curls bouncing. "Yes, dear, I know. But two of those six were lost during the Great Fire of 1811."

Frank chuckled. "Tibbits was kind of a hothead," he said. "It figures that while others were presenting silver to honor the birth of a child or give thanks for a safe voyage, Tibbits would make a donation in honor of the Declaration of Independence. I guess you'd call him a rabble-rouser; he was one of the first to call for revolution and to enlist, and afterwards, insisted on being called by his rank—colonel—for the rest of his life."

"Oh!" exclaimed Ginger as if she'd just thought of something delightful, "isn't Tibbits the one who wore a three-corner hat long after it was out of date, even as an old man?"

Frank grunted in the affirmative, his attention back on his book.

"So the church no longer has six tankards," I said.

"That's right," said Ginger. "In fact, I believe the two that were lost were the ones Tibbits donated."

I ran my finger lightly down the coarse paper. "Do we still have the other silver mentioned here? The baptismal font, the flagons, the patens?"

"Certainly," Ginger answered. "They're kept locked up in a vault and taken out only on special occasions. You've seen the baptismal font, haven't you? It's the basin Susan uses for dedicating children into the church."

"Oh, yes," I said, remembering. "It's a beautiful piece." We'd had the children dedicated when Max was a year old and Molly was an infant. I'd commented on the rich patina of the silver when Susan pulled the simple basin from its cloth bag and explained that the old silver tarnished slower than the new because of the methods craftsmen used back then.

"Do you know the font's history?" Ginger asked. I shook my head, and she smiled warmly. "In the early eighteen hundreds, the young mothers of the church donated silver dollars to be melted down and made into a basin for baptism. Isn't that a nice story?"

I agreed. "What about the flagons and patens? What are they?"

"They're all part of the communion service," explained Ginger. "The flagons are large drinking vessels with hinged lids; they're like the tankards only about twice the size. Patens are communion plates. Almost all the pieces were given during colonial times, and are excellent examples of local craftsmanship."

"If the church didn't burn, how were the tankards lost in the Great Fire?" I asked. "And how was the church spared? Wasn't everything else destroyed?"

"Pretty much," answered Frank. He was hunched over a scrapbook, fists pressed against his cheekbones, holding up his head. He didn't alter his position as he talked, just peered up over the rim of his glasses. "The fire started in a stable about where that women's clothing shop is now, and the wind swept it in the other direction, burning the city from this point eastward."

"I was just reading about it the other day," said Ginger, eagerly taking up the story. "Even though the fire began so close to the church, by some miracle not a single spark ignited it."

"No miracle," Frank corrected. "It was the wind, is all. Blew it the other way."

"Anyway," said Ginger, "when parishioners came to check on the church, they found two tankards missing—the silver was kept in the church back then. Some looter must have walked off with them."

"Why only two pieces stolen?" I asked. "Why not all of it?"

Frank raised his eyes again and I noticed how blue they were peering out from under a protruding wave of white hair. "They weren't with the rest," he said. "I can't remember why, but the two tankards were separate from the other silver."

"I'll find that article about the church and the fire for you, Andy," said Ginger. She bent over the sea chest and lifted out a large rectangular book. "Oh, look at this! The deeds to the pews from 1801 to 1830!"

"Deeds?" I asked, intrigued.

"Families bought their pews and passed them down to heirs," she explained.

"You mean parishioners actually owned their pews? Can I look at that?"

"Certainly." Ginger crossed the room, her sensible thick rubber soles squeaking on the varnished wood floor, and handed me the book. "There were still a few owned pews up through the 1930s." Then she clasped her hands up in front of her like a child. "Oh, Frank! Do you remember Jeannine Toole?"

"No," said Frank dourly.

"The prominent Tooles of Newburyport," Ginger explained for my benefit, "were ship owners and mayors and bank owners; one was even in the cabinet of President Pierce. And Miss Jeannine was the last of the line. She'd sit all by herself in her big side pew—number ten I think it was—ramrod straight, looking up at Reverend Hill." Ginger smiled at the memory. "I was a young girl then, and every week I'd look to see what fancy hat Miss Jeannine was wearing. They were always very colorful with lots of feathers," she giggled, "and never matched her dresses."

Frank frowned. "Why don't I remember her?"

"Women's styles have never impressed you," replied Ginger gently.

Frank looked at his wife for a moment as if trying to figure out what she meant by her comment, then went back to his work. Ginger winked at me and I grinned back. I was beginning to like the Van Amburgs.

We spent hours poring over the church records. There were tax books, Women's Alliance minutes, Sunday school records. There was a stack of slim volumes covered in marbleized paper, tied together with a faded blue ribbon and labeled Ladies Social Benevolent Society. Nice word, I thought: benevolent. A word that isn't in use enough today.

But the leather bound record books kept by the ministers of the 1700s and 1800s were the most interesting. In meticulous flowing script were recorded marriages, baptisms, meetings, and visits made to parishioners—firsthand accounts of daily life in the early years of the settlement of Newburyport. I set aside one that covered the first couple of decades of the 1800s—the Reverend Mr. Andrews' book—to take home, along with the records of the deeds to the pews.

Outside, the wind howled fiercely and inside, the heat having been cut back because it was a weekday, the room grew colder. The Oriental rug was thin padding under my backside and I rocked from one side to the other in discomfort. Looking up at the wall clock, I was surprised to see it was ten-thirty.

"This body has had about all the physical torture it can endure for one night," I said, getting to my numbed feet. "It's time to go home."

Which was the exact moment a shrieking crash overhead shook the building.

THREE

"GOOD GOD! What was that!" Frank exclaimed. We froze, faces raised to the ceiling like three Chicken Littles waiting for the sky to fall. Fingers of wind wriggled through the cracks in loose windows, took hold and shook them. The lights blinked off, then on. Then off again and stayed that way.

"It sounded like something big fell," Ginger said.

"Yeah, like the steeple," I said half-joking, then thought a moment. "Isn't that what's above us?"

"Yes," said Frank dourly, "but I don't think it fell off. The steeplejack's been working up there; maybe he left some loose boards around."

"That was more than loose boards," countered Ginger.

Nobody spoke for a few moments as we shuffled our things together in the dark. Then Frank said, "I should go check it out."

"What?" exclaimed Ginger. "Go up there tonight in the dark in this storm?"

"Susan needs to know as soon as possible if there's any serious damage."

"Frank's right," I said. "If the interior is exposed to the elements, somebody should take care of it immediately. I'll go with you, Frank."

"No, no," Frank protested. "Both of us don't need to climb up there."

"But it's not safe for you to go alone," I pointed out.

"Well, you're not leaving me here by myself," said Ginger. "We'll all go."

Frank grumbled something unintelligible, then said, "It'll be dark."

"I saw an emergency flashlight plugged into the wall some-where," Ginger said. "If I could only remember where it was."

"It's on the landing," he said. "The building committee in-stalled it last fall."

I went to look for the flashlight with Ginger behind me. Pale moonlight filtering through the windows allowed just enough vision to make my way safely through a brigade of music stands by the door, but once outside the choir room, I had to feel my way along the wall of the organ on the gallery landing.

"It's around here somewhere." Ginger's dark form brushed past me, and bent over, feeling alongside the baseboard. "Here it is." A circle of light illuminated the wall paneling. "Come on Frank!" she said. "Lead us onward and upward."

Frank grunted, but didn't protest. "You enter the steeple from behind the organ," he said, taking the flashlight from Ginger and shining it on the back corner of the organ's mahogany casing. Wedged between the instrument and the wall were narrow steep stairs.

"I never knew there were stairs there," I said in wonder.

"You can't see them until you're almost behind the organ," Frank said. He started up with Ginger and me close behind. At the top he opened a short door set into the wall. One by one, we ducked our heads as we stepped through it, then paused to let our eyes adjust to the greater degree of darkness.

"That's the attic above the sanctuary." Frank flicked his beam back and forth across a long expanse that spread out to one side of us. "We're in the base of the tower." Then he shined the light overhead. Highlighted against a murky background, a crude staircase twisted and turned at odd angles like the contorted vertebrae of a prehistoric creature, its head craning up beyond our sight. That should have been when we turned back, when somebody said this is too dangerous; who knows what condition these old stairs are in. But none of us did. As we hesitated, the electricity came back on, and light from the gallery streamed through the door.

"Well, that helps," I said in relief.

"Be careful," Frank warned over his shoulder, starting up the staircase.

Unnecessary words. Ginger and I gripped the thin handworn rail, which sagged between sparsely placed posts, as if it were a lifeline. We proceeded slowly, the steep rise of the steps challenging for Ginger's arthritic knees, the ascent into the unseeable overhead daunting for all of us.

We soon moved beyond the reach of illumination from the gallery, the last bits of light reflected on dust motes that spread out and dispersed into the dark like spent fireflies. Then there was nothing in the blackness except the narrow beam coming from the flashlight in Frank's hand, its wavering circle of light always just before us, beckoning us onward, then jerking ahead the moment we reached it. Sticking close together, hands gliding along the rail, feet sliding cautiously onto each step, we moved as one, the dark folding in on us from behind.

I concentrated on the back of Ginger's pleated skirt—the occasional brush of its swaying hemline against my knee bringing a bit of comfort—and tried to keep at bay the insistent feeling that the stairs were tipping and I was about to lose my balance.

"We're turning," warned Frank. He pivoted to the left and we followed suit. My hand met a corner post, trailed over the top of it, and took up the rail on the other side. I avoided looking down through the openings between the steps or over their sides into the growing abyss below.

Nobody suggested turning back. At one point I almost said

something. But by then we had gone far enough that the thought of retreat was equally intimidating as the thought of advancing. Besides, if two septuagenarians weren't crying chicken, I wasn't about to, either.

As my eyes continued to adjust, I saw gradients in the dark. We ascended two more flights, passed two more landings on our left that stretched into murky shadows. Our breathing had grown louder, more labored with the exertion. Once Frank stopped and flashed his beam behind him. "Watch that step. It's uneven," he said, offering his hand first to Ginger, then to me as we stepped over the warped tread.

"Whew!" Ginger said when we stopped on the last landing to rest. "This is a workout." She laughed nervously.

"How are you doing?" I asked at the same time Frank said, "Are you okay?"

"I'm fine," she said between audible inhales.

It had become damp and penetratingly cold. Drafts came in thin whispers that brushed cheeks and slunk around ankles. The musty smell of wood and the still, tight air overhead gave the impression we were getting close to the top.

"Are we almost there?" asked Ginger.

"The trapdoor is at the top of those steps." Frank shined the light on the last flight of stairs that was at an almost vertical pitch, its steps like ladder rungs.

"Oh, dear," Ginger said softly. "We'll have to go up one at a time."

Then loud splatters of rain struck the sides of the steeple and the wind picked up, coming in quick assaults that buffeted the tower. I pictured it breaking and falling off like the first church's steeple had done at Market Square back in the 1700s. "I hope it holds up," I said as the structure groaned and shuddered.

"Oh, it's sturdy," Frank reassured. "These wooden buildings

are constructed to give in high winds. But, maybe you should wait here, Ginger."

She shook her head. "No. I've come this far. I'll go the rest of the way."

Because it was less wide, we could now hold on to the rails on either side, which made up a little for its unnerving sheer rise. When Frank had climbed about five feet Ginger stepped onto the first rung. "Be careful," he called down.

"Go slow," I told her. I waited until Ginger, who was pulling herself up onto each rung one foot at a time, had moved above my head level, to start up. Because Frank was above and had to use both hands to climb anyway, his flashlight no longer lit the way for us: Ginger and I climbed by feel in the dark. I had gone only a couple of steps when Ginger gasped. Instinctively I tightened my grip on the rails just as she lost her footing and slid downward into me.

The half circle made by my arms on the ladder stopped Ginger's fall and prevented mine as well. For a moment we remained that way: my body pressing hers close to the rungs. "Are you okay?" I spoke over the thundering heartbeat in my ears. She nodded but I could feel her trembling.

"What happened?" Frank's voice boomed out from the dark overhead and the flashlight beam swung crazily out and then downward.

Ginger ducked her head away from the direct glare. I held up a hand to shield my eyes. "Frank," I said in sudden irritation, "shine that thing away from us."

Obediently, he raised the beam over our heads. "Are you hurt?"

"Nobody's hurt," I reassured him. "Ginger just missed a step." Then to Ginger, I said in a low voice, "We've gone far enough. Let's go back down."

"No," she whispered, determined. "I'd be all right if I could see."

I wondered why on earth I'd ever agreed to such a foolhardy venture; somebody was bound to get injured before it was over. But if Ginger was a bit unsteady on her feet, I knew she was solid in her determination. I sighed and called up to Frank, "Shine the light on the steps."

He ignored me. "Ginger! Are you okay?"

She took a long deliberate breath and called out in a clear strong voice, "I'm fine, Frank. Please just shine the light on the steps."

Frank obeyed then, angling the beam away from our eyes. I kept a few rungs behind Ginger this time, ready to catch her again if needed, but she climbed with renewed strength in her step. A few moments later we stopped behind Frank who surprised us by saying that we'd arrived at the top. He shone the flashlight on a door set in the ceiling a couple feet above his head, then pushed up against it with his free hand.

"There's a hook," Ginger noted when the door didn't budge. A few more moments were spent in Frank locating and fumbling with the hook at the side of the door. Standing still in the dark was worse than moving; the black space below pulled at me. I couldn't help thinking that if Frank lost his balance, we'd all tumble backward like dominoes and that we could fall three flights of stairs. Then, thankfully, I heard the trapdoor creak.

Yielding to Frank's force, the door swung upward, and then fell away to the left out of sight, landing with a soft thud against something unseen. High above was the white paneled ceiling of the belfry illuminated by flood lamps. Outdoor sounds sharpened: tires hissed on wet pavement, branches rattled in the wind, raindrops struck the roof in staccato.

"Do you see anything?" Ginger asked as Frank's upper body rose into the elements. Without answering, he crawled up through the opening and disappeared.

Ginger pulled herself up three steps and poked her head outside. "I can't see anything," she said, backing down the steps, "but you take a look, dear."

"Where's Frank?"

"Oh, he's right there, kneeling beside the opening."

I squeezed past her and climbed as far as the second step. The wind had momentarily died down and the rain had turned into a wet snow that eddied around my head as I came up through the opening. We'd reached the first stage of the steeple, the belfry, which was about fifteen feet square and, except for chicken wire stretched between the corner supports to keep out pigeons, open to the elements. The great bell—wrought by Paul Revere's sons and weighing around a thousand pounds, I recalled from my readings—was mounted on a massive yet simple wooden framework that took up most of the floor space, leaving an approximate four foot periphery between it and the edge. Above the belfry, I knew, there rose two more stages, octagonal in shape and enclosed by arched windows, which tapered gracefully to the spire topped by the proud gold-leafed rooster weather vane.

Suddenly I realized how foolhardy we were to be up there. "Frank!" I yelled as he moved out of sight beyond the bell. His answer was snatched away by a gust of wind before I could decipher it.

"Oh, dear," came Ginger's worried voice from below. "Once he gets going on something it's hard to stop him."

The wind whipped at my hair and slapped heavy wet snow flakes against my face as I strained to see around the bell. "I'm going out there," I said reluctantly.

"Oh, do you think you should, dear?"

"We'll be back in a minute," I reassured her. I crawled out onto the platform and stood up beside the bell, shiny black in its wetness. The floodlights at the edges of the platform shone up at the steeple, catching me in their bright rays. I took two timorous steps. Although the tar paper floor was icy in spots, it was coated with a gravelly surface and my boots gripped it well. I sidled around the bell, trailing a hand along it for assurance, keeping as far from the edge of the platform as possible. A sudden blast of wind surprised me and I fell against the bell, painfully banging my knee on its ungiving rim. I regained my balance, cursing the mammoth instrument as frigid wet seeped through my jeans leg. Once on the other side of the bell, I left its safety to move toward Frank who had his back to me, seemingly oblivious to the rain pelting him.

Airy graceful arches, formed by curved woodwork, spanned the underside of the ceiling between four boxed-in pillars, each about three and a half feet square, at the corners of the belfry. Three of these boxed-in pillars, which supported the upper tiers of the steeple, were intact. But the fourth—the one that now absorbed Frank—was split open, rotted wood lying in front of it. Next to it was an opening in the chicken wire, probably where the steeplejack went through, which was now gaping outward, debris caught in its edges as if something big had been hurled through.

A new concern occurred to me: how safe was the structure above us? With one support weakened, could the upper tiers of the steeple come crashing down?

"Frank, we need to go down immediately," I said urgently when I reached his side. "It could be very unsafe up here." I glanced upward nervously.

Frank kneeled in front of the damaged support. Water dripped steadily off the end of his nose and his white hair was plastered against his forehead as he craned forward and peered over the top of rain-flecked lenses. When he didn't answer me, I let my gaze follow to where his flashlight shined. Enough wood had broken away from one wall of the support to reveal a closet-like area about three feet square.

The circle of light was trained on what at first looked like a pile of old leaves pushed up against the back corner. Then I saw that it had a fabric-like texture; it was a blanket. A blanket wrapped around a form. As if looking at a page in a children's magazine with hidden pictures, my eyes suddenly saw what was there: a huddled body with its head ducked down, its eyes, or rather gaping eye sockets, staring out at us. Not a head. A skull.

Frank turned, surprised I was there. "It's a person," he said reverently.

"Oh my God," I whispered. "Oh my God."

"It's been here a long time. Look at that blanket." Frank crept closer, the beam of his flashlight narrowing on the figure. I moved forward with him. The form was leaning to the side in the corner, giving the impression of having gone to sleep sitting up and then falling against the wall. A coarsely woven blanket, its edges decayed to shreds, was pulled up around the figure.

"Who—" I stopped, startled by the squeak in my voice. I cleared my throat.

"And how," said Frank, "how did it get here?"

I bent closer to look at several small bones that were scattered around the floor. Even with a limited knowledge of anatomy, I recognized them as human toe bones. I shuddered and glanced at Frank to see if he'd noticed them, but he was leaning toward the figure, extending his left hand. I held my breath as he touched the fabric, expecting it to crumble. Then he slid a finger under the corner and lifted the edge slowly. Something glinted in his light.

"Wait!" I said. "I see something under there." I leaned forward to lift another section of the blanket and, in my excitement, clumsily bumped the figure with my hand. Repulsed, I pulled back and watched as the skull teetered on its neck as if shaking its head in disapproval, then fell off and landed in the folds of the blanket—the skeleton's lap—and leered toothily up at us. I shrieked at the same time Frank jerked sideways into me, knocking me onto my behind.

"Oh, I'm sorry. Are you okay?" He extended a hand, his attention momentarily turned to me, but I'd already regained my feet and was scrambling backwards.

"We should go down," I spoke breathlessly from a safe distance.

"Yes," he said as we both gazed at the sight in front of us. "You're right."

"We should go down because the steeple might not be safe—you know, because of the damage done." I made my voice sound normal.

Frank nodded. "And we should get somebody like the police." He was breathing hard and I worried that this was all too much for him. Heck, I thought as pulsing blood sledgehammered against my eardrums, it was too much for me. Finding a body in a steeple during a storm at night didn't belong in my world. A body, a skeleton, a corpse: the words whirled around my mind but they were mere codes that unlocked no meaning.

We edged backwards. A sudden wind gust swirled into the recessed opening and plucked at the blanket, teasing a corner free. We froze as the blanket flapped away from the shoulder of the body, swung across the front of it, and then caught on a piece of splintered wood on the opposite side, revealing the upper half of the body.

"Good God!" exclaimed Frank.

"It's so small," I whispered in wonder. "Is it—do you think it's a child? And those clothes—" The jacket on the torso was intact, the brownish rough material still held together by two large buttons. The exposed sleeve, however, had decayed considerably; mere scraps of fabric clung to a skeletal arm. My gaze followed down to where its bony fingers curled loosely around an object that was partly obscured by the skull in its lap. Curiosity overcame fear then, and we crept forward again and peeked over the top of the skull that was now, thankfully, covered by the blanket. The object in the skeleton's grasp was a large cup.

"Will you look at that!" Frank exclaimed, and I leaned in closer for a better look. The piece was not so badly tarnished that it failed to gleam in the light.

"It's a mug," I said. "A silver mug! And look, it has a lid."

Frank reached toward the mug, his fingers stopping just short of touching it. "Why, it's…it's a tankard!" he exclaimed.

FOUR

THE DESCENT WASN'T as bad as the climb had been. Familiarity with the terrain helped, as did knowing that the friendly, lit gallery awaited us. Other than telling Ginger that one of the corner supports was broken, we didn't speak until we reached the choir loft where Frank and I sank into pews and let Ginger fuss over us.

"Oh, just look at the two of you!" she scolded, handing a tissue to her husband. "You're both drenched. We have to get you home and dried off right away."

"Well, that's probably not possible," responded her husband as he mopped his forehead with the tissue. "We have something to take care of first."

"When you went out onto that roof all I could think of was tomorrow's *Daily News* headlines: MAN GETS BLOWN OFF STEEPLE," I said with a nervous giggle, "and then, when I saw what you were looking at, I almost fell off myself."

"What are you two talking about?" demanded Ginger.

As we related the story of our discovery, her eyes grew large and round. "But how did it get up there?" she wanted to know.

I shrugged. "It's been sealed inside that little hole for years."

"But the steeple has been worked on many times," Ginger protested. "If this…ah…skeleton is old, why didn't the steeplejack find it?"

"Good question," Frank said.

"Not just old." I wiped my face with the inside of the sweat-shirt I'd pulled off. "Ancient. Those clothes came from another century. And that silver cup—"

"What silver cup?" Ginger asked, and Frank told her about finding the cup in the skeleton's hand. Having just discussed the lost tankards, she at once seized upon the idea that it must be one of them. Frank insisted that the church's tankards were larger. I said it was too much of a coincidence to find some-thing that had been lost for almost two hundred years on the very night we'd been talking about it.

Abruptly, I turned to Frank. "You don't think that skeleton was up there for two hundred years, do you? A long time is one thing, but two hundred years?"

He started to shake his head, then stopped, frowning. "I don't know."

"We should call Susan," I said.

"And the police," said Frank seriously. "You have to report finding a body."

Frank went over to the church office to make the calls. I wedged the door open with the granite block so we could watch for the police. Before long, a white sedan, its door decorated with the logo of a clipper ship, arrived and two officers got out. One listened while the other jotted down our names and took notes in a small notebook as we explained about the crash, how we'd all gone up to investigate, and found the damage and the skeleton. Then they went back outside to confer with another officer who had just pulled up in his cruiser. The sum total of the nightly patrol was now converged upon the First Parish Church.

We shivered and stamped our numb feet in the cold vesti-bule while two of the policemen went up into the steeple. A little while later they descended, reassured us that the steeple wasn't in any immediate danger of toppling off, and strung yellow tape across both sets of gallery stairs. The first officer asked a few more questions, and Frank and I set up a time to come by the police station the next morning. After a second call to Susan to let her know everything was stable for the night, Frank locked up.

I was the last to drive away. From inside my car, I looked up at the lit spire, its three tiers rising majestically into the black sky, the damage not evident from the ground, and wondered how a body had gotten up there.

I woke Gus when I got home. Although groggy, he was attentive as I told him about our discovery and the police coming. We talked until I had unwound enough to be sleepy. The next morning I followed him from bathroom to bedroom to kitchen as he shaved, dressed, and ate breakfast, relating details that seemed unreal in the light of day. Now we were at the kitchen table, and he was lingering over coffee as we ruminated on how a skeleton might come to be in the steeple. Gus came up with possible scenarios: a wino who took the wrong stairs; a parishioner who fell asleep one too many times under the nose of a murderous minister. I'd added a couple of my own ideas, just as ridiculous, before we checked ourselves with the reminder that whatever had transpired, it had been no laughing matter.

It was at this point that an empty toilet paper roll shot down from the second floor and the plastic soles of two sets of blanket sleepers ssk-ssked down the hallway overhead. Amused, I took the message from the inside of the roll and read, "Wer not gone skol love Max and Molly," written in Max's best printing. I handed it to Gus who grinned that lopsided grin that had caused me to fall in love with him back in Psych 101.

I wrote "Come eat. Fruit Loops or Oatmeal? Love Mom," on the back of the paper and launched the missile back upstairs. A door opened and closed with a quick shuffling of feet in between, but no response, so I put water on for oatmeal.

"You're sure this skeleton is really old?" asked Gus. "It only takes a few months for a body to decompose under the right conditions."

"I'm sure. That blanket or whatever it was looked ready to disintegrate."

"Well, it had to be foul play. Even if he wanted to, nobody could wall himself into a steeple." Gus topped off his mug with the last of the coffee.

I took the carton of milk from the fridge and poured a dollop in his mug. "But why would anyone drag a body all the way up there? It doesn't make sense."

"Maybe he was killed inside the church."

"And another thing, wouldn't someone have smelled it…decaying?"

"It was way above street level," Gus pointed out. "All it would take to totally decay is a few months. Who else but the steeplejack ever goes up into the steeple?"

"Still, you'd think the bones would've been found long ago." I shook oatmeal from its box into the boiling water. "Ginger said the steeple was rebuilt in the fifties."

"So, if they took the steeple apart why wasn't it—he—found then?"

"Or she," I said. "It could be a woman. We don't know yet."

"Well, I've got to go." Gus rose and put his mug in the sink. "I've got negotiations after school today and then a school board meeting. I'll be late."

"Are you coming home in between for dinner?"

"Don't plan on me. I'll grab something. What are you doing today?"

"Meeting with Susan. Frank told her we'd come in to talk to her first thing. After that, volunteering in Molly's class, then probably grocery shopping."

"Well, have fun. I'll call later." He gave me a quick peck and grabbed up his briefcase. "'Bye you guys," he yelled on his way past the stairs.

From above came muffled giggling. I ladled oatmeal into two bowls and called them for breakfast. The response was another message shot down by Max who still had on his pajamas: "Wer not gone to skol today love Max and Molly."

The giggling now turned into high hilarity but I was no longer amused. "Max! Molly! Down here! Now!" I thundered. The voice that had once reined in a class full of rowdy eighth graders had about as much effect as a sneeze at Fenway Park on opening day. I moved into action, putting a foot heavily on the first step.

"She's coming!" squealed Molly in combined fear and delight. I heard them scuttle from his room into hers via the connecting door, then through the adjoining bathroom into the hallway at the other end, and pound down the front stairway. They'd rounded the corner from the living room and were sliding into their places at the table by the time I turned from the step. I gave them the Disapproving Look and slid two bowls of rapidly cooling oatmeal onto the table.

FIVE

I HAD ALMOST REACHED the door to the Parish Hall when I noticed that the debris hadn't been removed yet from the walk. I doubled back through the wrought iron gate and went next door to look at what I hadn't been able to see clearly the night before: bits and pieces of the steeple that the wind had sent hurtling out through the chicken wire. Behind a barricade of saw horses, the splintered wood—most of it small pieces blackened with age and rot on their unpainted undersides—was scattered over a good portion of the wide brick walk. There was one large piece about four feet long and three feet wide that had landed painted side up, a corner catching on the fence. I crouched down to look at it.

It wasn't a single piece but a series of tightly fit sections of paneling that interlocked every five inches or so. The broken edge revealed its marrow to be the honey color of new wood. The opposite side had come apart neatly along the seam, its mate most likely still standing in place up in the steeple. I felt along this smooth edge; there were no nails, no glue. How had it been attached? I ran my fingers down the back of the panel, over wood that had probably not seen daylight in more than two hundred years. At the bottom I felt an indentation.

I got down on my knees then and tilted my head to get a better look. A hank of hair fell forward and grazed water puddling on top of the bricks, but I ignored it, for I'd found something interesting. A wide groove, crooked yet uniform in width, had been cut along the bottom edge. I fit four fingers perfectly into it.

"Hello!"

I jerked upright, as if caught doing something forbidden, and scrambled to my feet, stuttering a greeting to a man who was grinning at me in amusement.

"A bit of work to be done, wouldn't you say?" Feet planted in the self-assured wide stance of a cowboy who'd just dismounted his steed, he wore a denim jacket and well-worn jeans that accentuated his lean build. He was handsome in a rugged boyish way with disheveled blond hair and an easygoing smile on a face reddened from exposure to the elements. From the fine lines around his eyes and mouth I guessed him to be in his late thirties, older than he had at first seemed.

"Yes. I was just looking at—uh, I was up there last night when the steeple—"

"Oh, yeah," he said, his grin widening. "Susan told me all about it."

I brushed off my pants, aware of the large damp spots on the knees and the ends of my hair that hung in wet clumps. "Andy Gammon," I said, summoning up some dignity. I stuck out my hand. "And you are?"

"Jason Snoud," he said, taking my hand in his rough, dry one. "Steeplejack."

"Oh, of course," I said, remembering the man I had watched dangle in near hurricane-force winds from the top of the steeple.

"Good thing nobody was on the sidewalk when that section came down." Snoud nodded at the piece I'd been looking at.

"Yes, it was," I said. "Actually, I'm glad you happened by. Being an expert on steeples, maybe you can explain a couple of curious details I found."

He shrugged but I could tell he was flattered. "Sure," he said. "Fire away."

"There's a cut out place under this section." I bent down and stuck my fingers into the groove. "See? It was done for some purpose—like maybe for a handle or something. But why would there be a handle in a stationary panel?"

Snoud squatted and ran his fingers along the bottom of the panel and then, as I had done, placed them into the groove. He looked up at me, the amused grin back in place. "Before factories, woodwork was done by hand," he said. "Craftsmen, being as thrifty as any other New England businessmen, often reused wood. This board here—" he thumped a knuckle on it "—could have originally been part of a piece of furniture or a structure, maybe even the first church they tore down."

"Oh." I thought about his answer for a moment, then filed it away for future speculation. "What about the way the paneling fits? Was it glued together?"

"Yeah, it would've been glued." He fingered a seam, then squinted as he looked up at the steeple. "That support seemed stable. It shouldn't've broken away."

"What about this side?" I touched the smooth edge of the board. "It's clean as a whistle. Did the glue evaporate?"

"There should be residue left." He frowned as he fingered the edge.

"Maybe it was never glued," I suggested.

"No. It would've been either glued or nailed." He got to his feet. "Well, I better go see firsthand what kind of damage we've got." He bestowed one last smile upon me. "Questions all answered?"

"All except how could a body have gotten up there?"

"Now, darlin'," he drawled, "that's the question of the day." He winked and strode off toward the church.

Frank was talking when I came in. "Here she is now," he interrupted himself.

"Good morning. Sorry I'm late."

"No, no, you're fine," Ginger assured me.

"We just got here, also," said Frank. His glasses, for once pushed up on his nose, magnified eyes that were bright and engaged.

"I want to say firstly that I'm impressed with your dedication to the church in investigating suspicious sounds," said Susan, a faint smile playing on her lips, "but I'm concerned that one of you might have been injured. That staircase is only marginally safe in the daytime."

"We were very careful," Frank assured her.

"Well, consider yourselves properly reprimanded." Susan made a show of brushing off her hands, then leaned forward. "Now, Andy, we have something to tell you." Under the straight line of bangs, her eyes crinkled up mischievously.

"Wait until you hear," said Ginger and Frank smiled knowingly. But before they could enlighten me, the phone rang.

Susan reached over a pile of books to snatch it up. "Reverend Tenney." She flashed a look our way. "Yes, that is correct." There was a pause during which Susan's eyebrows rose up underneath her bangs. "It sounds like you know about as much as we do, but if you want to come, you can." She returned the receiver to its cradle. "Well! Word travels fast. Barely nine in the morning and Don Santiago's calling from the *Daily News* wanting an interview about the body."

"How do you suppose he heard about it?" Ginger asked.

"He's a reporter: antennae are issued with the job," I quipped. "Now, what is this—" But before I could ask about the mysterious surprise that had been hinted at, the building shuddered with the forceful closing of the outside door and Nancy poked her blond head in the doorway.

"Mark Levenson—" she began.

"Good morning, everyone." Mark breezed past Nancy, who gave a little shrug and ducked back out. He grabbed a Windsor by its curved top and dragged it, screeching on the linoleum, up to Susan's desk. "I can't stay long. I have to open at ten," he said, checking his watch. "Now, tell me exactly how it was found."

"I didn't expect you this morning, Mark," Susan said pleasantly. Ginger darted a nervous look at Frank who was glaring at Mark, the muscles in his right temple twitching.

"This is an important historical find. I wish I had been called last night."

"But it had nothing to do with—" sputtered Frank.

Ginger put a hand on her husband's arm. "It was very late, Mark," she said, soothingly. "We didn't want to disturb you."

"Well," Mark said, mollified, as he fiddled with the back of his gold earring, "in the future I would like to be notified whenever something historically important is found, no matter what time of day or night."

"How did you hear about it so fast?" Frank demanded.

"I have a friend at the newspaper." Mark moved forward on his chair. "Now, tell me how you found it. Please," he added as an afterthought.

Ginger spoke up quickly. "The storm came," she began, "then there was a crash overhead. We climbed up into the steeple and then, Frank and Andy went out there with the wind blowing and the rain—"

"Go on," urged Mark, craning his neck like a greedy child waiting for a piece of candy.

"We shined the light on the broken support and inside was the skeleton," I finished for Ginger.

"And the missing tankard?" Mark prompted.

"The missing tankard?" I looked at Frank who pursed his lips.

"Andy, that's what we've been trying to tell you!" Ginger exclaimed.

"When Sergeant Wenninger came this morning to look at the body—er, skeleton—I examined the silver cup," Susan explained, "and I think there's a good chance that it could be one of the tankards that was lost during the fire of 1811."

"The silversmith has taken it away to determine for sure if it is!" said Ginger, barely containing her excitement.

"Then that person—whoever it is we found—could have been there—"

"Since 1811," Frank finished for me.

"But is that possible?" I asked. Frank shrugged but Susan shook her head.

"I don't see how," she said. "The steeple has been worked on so much throughout the years, including a complete restoration back in 1949; it just doesn't make sense that a secret closet wouldn't have been found before now."

Then Mark began asking questions. How was the body positioned, he wanted to know. Where exactly was the tankard? I answered most of Mark's questions, since Ginger hadn't been at the actual scene of discovery, and Frank, sitting stiffly with his arms crossed, refused to participate other than utter an affirming grunt here and there to back me up.

"Omigosh!" I said glancing up at the clock. "I have to run! I'm volunteering in Molly's class today." As if on cue, the Van Amburgs rose, also.

"I'll see you at the police station at eleven-thirty," I reminded Frank.

We trooped out of the office before Mark, surprised by the sudden desertion, could respond. Susan, a bemused look on her face, waggled her fingers in farewell.

SIX

ONCE A WEEK I attain VIP status simply by crossing the kindergarten threshold. It is not who I am that makes me important, but to whom I'm related. Upon my arrival, arguments break out over who's going to sit beside "Molly's Mom." I soak it up, fully aware of the years looming ahead when these same children will glance at me indifferently and Molly will undoubtedly scuttle, mortified, into a corner when I show my face on her turf. Still, sixty minutes a week is my limit for chasing after a gaggle of energetic six-year-olds who possess all the properties of playground balls.

"Oh look, class. Molly's mother is here to help!" God love Miss Cardigan with her disheveled curly hair and unlimited supply of theme aprons. A kindergarten teacher for twenty years, she still waxes believable enthusiasm when she sets out the crayons, scissors, and glue sticks.

While I helped sixteen sets of pudgy fingers cut, place, and glue construction paper pieces into sea animal collages I kept thinking about the steeple pieces lying on the sidewalk, specifically that panel of wood with the clean edge and the groove along the bottom. At eleven-twenty I excused myself to clean up. As I washed my sticky fingers, appreciating the tenacity of glue that was supposed to come off skin easily, I concluded that, even after two hundred years, there would be residue left on anything—paper or wood—that had once been glued. Jason Snoud was wrong; that side had never been glued. Moreover, I believed that panel had been altered—maybe even originally designed—with a grooved handle so it could be both removed from the outside and shoved open from the inside. A hiding place had been made in the support of the steeple with a purpose in mind.

"Mommy! Mommy!" Molly tackled me at the sink. "You're leaving early!"

When had she learned to tell time? "Just a few minutes, sweetie. I have an appointment." I gave up dabbing at dried glue on my jeans with wet brown paper toweling and gave her a quick hug. "I'll be back to pick you up in a little while."

At the police station I found Frank sitting alone on a slatted bench in the waiting room. Before I could sit down, a tall man with broad shoulders and the beginnings of a paunch approached.

"Mrs. Gammon, Mr. Van Amburg?" We acknowledged that we were and he curtly introduced himself as Sergeant Wenninger. He led us down a hallway to his office where we sat down on chairs with molded plastic seats. Noticing a crusty spot on my jeans above one knee I crossed the other leg over it. Wenninger eased himself into a worn upholstered office chair behind his desk, propped his elbows on the arms of the chair, and leaned back as if he were going to put his feet up, but didn't. "Okay," he said after the briefest of smiles. "Tell me about last night."

For the second time that day we related our story, with Frank doing the talking this time and Sergeant Wenninger nodding from time to time.

"It had been there for a long time," I added when Frank paused. "You can tell by that blanket or whatever it was wrapped in. And the bones, they looked gnawed."

"Mice," Wenninger said. "The place was once overrun by them."

"And it—he—was holding a silver cup," I said. "Reverend

Tenney thinks it might be one that was stolen in 1811. Could a person have been up there that long?"

Wenninger answered by raising his eyebrows and pulling his mouth into an inverted U: I don't know. "Anything else? Did either of you disturb the body?"

"No," said Frank at the same time I said, "Yes."

Wenninger looked at me. "I bumped it, remember?" Frank mouthed an "o" and nodded as I explained, "We saw something shiny under the blanket so I went to lift it but I bumped it and—" I shuddered, "the head fell off."

"So the skeleton was intact before you touched it." Wenninger stated it matter-of-factly, but I sensed reproach. He leaned forward and scribbled something on a pad of paper that lay on his desk. "Anything else I should know?"

Frank and I exchanged looks and then shook our heads. Wenninger pushed himself up out of the chair. "Thank you for coming in," he said. "If you think of anything else, call the desk and leave a message for me."

"Are you going to find out who the person was?" I asked.

He shrugged. "The state lab will determine how the person died. But if it's been as long as it appears, it'll be difficult to identity him."

"But they would try to, wouldn't they?" I pressed. "This person must have disappeared leaving people to worry about him."

Sergeant Wenninger smiled with exaggerated tolerance. "Anyone who may have been concerned over his disappearance would not be alive."

"I know that! But he—she—whoever—may have descendants still here in Newburyport. If it were me I would want to know whatever happened to Great-Great Uncle So and So who disappeared back in the eighteen hundreds."

The sergeant's smile was stiff. He glanced at the clock and shifted in his chair.

"What about the tankard?" asked Frank.

"What about it?" Wenninger said.

"Why did he have it?" I asked.

His answer was in the blank look on his face as he rose from his chair: who cares? Frank nudged me and we stood also.

"If you think of anything else give a call," Wenninger reiterated as he came around the desk and escorted us to the door. But the statement was for courtesy's sake. The implication was clear: a person who disappeared two hundred years ago was not a great concern of the Newburyport Police Department.

Outside on the sidewalk, we turned our backs to the wind that coursed down Green Street, funneled and intensified by the closeness of the buildings that lined its sides. "I can't believe this matters so little to him," I said, hunching my shoulders and stamping my feet for warmth. "We're talking about a human being. It shouldn't matter if he died yesterday or two hundred years ago."

"No, it shouldn't." Frank spoke into the collar of his coat.

"And if a crime was involved, efforts should be made to find out the culprit."

"Yes," Frank agreed, "an unsolved death like this could cast a shadow on the church, past and present."

I THOUGHT ABOUT what Frank had said on my drive home. He was right; if whatever had transpired in our steeple—which had culminated in a death—was ignored, there would always be a blight upon our parish. I took the idea a step further. That body and how it got there was now part of the church's past and, as historians appointed to update Frisch's book, Frank, Ginger, and I had the responsibility to find out the truth and add it to the written history.

I drove past the Historical Society on High Street. On a whim I did a U-turn and pulled up in front of the three story brick Federal style house that had belonged to a prominent ship owner whose descendants bequeathed it to the Society in 1955 to be used as their headquarters and museum. I pulled the bell knob next to the louvered door on the side of the house, the entrance commonly used, and was almost immediately greeted by a woman wearing a long flowered skirt that ended just above woolly gray socks and Birkenstock sandals.

She regarded me with polite interest as I stepped into the hallway and instinctively breathed in the essence of the house, a compressed mustiness caused by windows and doors kept shut against the menace of the outside environment. It's a smell I personally find pleasing, almost heady, and I often catch myself pausing in dank period buildings to drink in long drafts as if I'd just entered a florist shop.

I introduced myself and explained what I was looking for—records, diaries, letters, papers of any kind from the latter part of the 1700s to the beginning of the 1800s that would give information about members of the First Parish. Mary something—she said it so quickly I didn't get her last name—looked uneasy with my request. Or maybe it was all that sniffing she didn't like. Quickly, I explained my project for the church, leaving out, for the time being, any mention of a body.

"Are you a member of the Society?" she asked.

"I'm fairly new to town and haven't joined yet." Six years registered us as a newcomer in Mayta's book. "But I intend to," I assured Mary Something. "Soon."

"I'm just a volunteer so I don't know where papers from the 1700s would be," she said doubtfully. "We have boxes and boxes of personal papers and photographs and things that haven't been cataloged yet." She flapped her left hand backward at the room behind her, which looked like an office. "You would need permission from the director to go through them, anyway, and she's not in today."

"Oh." I looked with interest over Mary's shoulder where she'd indicated those boxes of things were, stalling to see if she would relent.

"I could give you a tour of the house," she offered as consolation.

"That would be lovely," I said at once, and dug out the admission price of three dollars. I passed a pleasurable half hour trailing Mary through three stories of rooms beautifully furnished in fine New England antiques. She was very knowledgeable, and pointed out unique pieces like a teak and ivory screen from the China trade in the living room, and a seventeenth century Dutch cradle at the foot of a canopied bed in an upstairs bedroom. Portraits of prominent Newburyporters of the seventeenth and eighteenth century hung throughout the house. I peered at the cards next to the paintings, looking for a familiar name. On the first landing of the front staircase, I found one.

Thomas Toole, ancestor, I was sure, of Jeannine Toole (whose feather hats and clashing clothes had entertained a young Ginger during long church services) had had his portrait painted in 1826. Toole was elderly at the time, his hair gray and his face jowly with an expression as somber as his clothes. His features were unremarkable other than an arrogant tilt of his chin. Noting my interest in the portrait, Mary pointed out Toole's hands resting on the arms of the chair in which he sat.

"Painting the hands with details of the fingers required a lot of work from the artist, and was therefore expensive," she explained. "You might have noticed that in many of the portraits the subjects have their hands behind them or tucked inside their jackets. Sometimes one hand is painted and the other one hidden. Both of Thomas Toole's hands are prominently featured, indicating that he was wealthy."

"What do you know about this man, Thomas Toole?"

"Oh, the Tooles were a very important family," she said. "Thomas was a ship owner. His grandfather, Nathaniel Toole, was one of the founding fathers of Newbury. One Toole was in the cabinet of President Pierce and one—I forget which—was mayor of Newburyport."

I murmured an appreciative sound. "Are any of the family around today?"

"That I don't know. Our curator might, though, if you come back."

We continued on our tour. Rooms that were not traditionally furnished held collections: clocks, ladies' fans, needlework, glass paperweights, silver. On the top floor, we lingered over a collection of nineteenth century toys. The third floor of a Federal house is a shortened story, and the cozy feeling of the lower ceiling and smaller windows with its happy and whimsical collection made the Toy Room a delightful place. On shelves perched stuffed dogs, monkeys, and bears with patches of fur loved off them, and missing odd eyes or ears. Tiny lead soldiers stood at attention next to a pair of colorful clowns, and fanciful dolls with painted china heads held court with their primitive rag counterparts. The more fragile toys were in glass cases, but most of the collection was displayed as if a child had arranged them, lovingly, democratically, with no regard to individual prestige.

"My favorite room," Mary said with warmth.

"It's charming!" I exclaimed, kneeling to inspect a miniature tea party in progress. Mary became more talkative then, pointing out a doll's minute sewing basket complete with threads and tiny needle, a "magic lantern," clay marbles, a tiny wooden barn with lead animals, a mechanical monkey. We oohed and ahhed over each trinket, and then mused over a child's life in the nineteenth century: the hardships, certainly, but also the pleasures, especially if a child's father could afford such delightful playthings. We might have continued chatting up there in that little room encapsulated in the nineteenth century for another half hour but the downstairs bell sounded. Reluctantly, we descended to the first floor.

"The director is usually here between ten and four," Mary said. "She can help you find what you're looking for." She picked up a brochure from the hallway table. "This tells about the Historical Society. The application for membership is on the back."

I thanked her and stood back to admit a man through the door before exiting.

"Good morning, Mary." His voice was familiar.

"Good morning to you, Ben," Mary replied. "What brings you here today?"

I placed the voice then: Benjamin Barrett, mayoral candidate, ex schoolmate of Mayta. He glanced at me and we exchanged polite smiles as I slipped out the door.

SEVEN

"WHAT'S A BEN BART?" asked Max over his hamburger. He shifted his eyes from a point beyond my left shoulder to my face so that I couldn't tell where he'd seen the words and read them for myself. It was his way of testing himself to see how well he could read and of testing me to see how well I recognized how well he could read.

I let him down; before I could check myself, I glanced over my shoulder out the big McDonald's window. Driving across the plaza parking lot, a red van decorated with balloons and streamers and a banner that proclaimed Ben Barrett for Mayor provided a colorful spot in the bleak setting. "Ben Barrett. He's running for mayor of the city," I explained to Max.

"You looked!" Max accused.

"I'm sorry, sweetie; I didn't mean to. You did a great job reading the banner!" But Max kicked the underside of the table and pouted. It didn't count unless I understood what he read without looking. Next to him in the booth Molly wiggled.

"Stop it!" Max rammed her shoulder with his. Molly screamed in protest and rammed him back. And then arms were flailing and French fries were airborne. The others in the restaurant, mostly senior citizens at that time of the day—mid-afternoon—watched us surreptitiously while I dived over Happy Meal boxes and grabbed for whatever body parts I could make contact with. I surfaced holding aloft Molly's wrist and Max's empty jacket sleeve, which still rendered him incapable of moving as he wasn't able to disengage himself from the rest of the jacket. Then I stared at them in shock, an expression meant to impress upon our audience that outlandish behavior on the part of my children was a rare occurrence. After uttering low, terse threats that included corporal punishment and denial of TV for the rest of the century, we settled back down to our meal.

"Mommy, can we have a balloon?" asked Molly.

"We'll see," I said, wiping ketchup off the sleeve of my coat with a napkin. "You'll have to be very good for the rest of your dinner."

When we emerged from McDonald's, a light snow was melting into oily little puddles on the asphalt. In the middle of the parking lot, equidistant to McDonald's, Shaw's Supermarket, and Kmart, the campaign van had set up shop. A handful of perky young men and women were greeting and handing out balloons to passersby.

"Come on, Mommy, let's get a balloon," begged Molly, pulling on my hand.

We crossed the parking lot and waited in a small group of other moms with children. I hoped Mayta hadn't picked this time to do her grocery shopping. I'd be hung out to dry if she saw me standing in front of a Ben Barrett campaign van.

"Ben Barrett for mayor!" exclaimed a red cheeked girl, handing a balloon each to Max and Molly and thrusting a brochure into my hand.

On the way home we stopped at the library. I settled the kids down with a pile of books on the carpeted floor of the children's room and dashed downstairs to find the article about the fire that Ginger had mentioned.

Staffed by volunteers, the Newburyport Room is only open when someone has signed up to work there. I entered the room with a whoosh of its hermetically sealed door and, as luck would have it, found that not only was there a volunteer on duty but it was someone who knew where to find information on the Great Fire of 1811. In no time at all I had a copy of the article Ginger had recommended and was back upstairs just as the tenuous peace between Max and Molly was broken. I took away the picture book they were both tugging at, and whisked them into jackets and out the door under the tolerant but watchful eye of the children's librarian.

The light was flashing twice on the answering machine when we got home. "Okay, where are you now?" I punched the button.

"Hi, it's me," said my husband's voice. "We're going to be tied up with negotiations later than I thought and I'll have to go straight to the school board meeting from here. I'll be home in time to tuck everyone in. Love you!"

Click. Beep. And a second message came on. "Hi Andy. This is Frank Van Amburg. It's about five-thirty. Please give me a call at my home tonight."

I chased the kids upstairs to get into their pajamas early with the promise of half an hour of TV if they didn't complain. Then I looked up Frank's number in the church directory. He answered on the first ring. "Frank, it's Andy."

"Oh, Andy!" He sounded as if he'd run to catch the phone. "Thanks for calling back. I wanted to update you."

"Sure," I said. "Shoot."

"The state police came this afternoon. They took pictures and removed the body to Salem. Because of its age—you were right about it being at least a century old—they're calling in a forensic anthropologist."

"Can they tell anything yet?" I asked. "Like male or female, age, cause of death?"

"No. Other than to say it had been up there more than a hundred years, they didn't comment. They were real professional."

"Wow! Think of that—all that time holed up there and nobody knew."

"Hard to believe, huh?"

"Well, you've been a busy bee since I saw you this morning," I said. "Have you been at church all day?"

He laughed. "I went back after lunch and helped Nancy put together the newsletter for the week. It was just an excuse to hang around," he admitted.

"What about the silver cup? Anything new on it?"

"It's still being analyzed by the silversmith. But it matches one of the others in the collection, so I'm betting that it's one of the missing ones."

"Don't they all match? I thought they were a set."

"No. The tankards were acquired over a period of years. Only rarely did a parishioner give more than one piece of silver at a time—the expense, you know—so most of them are slightly different in size or ornamentation," he explained. "It's unusual that the two lost tankards were a matched pair given by Merriman Tibbits in 1776. And what's even more unusual is that, according to the records, they matched another lidded tankard that was given to the church the same year. So we're able to compare the one we just found with one in our possession."

"I'd love to see all of the church silver," I mused. "Where is it kept?"

"In a bank vault nowadays," said Frank. "But Susan and I were discussing the possibility of putting the silver plate on display during a service sometime soon."

"As a kind of celebration?"

"Yes, something like that," said Frank. "It's just so fantastic that we should find one of the lost tankards after all these years."

"What do you think, Frank? Has Mr. Bones been up there since 1811?"

"It's beginning to look that way."

"I'm dying of curiosity," I said. "Who was he and how did he get up there? Why did he have the tankard? Where's the other lost tankard?"

"Good questions."

"Yeah," I said. "Maybe we could find out the answers."

"We? What do you mean?"

"You talked to Sergeant Wenninger today, Frank. How much investigation do you think he's going to do into the mystery of Mr. Bones?"

"Not much, but the state police—"

"Will perhaps find out the age, sex, cause of death, and some other particulars about the bones," I said. "But neither Sergeant Wenninger or the state police will try to figure out who that person was or why he was there. Whatever happened is too long ago to matter to them. They have more pressing recent crimes to solve."

"You're probably right," said Frank.

"If we want to know who Mr. Bones was and how he came to be in the steeple clutching a tankard that's been missing for a couple of centuries, we'll have to find out for ourselves," I pointed out. "After all, it's our task to learn as much as possible about the background of the church for the new edition of the history."

"And whatever took place in the steeple is part of that history," he agreed. "I'll look in the records for any mention on the construction of the steeple, specifically why one support might have a hidden compartment."

"And I'll go to the library tomorrow to see what I can find out about missing persons in 1811," I said. "I'd like to get a look at that support in the daylight."

"I would, too."

"Okay, then, how about tomorrow morning during kindergarten time?"

Frank sighed. "I have a physical."

"Oh. Well, how about Monday, then?"

There was a pause during which I presumed he checked his calendar. "Yes, Monday is free. What time?"

"Nine?"

"Sounds good. I'll see you at the church then."

IT WAS GUS'S TURN to be all keyed up when he got in that night—too late to tuck anybody but me into bed—so I poured us some wine and we perched on stools at the kitchen counter. I was patient while he talked about negotiations for the new contract. With a balky school committee and a slow economy, it was going to be a tough fight this year just to keep the benefits they already had, never mind salary increases.

When he paused for breath, I took my turn. "Remember that silver mug we found with the skeleton?" I told him about the speculation on the tankard.

"When will they know something?"

"The tankard is being analyzed now, but it could be a while before we have definite information on the bones. And even then, information about the person—age, how long dead, that kind of thing—won't tell us who he or she was or what happened." I sipped my wine. "So Frank and I are going to investigate on our own."

"What do you mean, 'investigate'?"

"You know—do some research to figure out who he was. I'm going to look for missing persons of the time. Frank's going to check out the history of the steeple."

"I don't know if you should do that." Gus set his glass down with a sharp clink of stem base against counter top. "Maybe you should leave it to the police."

"Gus Gammon, I'm surprised at you! We're talking about our church." For the second time that day I found myself expounding upon my rights as parishioner. "Whatever happened in that steeple, including the identity of the person who died there, is our business. I was asked to research the history of the First Parish—specifically the current building—and the steeple is part of what I'm supposed to research."

"All I'm saying is that Lew Wenninger might not appreciate civilians trespassing on his turf. Finding a dead person makes it a police matter."

"It's our matter, also, and I intend to find out who that person was. Wenninger won't—he as much as said so this morning—and it's not right for somebody to die anonymously. He should be buried properly with a name on his grave."

Gus raised his eyebrows but didn't say what he was thinking. Instead, after a beat he said, "How can you find out who it was after all these years?"

"There are ways." I raised my eyebrows back at him. "I didn't spend all those years in college archives for nothing."

"Well, good luck," he said, rising from the counter. He picked up the wine glasses and set them in the sink. I followed Gus upstairs where he first batted a deflating balloon out of his way, then grabbed the dangling ribbon and pulled the balloon up in front of him. "Ben Barrett!" he exclaimed, reading the lettering.

"Hugh! You'll wake the kids."

"Do you realize this is the guy who wants to cut our benefits?"

"Shhh! What do you mean?"

"He's on the school committee! Didn't you know?" Gus's voice had lowered but the words came out with the same vehemence. "He wants to cut programs—"

"Oh for Pete's sake, Gus, it's just a balloon. They were handing them out up at the plaza. It doesn't mean I'm going to vote for him."

"If he becomes mayor of Newburyport," Gus sputtered, reminding me at that moment of his mother, "our school system is going to suffer!"

EIGHT

THE KIDS WERE still sleeping when Gus kissed them and left early the next morning to get some planning done before classes. On his way out he said there might be another meeting after school. I protested; it was Friday, after all. He assured me it would be a short meeting if there even was one. With Gus as building rep for the Teacher's Association I could see the handwriting on the wall.

"Don't get home too late," I called after him. "Mayta's taking the kids overnight and I thought maybe we could catch a movie or something."

"Great!" He waved a hand as he tossed his briefcase into the passenger's seat.

Although it was windy and raw, the sun had come out so I bundled up the kids and let them walk the three blocks to school. Then I stacked the breakfast dishes in the sink, poured a fresh cup of coffee, and curled up on the couch with the church history, Mayta's books, a pencil, and a legal pad. Since the library didn't open until almost the time I had to pick up Molly from kindergarten, I'd have to save my side research (who was Mr. Bones?) until after school when Mayta would have the kids.

I opened Etta Mae Frisch's book and skimmed through the early parish history, starting with the "nonconformists" who, in order to escape the persecutions of Charles I, came to the New World and established the Parish of Newbury in 1635.

I could envision that first settlement hugging the banks of the Parker River at the edge of a vast and hostile wilderness, its inhabitants reluctant to sever the watery connection to their homeland. I could see them muddying their heels and hems as they somberly trudged back and forth between mean houses with stingy windows that let in scant patches of light and the crude meeting house that would have been the center of the community. Even though the sky was just as blue, the snow as white, and grass as green as they are now, I always picture colonial times in gradients of gray: the color of weathered wood, angry seas, snowless winters.

I took a sip of coffee and read on. Before the days of separation of church and state, parishes levied taxes to support public worship and education and to erect public buildings. When colonists in western Newbury demanded the right to establish their own parish, Newbury initially refused, not wanting to lose taxpayers. Eventually the separatists won out and the West Newbury Parish was established. This paved the way for another settlement that had developed at the mouth of the Merrimack River, and had grown greatly in commerce and shipbuilding, to present a demand for its own meeting house. Once again, the request was reluctantly granted and a third parish, Newburyport, was carved out of the original tract.

In 1725 the Newburyport meeting house was built, its steeple rising amid the masts of ships docked at the wharves on the Merrimack River. With its first minister, Jacob Lovell, a long tradition of liberalism began. By now I was beginning to recognize recurring names. A Tibbits—William—was among the first colonists, it was a Tibbits, along with others, who petitioned for the separation of Newburyport from Newbury and—skipping ahead—I found a Tibbits who spoke at the 150th anniversary of the founding of the parish.

Likewise, Rands, Browns, and Tooles, among others, were

sprinkled throughout the history. On impulse I took out the telephone book and sure enough, I found a smattering of the same surnames listed, preceded by Thomas or Linda instead of Tristram or Asa. Idly, I wondered if there were any Tibbitses or Rands in the present congregation. I made a mental note to check the church directory at a later date, and settled back down with the Frisch book, taking up with the 1700s.

Life in the new parish was full of anxiety: belief in witches lingered, deadly epidemics struck with fair regularity, Indian attacks were still a danger, and, with Canada so close, there was the threat of French encroachment. The northern lights were first observed—and feared—around this time. A host of natural disasters—earthquakes, droughts, snow in summer, and swarms of caterpillars and other pests that destroyed crops—led to a rise of religious hysteria. An English zealot who spoke at the meeting house in the 1740s charged the congregation with evilness, and took away with him 143 members, much to the dismay of Reverend Lovell. Nevertheless, the parish continued to grow. The meeting house was enlarged once, and by the late 1700s there was talk about building a new one.

Thus far there had been nothing on the silver tankards, although I recalled they had been acquired during this period. Figuring that Frisch might address it in a later chapter and, as there was no index at the end of the book, I decided to continue on page by page, as I had been doing.

The town grew up around the old meeting house on the waterfront. The market place evolved next door, while at the wharves Newburyport's shipbuilding industry matured to world prominence. The meeting house itself became part of American history when its spire was shattered by lightning and Ben Franklin came to study it (which led to his presentation on electricity in London). The bell in its steeple rang for liberty from the British and announced the visits to Newburyport of

John Hancock and George Washington. Its pews held patriots who cried out for revolution. Tea was burned in protest on its doorstep, and just beyond its windows troops drilled and men marched to war. It must have been heart wrenching when the congregation made the decision to raze the shabby building, sell the lot to the town, and rebuild on a newly laid out street away from the waterfront.

This brought me up to the present meeting house, built in 1801, which came to be known as the First Parish meeting house, the one I needed to focus on for my research but before I could start reading, Mayta stopped by. A slight chemical smell wafted through the door as she breezed by me on her way to the kitchen. Her hair was freshly silvered, with perfect nickel sized curls covering her head.

"Nice 'do," I commented.

She gave me a murderous look that ended the subject.

I poked my nose in the small bag she'd plunked on the table. "What's this?"

"Chocolate croissants from that new bakery," she said, a bit crankily.

I wiped breakfast crumbs off the table and put on water for tea. Mayta immediately brought up the skeleton, making the point that she'd heard about it from her hairdresser, which clued me in that it wasn't just her hair she was peeved about.

"I called yesterday and you were out," I said in defense. "If you had an answering machine I could have left a message."

"You could've called back or come out. The door's always unlocked and I'm never gone long." She bit into her croissant.

"I was going to try this morning until I remembered your hair appointment."

"Don't bring that up again," she warned. And then, because she'd spent enough time admonishing me and was anxious to hear about the skeleton, she said grudgingly, "Okay. Now tell me all about it." And instantly her good humor, always just under the crustiness that is Mayta, was revived.

So I told her everything.

"You touched it?"

"Well, yeah. Accidentally."

"They had contagious diseases back then. What if you got infected?"

"I didn't get infected."

She squirted honey out of a plastic bear into her tea. "It coulda been someone accused of witchcraft. Perfect place for a witch to hide—in a church."

I licked a chocolatey finger and looked askance at her. "That was Salem."

"In the seventeen hundreds we had a convicted witch here in town. She was kept under house arrest for the rest of her life. It was in the newspaper a couple of years back."

"Yeah, well, the witch craze was over long before the church was built."

"What about the Underground Railroad?" She pushed the honey bear in my direction and fingered the contents of the fruit basket in the middle of the table. "They hid escaped slaves in houses around here. Maybe churches hid 'em too."

I stirred my tea and considered it. "One of the ministers was an abolitionist. He wasn't popular and didn't last long but maybe they hid slaves during that time."

"That could explain why there was a hiding place up there." She pointed at some peaches with shriveling skins. "What are you going to do with these?"

"Oh, nothing, I guess. They're too ripe," I answered distract-edly. "But why would somebody have been left up there? And there's still the question of the tankard that was lost years before—in 1811. How did it get there?"

"Maybe it was found by the person who got himself locked

in and couldn't get out—or was killed and stuffed in there."
Mayta picked up the peaches. "Mind if I take these? I'll make
Peach Brown Betty for dessert tonight. You coming for
dinner?"

"Sure," I said in answer to both questions.

"The kids are still staying over, aren't they?"

"You bet," I assured her. An offer of overnight babysitting
on a Friday night; I'd back out on a deal like that?

"I'll cook early so you and Gus can go out afterwards. See
a movie or something. I know you haven't had much time
together lately."

"You've got that right! The association is negotiating a new
contract and Gus has been so busy with meetings, you'd think
I was married to a Boston executive."

She shook her curls in disgust. They glinted in a ray of
sunlight like newly minted coins. "They'll have to fight tooth
and nail to get a pittance of a raise."

I uttered a noncommittal, "Hmmm." Mayta had enough fuel
to feed her fire.

"Well, they better settle their contract before the mayoral
race in the fall," she continued. "Ben Barrett's running on a
platform of cutting the budget, you know."

"That reminds me, what were you hinting at the other day
about him? The kids aren't around now so you have no excuse
not to tell me."

"I wasn't making up any excuses," Mayta rebuked.

"Okay, okay. So tell me."

She leaned forward and rested her arms on the table,
drumming gnarled fingers on its surface. "Back in the seventies, before Barrett was mayor for his first term, a committee
was formed to restore downtown. You wouldn'ta known Newburyport back then; the old brick buildings were in shambles
and some were abandoned. Train service had been cut off

'cause there weren't enough people using it. Once restoration of the town got going there was interest in bringing back the train and Barrett was the leader of a group that began working on it. That's how he got elected: he promised to get state monies to repair the tracks and build a new station."

"Sounds good to me," I said. "I would've voted for him."

"Yep, we all voted for him," Mayta twisted her mouth to one side and nodded slowly. "When Barrett became mayor, his committee, with his brother Richard as new chairperson, set about applying for grants and loans. Then, when everything was going along nicely—they were getting donations and a state grant came through an ad hoc committee of people who felt that the mayor's committee wasn't moving fast enough, formed." Mayta drummed her fingers again, faster and louder.

"Okay, so what happened to cause Barrett's fall from grace?" I prompted.

"The chairman of the ad hoc committee—I forget his name—challenged the mayor's committee to account for their funds. Everybody thought this guy was just being petty 'cause his group hadn't gotten the donations that the mayor's committee was now getting. But then the mayor's committee couldn't account for a good portion of the money and people got mad. Barrett kept covering for his committee, looking like a fool, until suddenly the money was all accounted for. Just like that. It's missing and then it's there." Mayta slapped the palm of her hand on the table.

"So where had it been? Was it an error in bookkeeping?"

Mayta put on a knowing look and shook her head slightly. "There was some story about entries that mistakenly weren't made, which was believable enough except that half of the mayor's committee—the ones who weren't his cronies—quit in anger. Made the public think that they knew something we didn't, like maybe Barrett was covering for himself or his brother." Mayta reached over and picked the peaches out of the basket, then rose to her feet, using the table for support.

"There were never any formal charges made, but a lot of us thought that one of them—Ben or Richard Barrett—had been playing around with the committee's funds. Richard Barrett moved away some time after that, so maybe it was him. I don't know. I've just never completely trusted Ben Barrett since, even though he got reelected, and what was left of his committee joined with the ad hoc committee after its chairman—the guy who'd first made the accusation—left, and the train and tracks did eventually get restored. Seemed like Barrett lost steam after that and started digging in his heels against growth and change."

I gave her a bag to put the peaches in and walked her to the door, digesting what she'd said. "But everything turned out okay."

"Yeah, I guess it did," Mayta said grudgingly. "How about I come by around three-thirty to get the kids? Then you can get to the library before Gus comes home."

"You don't have to do that. I'll bring them out."

"I've got an errand to do in town this afternoon, anyway. We'll have dinner at five. Sound okay?"

"Sounds great," I said.

I called school and left a message for Gus to meet us at Mayta's for dinner. Then I took up where I'd left off in the Etta Mae Frisch book—the chapter that described the building of the 1801 meeting house. I read about architectural details that I'd taken for granted, having never separated them from the overall beauty and grace of the Colonial style building: the Corinthian pilasters and Ionic columns, the fanlight over the center door and the elegant spire that has been called the most beautiful in New England, all crafted by skilled ships' carpenters and finishers.

I'd just begun the section on the layout of the pews, how they were numbered, divided into classes, and valued monetarily according to desirability of location, when the telephone rang. My intention to let the machine take a message was aborted when I recognized the voice of the school nurse.

I snatched up the receiver fearing the worst: Molly had tumbled off the climbing structure and broken an arm; Max had fallen on the pavement and knocked out a tooth.

NINE

THINKING BACK TO the morning, I should have paid attention to indicators foretelling that forces in the universe were unbalanced. If I didn't catch on when I got out of bed and felt the fat in my thighs slide down towards my knees, I should have definitely known it was a Gravity Day at breakfast when Molly bumped her cereal bowl off the table with her elbow less than three minutes after Max tipped over his cup of juice for the second time.

Thankfully, the nurse hadn't called to notify me of a broken arm or a knocked out tooth. It was, however, a pussy willow lodged in Max's ear. It seemed that, while making a nature collage, Max rubbed a soft furry bloom on his cheek and it "fell" in. Once in a while I believe my children when they tell me these things and this was one of those times; I knew gravity had sucked that pussy willow down his ear canal.

I picked up a scared little boy and took him to Dr. Janes who peered in, made one mining attempt with a long skinny instrument, then sent us to the ear, nose, and throat specialist down the hall. This was not going to be simple.

What followed was an hour of high tech torture in a cubicle that looked like the cockpit of an Army bomber during which the doctor picked and flushed and clucked and shook his head. Every flinch poor Max made and every tear that rolled down his cheek tore at my heart. At last the pussy willow was flushed out intact and, after a final admonishing on the dangers of putting objects in body orifices, we escaped, limp as a couple of overcooked noodles.

We decided to blow off school for the rest of the day and celebrate our survival of the ordeal with two hot fudge sundaes at the ice cream shop. By the time we were scraping our spoons against the bottom of our tulip glasses, Max had happily recounted his pussy willow experience to the waitress, an elderly couple in a nearby booth, and was now telling it to me as if I hadn't been there. I knew he was practicing the story to tell his friends in school on Monday. The ordeal was an adventure now that it was in the past.

"Andy, Max! Hello!" Susan Tenney slid onto the stool next to Max.

"Oh, hi, Susan. On your lunch hour?" I asked before realizing it was almost two o'clock.

"No. I just came over for coffee. Nancy and I take turns getting it. We could make coffee in the kitchen but this gives us a chance to get outside on these nice days." She raised a hand for the waitress and then turned her attention to Max. "What are you doing out of school?"

That launched Max into telling his now perfected story. I cut him off when he began to embellish it with details inappropriate for the ice cream counter. Susan was duly impressed and, thankfully, did not come back with a tale about an acquaintance who stuck a bean in his nose or got a fly in her ear the way some listeners had.

The waitress came over then and scribbled Susan's order onto her pad. When she left I asked Susan about the tankard.

"Oh, yes!" She leaned in front of Max who was now rotating in complete circles on his stool. "Ben Worthy at Silvercrafters has determined that it is indeed the mate to one of the tankards in our collection. He's going to polish it up." She lowered her voice and leaned closer. "Do you realize what a valuable find this is?"

"It must be worth thousands of dollars."

"Oh, many thousands of dollars," Susan said. "But that's not what I meant. You and Frank have recovered a priceless relic from our past."

"The other tankard that's missing—it matched the one we found, didn't it?"

"Yes, they were lost at the same time."

"Frank said they weren't with the other silver that night," I said. Max was now spinning on his stool, a celestial body whirling on its axis, threatening to propel itself out of its orbit. I grabbed a flying elbow and brought him back to planet Earth. "Do you know why?" I asked over his bobbing head.

"I looked it up today," she said, giving Max an amused smile. "Apparently they'd been put in the pulpit for some reason that is no longer known—perhaps the minister, Reverend Andrews, used them in a ceremony. Then, before they could be put back safely, there was the commotion of the fire and they disappeared."

"When did they discover the tankards were gone?"

"Right away. Members came at the onset of the fire—within the hour—to remove valuables and found them missing. Oh!" Susan reached into her skirt pocket and brought out a triangular scrap of paper that she laid on the counter. "Ben found this inside the tankard." The scrap, a corner torn from a larger piece, had the letters LL written in large slashing strokes, the ink faded brown with age.

I picked it up and turned it over, feeling the paper's heaviness and rough texture. There was nothing on the other side. "I wonder what LL means."

"That'll be a dollar sixty." The waitress set a small bag on the counter and watched Susan curiously as she dug into her pocketbook. When Susan handed her the money, she said, "Are you the minister of the church that found the skeleton?"

A corner of Susan's mouth turned up in amusement. "Well, yes I am."

The girl wet the middle of her top lip with her tongue. "Is it true he was murdered?"

"We don't know the cause of death yet," Susan said firmly.

"It's what they're saying." The waitress shrugged and turned on her heel, her ponytail swishing across her shoulders.

"Who was murdered?" Max said in his high clear voice. He'd frozen in mid-twirl and was now the model of attentiveness. "Was it the dead man you found in the steeple, Mommy?" Several heads turned our way.

"Max," I said in distress, "how did you hear about that?"

"Everybody at school knows it."

"We found somebody who died a very long time ago," Susan told him quietly. "The person might have died of an accident or sickness."

"Then, how come—" Max started.

"Goodness, look at the time!" I exclaimed. "Molly got out five minutes ago. We've got to run!" I slapped some bills on the counter, along with some change, and grabbed Max's hand. We said goodbye to Susan, and ran all the way to the parking lot. At the car I found that I still had the scrap of paper in my hand. I shoved it into my jeans pocket, thinking I'd give it back to Susan the next time I saw her.

WHIP-WHIP-WHIP. The microfilm spun forward, its sound rising in pitch with the speed. I released the knob and the film squealed to a stop. I checked the date. Then I twisted the knob to the forward position—whip-whip-whip—again. Too far forward. I reversed it with short whining starts and stops until I found what I wanted. The *Herald* of May 31, 1811 consisted of short articles and announcements separated from each other by lines that paraded down three columns on two pages. There were no drawings, logos, or large eye-catching headlines.

In the hours before the Great Fire of 1811, Newburyport's greatest catastrophe, its citizens were reading about ships that had arrived in port, what was happening in the Massachusetts Legislature, and a Virginia woman who committed suicide by taking a "considerable quantity of laudanum procured through the means of a child from an apothecary." With minor alterations in vocabulary, I could have been reading modern day news.

I skimmed one article titled "Be prepared for WAR," an account—punctuated liberally with exclamation points—of an incident in which a British sloop of war boarded an American vessel off Cape Cod and took men, forcing them into the British navy. The author of the article blamed mercantile hardships on Jefferson's Embargo Act of 1807, which had forbidden American vessels to dock (and therefore trade) at foreign ports. Its ships languishing at the wharves, Newburyport had suffered greatly during the ensuing two years before the embargo was lifted. By 1811, problems at sea with Great Britain had escalated until war seemed imminent.

I scanned ominous words that were first read by nineteenth century butchers, lawyers, and shopkeepers pausing in their daily routines to tut-tut about a suicide or shake their heads at the impending War of 1812 (as it would be called), unaware that within a matter of hours they would personally suffer a catastrophe of a far more ruinous nature.

I whirred the film ahead one frame at a time. The next edition of the *Herald* was three days later. Had the publication shut down in the aftermath of the fire or had a copy not survived to be put on microfilm? An announcement, presumably from the editor, explained that foreign and domestic news had to be excluded from the paper because "in short, the gloom that overspreads our citizens occasioned by the late dreadful calamity, hardly permits them to enquire the news of the day."

Two columns were devoted to short thank you notes from private citizens to others in general, sometimes in specific, for assistance given in saving or attempting to save property from the fire. The town clerk thanked the people of Salem for their "spirited exertions" in coming to Newburyport's aid. Bravely looking to the future, a meeting to discuss new fire regulations to be adopted with regards to rebuilding was announced. There was a request that a green leathern bucket belonging to one J. Daniels, missing since the night of the fire, be returned. Then a heading caught my eye: "One Thousand Dollars Reward."

"Whereas there is reason to fear that the great and distressing conflagration of Friday night last, in this town, was occasioned by the wicked design of some incendiary, the Selectmen, at the request of some of their Fellow-Citizens, hereby offer a reward of ONE THOUSAND DOLLARS to be paid to the person or persons who shall discover and bring to justice the perpetrator."

The item was signed by selectmen of the city: Eleazar Rand, Thomas Toole, and Merriman Tibbits.

"The wicked design of some incendiary"—it was the first I'd heard that the Fire of 1811 was considered anything but an accident. What had given these selectmen "reason to fear" the fire had been set? Had they found evidence of arson? Eagerly, I forwarded the film, skimming through following editions for the next few weeks, months, the remainder of the year. The reward offer was not repeated and apparently nobody came forward with information on a perpetrator. No other mention or speculations were made nor details given to support the suspicion; if the fire was determined to be intentional, it was never addressed in print. Local news became focused on the future, on the rebuilding of the business section for those who were not so ruined that they were able to do so.

What had caused the initial suspicions of arson? Was it a frustrated attempt to place blame on someone or did it have basis in evidence? Why, after the published reward, was there no more mention of it?

"Excuse me, Andy, but the Newburyport Room will be closing in ten minutes." Gloria Trainor, the research librarian who had helped me find the reels I'd needed, touched my shoulder. I looked up at the wall clock and saw with surprise that it was almost six o'clock. Mayta would have served dinner to Max and Molly and to Gus, if he'd gotten my message to meet him there.

"I didn't realize it was so late," I said, handing her the two books I'd taken from the room. Gloria smiled apologetically and moved on to a round table where two high school kids were absorbed in research books and spiral notepads.

Since I'd gotten sidetracked and had forgotten to look for a missing person around the time of the fire, I quickly rewound the film to the first edition after the fire. I set the machine in forward slow motion and skimmed the columns once again. Two weeks after the fire, on June 13, I found what I was looking for:

RUNAWAY

From the subscriber an indentured apprentice to the bakery business, named Peter Chambers, 14 years of age, missing since the fire on May 31.

Whoever will return said boy shall receive a reward of ten dollars from James Stockwell.

They had saved me a plate of food and—oh joy!—some Peach Brown Betty, made from the fruit Mayta had taken from my house. Gus hadn't put in an appearance so I called and left a message at home in case he'd missed the two I'd left for him at school (concerning the pussy willow ordeal). Then, after apologizing profusely for being late, I filled Mayta in on the parts of Max's ear story he had skipped, and then my research work, while scarfing down a wonderful dinner.

"Did you know that there was suspicion that the Fire of 1811 was set deliberately?" I asked as an elated squeal came from the next room where the kids were watching TV.

She frowned. "I don't remember if I did. Did they arrest anybody?"

"No, but three days after the fire a thousand dollar reward was offered for information."

Mayta gave a low whistle. "That was a lot of money back then."

"Yeah. Something else interesting is that a fourteen-year-old boy ran away on the day of the fire. A baker's apprentice. There was a reward for him, too—ten dollars." I took a bite of dessert, letting peach, crispy brown sugar topping, and ice cream melt together in my mouth. Heaven!

"Ten dollars was also a decent amount of money back then."

"Mm-hmm."

"Oh, I get it," Mayta said after a moment. "You think he's your skeleton."

"Could be. It's somewhere to start."

"It would be coincidental for him to choose the day of the fire take off. Or maybe not," she countered herself. "He could have been waiting for the perfect time to run away and the fire provided it. Was the skeleton an adult?"

"I don't know."

"'Course a teenager could be as big as a man." Mayta handed me a mug of coffee and sat down across the table. "Supposing that's who it was, why would a baker's apprentice crawl up into a church steeple with a piece of church silver and die?"

"He could have been looting the church and hid in the steeple when somebody came in, then died because he was trapped or got overcome by the smoke."

Mayta looked thoughtful. "That would make sense."

I helped finish up the dishes and accepted a second cup of coffee. Then I dug out my notebook from my purse and flipped it open. "I've been meaning to ask you about some names I keep running across," I said. "Moody, Rand, Toole, Tibbits…"

"Old names in town," said Mayta, curling arthritic gnarled fingers around the base of her mug. "Toole, Rand, and Tibbits were founding families, I believe."

"Ginger Van Amburg remembers Jeannine Toole from her childhood."

"Hmmm." Mayta nodded. "One of the last High Street society ladies."

"Do any of their descendants still belong to the church?"

Mayta pondered a moment. "Let's see. Frieda Cole was a Rand and I think there are still some Tibbitses at church." She went over to the sideboard, opened a drawer, and shuffled through a mishmash of coupons, potholders, and kitchen utensils, then held up a sheaf of stapled pages. "Here it is. The church directory."

We flipped through it, finding two Rands, but no Tibbits or any of the other surnames in my notes. "These are new people." Mayta tapped a page with the side of her bent finger. "Jill and Eric Rand. They're from out west somewhere."

"Well, I guess *they* couldn't possibly be old Colonial stock, then," I playfully mimicked Mayta's dismissive tone. She shot me a sideways look that I ignored.

"I'll introduce you to the Coles. Frieda's father was a Rand."

"That would be great." I put my mug in the sink and glanced at the clock: seven-thirty. "I better go see if I can find my husband."

"What was it today, another association meeting?"

"Yeah, I don't think they're getting any closer on a contract." I leaned through the wide arch into the living room. "Come give me a kiss, guys. I'm leaving now."

"Just a minute, Mom. It's almost over." With their backs to me, it was impossible to tell which one had spoken. They were sitting side by side on the floor three feet from the TV perched on an old wicker foot stool. At home I would have told them to back up, but on Mayta's tiny TV screen the cartoon characters they were watching would take on the proportion of ants if they were any further away.

They hugged me and promised to be on their absolute best behavior and I thanked Mayta for dinner. Out on the porch, Mayta had me wait while she dashed back inside. A moment later, she handed me a gray booklet with bent corners.

"Almost forgot this. It had fallen behind the books." I looked blank so she added, "The booklet on the fire I told you about."

"Oh! Thanks." We had kisses around again before I left.

At home I found Gus asleep on the couch. Across the room the answering machine blinked three messages. The first was Don Santiago of the *Daily News* wanting me to call him before four o'clock, then mine asking Gus to meet us at Mayta's. Exasperated, I shook his arm but he just mumbled something and rolled over. I went to shake him again, then stopped to listen to the last message. It was from Mayta, saying she'd remembered something right after I left and had looked it up to be sure. William Tibbits, one of the founding fathers of Newbury, had a direct descendant who was a current member of our church: the mayoral candidate Benjamin Barrett.

TEN

HUMAN BONES FOUND IN STEEPLE. If there was anybody in Newburyport and its surrounding areas that didn't know that a skeleton had been found in the city's most picturesque steeple, he or she was now duly informed. The headlines were double their usual size, a clue that this was not the customary breaking-news story in Newburyport (a hike in the sewer bill, a row between members of the school committee or city council, a rabid raccoon sighting). Reading the Newburyport *Daily News* is not exactly like reading the *Detroit News,* for which I am exceedingly thankful. Still, HUMAN BONES FOUND IN STEEPLE sounded, on the surface anyway, like a distant cousin to MOB KINGPIN GUNNED DOWN IN STREET and I felt a bit queasy reading the splashy words on the top of my adoptive town's paper.

Don Santiago, on the other hand, had obviously relished his topic. Beneath a big color picture of the First Parish's steeple taken at street level, the bell platform prominent in the foreground, spire tapering to the weathercock against a backdrop of puffy white clouds in a blue sky, was his article outlined in red. It took up a good third of the page and was continued on the back page.

Santiago had interviewed the policeman who'd responded to the call, and Susan who said no, there weren't any plans to re-consecrate the steeple after the discovery of human remains. Then he interviewed Mark Levenson, who made some vague statement about our historical heritage, and Jason Snoud, the steeplejack, who said that maybe the skeleton hadn't been found during previous restorations because that part of the steeple had been lifted off intact. The bulk of the article was devoted to Frank's account describing in exciting detail how we had climbed the dark stairs in the storm and made the discovery. In conclusion, Santiago quoted Dr. Denise Fitzpatrick, a forensic anthropologist connected with the state lab where the skeleton had been taken, who said that—no revelation here—on preliminary examination, the bones appeared to be very old and that she couldn't comment further until tests were completed. I jotted down Dr. Denise Fitzpatrick, State Police Lab, Salem on a scrap of paper and stuck it on the refrigerator with a magnet.

"Good morning!" Startled, I jumped. Gus had come down the back staircase, footsteps soundless in his slippers.

"Good morning yourself," I said. "Sleep well?"

"Yeah." He looked sheepish as he put his arms around me. "Listen, I'm sorry about last night. I was just going to lay down and watch the news but I guess I fell asleep. I completely forgot that Mayta was taking the kids overnight."

"I left two messages at school," I said reproachfully into his terrycloth robe.

"I was out at a meeting for part of the day and when I got back, things were crazy in the office so I guess they forgot to give them to me."

"And I left you—"

"I know, I know. I should have checked the machine. I always forget about that darn thing." He held me tighter, as if to squeeze out the last vestiges of anger. Then we kissed and he released me. "So, what's new?"

I told him about Max and the pussy willow, reassuring him that Max was now in good form, and about the rest of my day including dinner at Mayta's. Then, because I couldn't resist it, I gave one last parting shot. "We could've had a night out."

"Andy, when things get calmer, we'll go out, I promise you. Mom's always begging to have the kids over." He took a mug out of the dishwasher, poured the remainder of the morning's coffee into it, and put it in the microwave. "Max is fine, then? No residual problems with the ear?"

"None."

"How's Mom?" He sat down at the table and I sat down across from him.

"Ticked off at you for not showing up for dinner, but otherwise good," I said. "You might want to give her a call. How are negotiations going?"

He rolled his eyes. "You don't want to know."

I tried a new subject. "Did you see last night's paper?"

Gus took the newspaper, which was turned to where I'd just finished reading. He turned the section over, shuffled the pages into order, then, noticing the headlines, began reading. I put away the milk, rinsed out the coffee pot, and wiped the counter, waiting for his reaction. He flipped to the back page and snickered once.

Finally, I said, "So! What do you think?"

"I think Santiago is plugging for a job as investigative reporter for the *Globe*."

"I was talking about the content of the article," I said. "Murdering somebody and stuffing him into a steeple isn't a joke. And just because it happened a long time ago doesn't make it any less of a crime."

"Aw, come on, Andy! You're being a bit dramatic." He shook out the paper and then turned to the sports section. "It hasn't been determined that anybody was murdered. And, yeah, it does make a difference that it happened long ago." He grinned. "The perpetrator isn't likely to be around."

I threw the dishcloth at him. "I give up. My own husband

doesn't take me seriously. You have to go out to the island to pick up the kids because I'm going to the library this morning. And while you're out there you can apologize to your mother for standing her up last night."

WHIP-WHIP-WHIR. I was seated back in front of the microfilm machine in my trusty old chair, the gray padded one with a broken spring on one side that goosed me whenever I forgot and shifted my weight dead center. By the time I was done with this project the library would be dedicating the chair to me.

I started with the *Newburyport Herald* of June 13, 1811, the edition in which the notice for the missing baker's apprentice had appeared. I reread the short paragraph, dropped a quarter into a slot on the side and made a copy of the page. Then I twisted the knob and the film crept forward. I scanned the columns for mention of the apprentice, Peter Chambers. The notice was repeated a week later, June 20, and then there was nothing else. If the boy had been returned it went unheralded in the news, which wasn't surprising. A returned baker's apprentice would not have been earth-shattering news. I'd have to go about this in a different way.

I set the microfilm again on the *Herald* of June 13. This time I moved backwards tediously, frame by frame, searching for anything that fit a pattern, anything that gave a clue as to why the fire seemed suspicious to its investigators.

Then, about three weeks before the Great Fire, at the beginning of May, there was a short article on an inside page near the bottom that was blurry and difficult to read. But I had caught the word "fire" so I moved the page higher on the frame and brought it into focus with the knob. It was an account of a small fire in an empty warehouse on Market Square. Luckily, a sailor had passed by and doused the flames before much damage had occurred. The fire marshal determined that the fire had been deliberately set and expressed concern that this was the second fire that had been started within the month.

Second fire! Bingo! With renewed focus I continued the tedious process backwards, looking for some mention of an earlier fire. And suddenly, there it was: an article written three weeks prior to the first one covering a small fire that had been caught before it became a catastrophe. As in the second case and the third one (the Great Fire), this fire had started in an empty building—a ramshackle tool shed this time—in the downtown section of the city. And again, as in the other two fires, the fire marshal labeled it suspicious. A pattern. Could there have been a firebug?

"Excuse me, Andy. I hate to bother you…" Gloria smiled apologetically. Behind her stood a tall gangly boy of high school age, an impatient look on his face.

"Oh, sure, be off in a sec," I assured them and copied off the page.

I PLUNKED TWO CUPS of apple juice on the table in front of Molly and her little friend, Courtney, then grabbed up the telephone which had begun ringing the instant the girls had come in from playing outside, shedding coats and demanding a snack. "Hello," I said into the receiver wedged between my shoulder and chin. "Oh, hi, Ginger. Just a sec, okay? Banana? Grapes?" I offered to the girls. In unison, they shook their heads no.

"Cookies! We want cookies!" Molly demanded loudly and then Courtney took up the chant. "Cookies, cookies, cookies!"

"Shhhh!" I reprimanded but made rapid movement toward the cookie jar, knowing that under general child law a parent on the phone is fair game. They continued their chant until I'd divvied out oatmeal raisin cookies onto two napkins.

"I'm sorry, Ginger," I said again when it was quiet. "You were saying something about the records—"

"I just came up here to the choir room and opened the chest," Ginger's voice was shaking with indignation, "and found it all in a mess."

"Is anything damaged?"

"I don't believe so. But one of the minister's journals was left open and on top with the lid resting on it. The binding is weak and could easily have broken."

A chilling notion occurred to me. "Is anything missing?"

"Oh dear me, I hadn't even thought of that. I'm still in the choir room—I brought the portable phone over here—so let me look again." She set the receiver down and while I waited I got the dishcloth from the sink and wiped up crumbs muddied by apple juice, creating swaths of clean surface around each girl's place.

A few moments later Ginger was back on the line. "The papers are out of order, some are folded over and the books are piled in every which way," she said, "but it doesn't appear that anything is actually damaged or missing. Although I can't tell for certain about missing because I can't remember everything—wait a minute." There was another pause during which I heard dry shuffling sounds because this time Ginger hadn't set down the receiver. "Oh, dear!" Her voice rose in anxiety. "I don't see the deeds to the pews record. You know, that big book?"

"I have it," I said quickly. "I took it the other night, remember?" I moved into the dining room to get away from Molly's and Courtney's excited chatter that was escalating into little girl falsetto. "I also have Reverend Andrew's book."

"Oh. Then it's probably nothing to worry about," Ginger said diffidently. "I was overreacting. Most likely it was somebody on the Historical Committee."

"Hmmm," I agreed. But I was thinking—and I knew she was, too—that nobody on the Historical Committee would have been so careless. Which raised the question: who else would be interested in a pile of old papers and books? "Maybe we should move the chest to a room that can be locked up," I suggested.

Ginger hesitated. "I hate to think we have to lock up our church records."

"We can't afford such a casual attitude if we want to preserve them," I pointed out. And then, since I'd begun it, I went ahead and expanded upon something that had been bothering me since we'd started this project. "These firsthand accounts are being stored as if they were last year's bestsellers stacked away in a box, exposed to humidity, temperature, pests, and handling by anyone on a whim."

"I guess we still think of them as ongoing rather than historical records."

I continued in a gentler vein, "What we have in that chest is a gold mine of handwritten history. I was reading in a newspaper the other day how people are relying more and more on computers and fax machines. Handwritten letters, journals, and rough drafts—expressions free from technological interference, fresh and revealing in their imperfections—are going to be as rare as hen's teeth in the future."

"You're right, Andy," Ginger said. "We've taken our history for granted. I bet where you come from they'd put all this stuff under glass in a museum."

"Records from the sixteen hundreds don't exist in the Midwest," I said dryly.

"Yes, well, let's hope our new Historical Committee finds a better way to store them. In the meantime I'll see about moving them to a room that can be locked."

After their snack the girls went up to Molly's room to play and I brought out my research. I opened the deeds book, and thought about my conversation with Ginger. It occurred to me that, as I'd been reading history of the church through the handwriting of its forefathers—the differing slants, sizes, spellings, and choices of words that gave clues to their unique personalities—these men and women had become individuals to me. The painstaking regular script that flowed unerringly onto page after page of the Women's Alliance minutes from 1880 to 1890 summoned up a picture of Miss Bettyann Luther, secretary of the committee. I was sure she'd been just as precise and modest in life, probably one of those nondescript persons often overlooked who, for anyone bothering to find out, glittered like a jewel underneath.

Likewise, I had a pretty clear picture of Colonel Merriman Tibbits, wealthy ship owner, whose bold strokes and choice of legal words dominated the pages of the tax books in the late 1790s. I could see him strutting around with his cane in his fancy breeches and white hair, persisting in wearing a three-cornered hat decades after it was out of fashion to show he'd been a colonel in the Revolution.

There were others, too, who'd begun to come to life through the written words they'd left. I wondered what future generations would glean from my generation's leavings. How much will computer printouts tell about us as a society? As individuals?

ELEVEN

THE FINAL DRAWN-OUT chord of the prelude, which had filled the church to its rafters and then spilled out the front doors onto Pleasant Street, cut off abruptly and was still reverberating in the air as I met up with Gus and Mayta after delivering the kids to their Sunday school classes. I had only glimpsed the back of Betsy Watson seated at the huge old pipe organ whenever I strained my neck to see up into the choir loft, yet I always imagined that she had an expression of pure joy as she whomped the keys fortissimo. I suspected her intent was to reach Sunday morning clammers on the flats down in the south end of town.

We hurried through the double doors of the sanctuary, took two orders of service from the greeter, and scurried into a pew as Susan took the pulpit and began the announcements. The pew, which already held four people, none of whom I recognized, was made more crowded by the fact that Mayta was wearing a wide-brimmed hat. I figured she was still a bit touchy about her hair.

"Good morning. We welcome you to our service and invite all to join in the social hour which will take place next door at the Parish Hall at the close of this morning's service," Susan's amplified voice informed us. "The Ladies Auxiliary meeting will be held this Wednesday at Frances Fenster's house."

My mind wandered as Susan continued. I noted that the sanctuary was almost filled. There were even a few people up in the gallery—unusual except during Christmas Candlelight and Easter services. A skeleton in the steeple was obviously good for business. My attention was drawn back to Susan's words: "So I hope you will come down front at the close of the service and look at our heritage, our silver, which the Historical Committee has put on display."

I sat up taller, trying to see over the heads to the front. "What's on display?" I whispered loudly to Gus. Nancy Freeman, her precision-cut blond hair brushing the collar of her navy suit trimmed in white piping, sat directly in front of us. She turned at my voice, mouthed "hi" and fluttered the three middle fingers of one hand at me. I smiled in a return greeting.

Gus put his mouth close to my ear and said in a low voice, "They shined up the silver and put it on display up front, along with the tankard you guys found."

I strained to see through the heads again. On the mahogany table, which usually held a flower arrangement, I caught a glimpse of a tall silver vase. The first hymn was announced and I stood quickly. Before my view was obliterated by the rising congregation, I was able to see the whole array of shining silver tankards and lidded flagons, along with other various low pieces I couldn't make out clearly.

Since I was in the middle, Mayta handed me the hymnal to hold for the three of us. I opened it to one of the revised hymns whose words were now gender and politically appropriate ("author of creation") but which, for me at least, had lost some of the spirit of the original version ("Lord, God almighty"). I had a hard time picturing the Methodist congregation of my youth belting out some of these new verses, but I supposed that they'd probably updated their hymnals by now, also.

As I sang with tepid interest, I looked around at the filled sanctuary. Close to the front was Frank, rising a head above others around him, his body canted to the left in order to share his hymnal with someone shorter—Ginger—although I couldn't see her. Also in the front, on the other side of the aisle was Mark Levenson, standing alone and erect, his long brown ponytail trailing down the back of a black vest. Idly, I wondered if the vest was leather.

"Pssst!" Mayta hissed at the end of the last verse, her hat brim knocking into the side of my head, "Do you see Barrett? He hasn't been to church in a while."

"How would you know? You're hardly ever here either," I whispered back.

She ignored the comment. "Probably knew there would be a crowd today and came to be seen. Maybe do a little campaigning."

I'd only seen him that one time at the Historical Society but I located Barrett right away standing next to an elderly woman and a young man three pews ahead.

"His mother and his son," said Mayta. "His wife died of cancer years ago."

Barrett looked like a mayor; there was a dignified set to his wide shoulders, and his thick dark hair grayed handsomely at the temples. Although heavy, he was someone you would call portly rather than fat. As he lowered himself into his pew he spotted Mayta and nodded, smiling.

"He sees you," I said under the commotion of everyone taking their seats.

"Old coot." Mayta tilted her face to the pulpit where Susan stood, ready to begin the morning's readings.

Later, while the collection was being taken, I watched Barrett share comments and good-natured grins with his neighbors. I thought back over the things Mayta had told me about him. Had he taken money from his committee? Or had someone else, like his brother, been responsible? The fact that

Barrett was reelected after the incident indicated that a majority of the voters had their faith in him restored. Or maybe they just cared more about Barrett's promise to cut taxes.

"Are you coming out to the island for brunch afterwards?" Mayta inclined her head to see Gus on my other side and her hat shifted so that it was cockeyed.

"No, we're taking you out," Gus said firmly. "And you're going to let us."

Mayta snorted but I could tell she was pleased. "I don't want to go to The Garden Restaurant. They serve rubbery eggs and the bread isn't homemade."

Gus sighed and we exchanged amused looks, recalling the last time we took her out for breakfast. "We thought we'd take you to Maxine's—your favorite," I said.

Then Susan began the sermon and I made a concentrated effort to pay attention. Not that I usually need to make an effort to listen to Susan; I enjoy the way she adds humor and a genuine down-to-earth compassion to her messages, often highlighting them with quotes from Thoreau and Emerson as well as contemporary thinkers. But for some reason, on this particular Sunday, my mind kept buzzing with thoughts. First of Ben Barrett and now of Mr. Bones. Who was he? How did he get up in the steeple? If he was the missing apprentice what was he doing in the church? Was he trying to escape the fire? Why did he have the tankard? And what about the letters on the scrap of paper—LL—what did it mean?

Gus bumped my elbow. It was time to sing the final hymn. Guiltily, I realized I had missed the last half of the sermon. As we rose to sing, I glanced over at Mark Levenson again and noticed that his pants matched his vest. I wondered if they were leather too. Stop it! I reprimanded myself sternly. But my thoughts were shooting stars, darting all over the place, eventually coming back to Mark. Then, something halted my flitting mind, pinpointing it at one spot with one hundred percent of my attention. There, at the junction of Mark Levenson's pants (leather or not) and his vest was the rail of the box pew and just below the rail next to the door was a brass number—seventy-eight. Suddenly, I had a thought; could LL be 77? I craned my neck to see the pew number in front of him—seventy-seven. I gave a small whoop that fortunately coincided with Betsy Watson's first exuberant chord of the recessional so nobody but Mayta and Gus, who whipped their heads in my direction in unison, heard me. Could the number on the scrap of paper refer to the number of a box pew? I rose and impatiently waited to exit the pew.

"Where are you going?" Gus asked as I pushed past him in the aisle.

"Up front to see the silver." Since most people either didn't stay to view the silver or paused for only a cursory look, I moved against a tide that streamed out to the vestibule. Close to the front, I stepped into pew seventy-seven, now vacated, and pulled the door closed behind me. Because of its location, it would have been one of the more expensive ones at the time of Mr. Bones' demise.

Most of the box pews are about eight feet long with roughly four feet of floor space in front of the bench. Some are equipped with built-in breadboards from the days when services lasted for hours and families brought their midday meals with them. Others have individual touches like foot stools or cushions. Number seventy-seven had a long, narrow box with a hinged cover, built under the seat of the pew in front, which had been used—according to Frank—for captains' brass spittoons. I bent down, raised the lid, and looked inside as if I might find something hidden there from two centuries before. Then I peeked under the bench seat, wishing the floorboards would talk to me. Other than the hymnal holders on the back of the bench ahead, there was nothing more to see. I slipped out of the pew and moved forward to join the small group at the front.

Frank allowed us time to look over the display, arranged on the damask-covered table, before beginning. Because none of the pieces except the baptismal bowl was used anymore, it was the first time most of us had ever seen the antique silver. We circled the table, admiring its rich patina, a soft glow unlike the brilliance of new silver. A matched pair of lidded flagons, about fifteen inches tall, flanked the display with the shorter items— the tankards, a vase, two large communion plates, and flatware— arranged artfully between. Most of the pieces were simple, their only ornamentation a fancy knob on a lid or an inscription.

"The silver was given individually or in pairs by some of our most influential early members. You'll recognize the names: Toole, Rand, Moody, Tibbits," Frank began, with a sweeping wave over the table. "The five tankards are the oldest pieces. They predate the signing of the Declaration of Independence." As Frank talked I picked out the tankard we'd found in the steeple. I read the graceful script on the pieces that were inscribed: "Gift of Nathaniel Toole to the First Parish of Newburyport, April, 1712"; "Presented to the First Parish of Newburyport by Eleazar Rand, on the occasion of the birth of his son, Eleazar Rand II, January 15, 1775." I dug out a pencil and scribbled on the back of my order of service.

"Fascinating, isn't it?"

Startled, I turned and found myself face to face with Mark Levenson. "Yes, it is," I said, stuffing the order of service into my pocket. "You read about these pieces but it's something entirely different to see them displayed like this." Why did this man make me nervous? Since I already sounded foolish I went ahead and asked, "By the way, did you happen to go through the records in the sea chest the other day? Ginger said it looked like someone other than us had gone through them."

Mark looked at me quizzically and gave a curt shake of his head. I turned back and was immediately caught up in a story Frank was relating about a sea captain, Nathaniel Toole, who, believing that he might die at sea during a pending voyage, vowed to give a gift to the church if his life was spared. The deal must have been acceptable to the Almighty as evidenced by two magnificent flagons, the most ostentatious pieces of the collection, now adorning the table. Frank paused a beat before adding wryly that a few years later, on another voyage, Toole had, alas, died at sea.

"Guess the bargain only worked once." The voice in my ear this time was Gus. I grinned at him and he draped an arm loosely around my shoulders. Scanning the small group, I saw that Mark had left.

Out front Max and Molly were sidestepping along the bottom rail of the iron fence. Gus and I joined Mayta who was chatting with an elderly couple.

"Frieda and Herb Cole, this is my daughter-in-law, Andy." Mayta beamed at me from under her ridiculous hat, then waved the back of her hand in Gus's direction. "You remember Gus, of course."

"Hello, Gus. Nice to meet you, Andy." I could've sworn they said it in unison.

"Andy is working on the Tricentennial Committee with Frank," Mayta said. "They're putting together a new book on the history of the church."

"It's more of an addition to Frisch's book," I explained. The Coles watched with wide expectant eyes, reminding me of a pair of chickadees. "We're adding to parts of it, especially from 1930—when the book was written—onward."

"Oh, that's just wonderful!" Frieda said eagerly and Herb bobbed his head.

"Andy, Frieda is a Rand descendant," Mayta said, giving her

words emphasis. "You asked if I knew any descendants of the founding fathers, remember?"

"Oh, yes!" I said. Then, recalling an inscription I'd just written down, added, "Didn't a Rand give a piece of silver to the church?"

Frieda pulled herself up so that she stood a smidgen taller than her mate. "That's right. Eleazar Rand presented a tankard in honor of his first born son. But there were Rands here long before. Amos Rand was an original settler of Newbury. If you would like, I could show you the family papers." She glanced at Herb and they both smiled. "We've been doing some genealogy."

"I'd love it," I said, knowing I didn't dare say anything else. Interesting as they might be, I doubted family papers would give me the information I needed on the church. Still, I made an engagement for afternoon tea at the Coles' house for a week from the upcoming Wednesday.

TWELVE

"Oops! Sorry. I didn't realize you had somebody—" I backed out of the doorway I'd just rushed through.

"Come in, Andy, come in." As she stood up, Susan bumped her desk and a tower of books swayed precariously. Steadying the stack with one hand, she waved me in with the other, and then gestured toward the man standing in front of her, whose tall lean build and tousled blond hair I recognized before he turned. "I believe you've met Jason Snoud, our steeplejack."

"Hi, Jason," I said. "How's work going on the steeple?"

"Haven't started any real work yet—I've just been stabilizing it," he said, smiling as he gave me a quick once-over, his eyes flicking down and up, taking measure. "That support's been rotting for some time," he said, turning back to Susan. "If it hadn't gone in this storm it would've gone in the next one or the one after that."

Susan frowned. "What about the other supports—are they rotting, too?"

"Nope, everything else seems stable."

"Why did that one deteriorate faster than the others?" I asked.

He shifted his weight, leaned one thigh against the edge of Susan's desk, and crossed his arms. "Could be 'cause it's the side that gets the brunt of the weather coming off the ocean, and more moisture got inside that loose panel."

"You would have thought that at some point during all these

years somebody would have found that loose board," I said, then added, "and what was inside."

Lines creased his forehead, then he shrugged and curled his lips into an engaging grin that I figured served him when words didn't.

"Maybe it wasn't loose until recently," Susan suggested. "When the steeple was rebuilt in 1949 the supports were fine so they removed the top part intact, by crane, to work on the section below it."

"Well, I just stopped by to see if Frank was here yet," I said, edging toward the door. "I'll go on over to the church. We want to see the damage in the daylight."

"It's unsafe," Jason said quickly. "Only authorized personnel can go up there."

"Do you suppose we could be authorized for long enough to take a quick look?" I smiled in what I hoped was a winning manner. "We'll be careful."

"Jason's right," said Susan soberly. "Until he's finished inspecting it completely, I shouldn't allow anyone to go up there. But," she hesitated as Jason shook his head disapprovingly, "I know you and Frank will be careful."

"Thanks, Susan. If Frank pops in will you please tell him where I am?"

"Oh, why don't you wait here?" Susan urged. "We can chat until he comes."

Feeling that I couldn't refuse without appearing rude, I sat down in one of the Windsor chairs while Susan finished her business with Jason. She fished around in her top drawer and handed him a key. "This is the only one I have at the moment, so I'll need it back when you leave for the day. I'll have more copies made soon."

"Aw, that's okay, I don't need a copy," Jason said, including me with a wink as part of his listening audience. "Mine'll show up somewhere—probably at home."

"You can leave it with Nancy if I'm out." Susan glanced at the door where Nancy had appeared, wearing a greenish-blue pantsuit with a short fitted jacket that showed off her trim waistline.

"Sure, okay," Jason said, but his attention had shifted. "Hi, Nance."

"Hi, all." She gave a dazzling smile, tilting her head so that a silky strand of blond hair fell across her cheek. "Andy, Frank said to tell you he's in the church."

"Oh, good. Thanks." I rose from my chair.

Jason's gaze followed Nancy out before returning to Susan. "I'll be back around noon," he said. He gave me a nod and left.

"Nancy's looking good these days," I commented, "new clothes, new hairstyle, looks like she's lost weight."

"Yes, she does look good," said Susan, hesitantly. "She's been working out regularly at the gym since her separation from Keith. It's a step in the right direction, I guess."

On the way over to the church I thought about Susan's comment. It was like her to be worried about something the rest of us didn't see; obviously Nancy wasn't coping as well with her divorce as it seemed.

The large paneled door to the church was wedged open about six inches with a granite paving block. In the foyer a woman I recognized but didn't know was holding a large painting of pale purple irises in a gilt frame. Ten more watercolors, each depicting a different flower, were lined up on the floor, leaning against the wall.

"I'm trying to place complementary colors together so I opened the door a little to get some natural light," she explained. "I hope you don't mind the cold."

"Oh, I don't mind," I said. "I'll be upstairs. Are all these yours?"

"Yes. I was flattered when Susan asked me to display my work this month."

"They're very good," I told her. "I like the lilacs next to the pink geraniums."

"Thank you. I'm just an amateur, though. Where do you think this one should go?" She meant the irises in her hands.

I studied the row of watercolors in pale and medium tones of color. "What about between the orange daylilies and the daisies?"

"Here?" She set the picture down and stepped back. "Yes, I like that. Thanks."

I found Frank in the choir room seated behind the long folding table, bent over a book swollen and mottled from moisture and age. He looked up as I entered, and shut the book soundlessly, its pages having lost their crispness more than a century before. "Good morning!"

"Where's the chest?" I asked after returning his greeting.

"We decided to keep it locked in the closet." He waved at the opposite wall.

"Good idea," I said. "I just saw Jason over in Susan's office. He was talking about the damage to the steeple."

"Oh, yes, I was hoping to run into him today. What did he have to say?"

"He said that side gets the brunt of the storms, and that the loose panel in the support must've allowed moisture to come in." I fingered the suede-like cover of the book in front of Frank, one of the early minister's journals. "I think it was never glued. I think somebody built or altered that support to make a hiding place."

"It's possible. There were abolitionists in the congregation back during slavery times; they even had an abolitionist minister for a while." He pursed his lips. "It's not likely they would have hidden slaves in the steeple, though—too risky."

I told him what I'd found out in the library, that a baker's apprentice had run away on the day of the fire and was never found. "It's a long shot, but maybe our Mr. Bones is this apprentice." He nodded thoughtfully. Then, watching for his reaction, I mentioned the reward for information on the perpetrator of the fire.

"They suspected arson?" he asked in surprise.

"So you'd never heard that, either," I commented. "I'll bring in the article to show you." I checked my watch. "Are you ready to go up in the steeple?"

The daylight helped immensely; I climbed out onto the belfry this time with less heart-hammering fear. There was a slight wind but the day was clear, enabling us to see out over the entire city laid out in a patchwork of odd sized parcels created by streets and roads that crisscrossed to form every conceivable geometric shape. A wide band of blue bordered one side where the Merrimack River, fat and sluggish at the end of its route from mountains to sea, met the incoming tide of the Atlantic.

I looked closely at the construction of the belfry. The upper tiers of the steeple rose above us, supported by four bases that curved upward from the corners of the bell platform to the ceiling, forming graceful arches along the sides. Each base was boxed in, giving a finished appearance from the belfry as well as from below. Skirting the bell, I joined Frank in front of the damaged support and peeked inside. There was just enough room to accommodate one average-sized person, more than enough room to hold the small person who had been entombed there. The interior was braced with new two by fours, their whitish color contrasting with the dark rotting wood. The floor, blackened with water stains, sloped down toward the back corner of the triangular space where it had broken away, creating a gaping aperture a couple feet long and about eight inches wide between floor and wall.

"No wonder the skull toppled off so easily," I said. "The skeleton was tilted to such a degree that all it had taken was my touch to upset its balance."

But Frank had moved to one of the other supports where he knelt. "The tongue-and-groove panels are so finely crafted you can hardly see where they meet," he said. "If you got one out, you could fit it back in place so that nobody could tell."

I ran my hand over the paneling, its seams tight. "You'd have to know the exact spot on which to pull." I felt along the bottom edge. I stuck my fingertips into a slight space between floor and board and tugged without success. "Just one of these boards would give enough space for a person to squeeze—or a body to be squeezed through."

"Hmm," Frank acknowledged. "Which brings us back to the question: did he put himself there or was he put here?"

"Was it accidental death," I said, coming to the point, "or was it murder?"

I HAD BEEN GIVEN a gift of two additional childless hours. Molly was invited to play at Courtney's house after kindergarten so I headed for the library, wasting no time in gathering the usual books—plus a new one that Gloria had found for me—and parking myself at a round table in the corner of the reference section.

I picked up the book Gloria had given me. Emmaline Samuels was eight years old at the time of the Great Fire of 1811, and more than eighty in 1887 when she wrote her memoirs, *Miss Samuels Remembers*. It was a copy of the third printing—1930—that I now held in my hands. Pasted inside the cover was a flap from the original book jacket, describing the author simply as an unmarried minister's daughter who wrote children's stories. In addition to having possessed an impressive memory, Samuels had been a good observer. Her vignettes painted with meticulous strokes characters, events, and traditions of the 1800s, imparting details that would have been overlooked by a less discerning chronicler. But I only skimmed most of the book; it was her account of the Great Fire in which I was primarily interested:

During the previous year there had been frequent occurrences of fires. Someone of evil intent was plotting mischief and the citizens of Newburyport had become watchful over their city. The stable where the Great Fire of 1811 commenced had been set ablaze twice before, but the flames had been doused in time without having to sound an alarm.

One of them happened this way: Upon arriving at Mr. Clemens' shop during the dinner hour, Sanborne Brown sat down outside to wait for the men to come back to shoe his horse. Mr. Brown saw a boy dart around the side of the stable and run towards the wharf. Immediately afterwards, he saw smoke coming from the stable's window. Jumping up quickly, Mr. Brown grabbed a bushel measure that lay next to the pump, filled it, and ran. Inside, the stable was empty except for one corner where a pile of hay was burning. Mr. Brown doused water on the flames that sufficed to quench the fire.

I read the section again to be sure I understood it correctly. *The stable where the Great Fire commenced had been set ablaze twice before;* if true, why hadn't it been mentioned in the newspaper reports after the fire? Were both earlier fires set by the same person—a boy? Had the Great Fire been set by this boy also? I read on.

In March of that fateful year the incendiary succeeded in burning Whitey Gilbert's crockery shop. The church bells gave the alarm at 8:00 p.m. but the building was enveloped in flames by the time the fire wagons arrived and the shop was lost. Nearby Market Square was untouched. Another fire, set about a month later in a tool shed, was put out quickly. Therefore, on Friday evening, May 31, 1811, when the cry of *Fire!* went up, the town couldn't have responded more quickly, having been on the alert after five occurrences within a year, three of them within a few months. But by the time the fire brigades were organized, the stable was consumed by flames. Soon after, the fire extended to the market and to State Street, fed and guided by a brisk wind.

FIVE ARSON ATTEMPTS before the Great Fire! And I'd found mention of only two previous fires—the tool shed and the warehouse—in the newspaper. I looked up and gazed at the tall mahogany bookshelves on the opposite wall without seeing them. I was visualizing scenes: wary businessmen locking up each night, entrusting the safety of their properties to the town-watch and his metered click of heel against cobblestone as he made his lonely rounds in the dark. Then those same businessmen giving an internal sigh of relief the next morning—in the days before insurance when a destructive fire meant sure ruin—at the sight of unharmed shops and businesses. Recalling a story of a raging fire in a Boston apartment building on the news the night before, I thought how this elemental catastrophe—fire—is held in as much fear and awe now as when primitive man first witnessed lightning strike a tree.

From my canvas bag, I pulled a steno pad along with the manila folder that held photocopied newspaper accounts. I laid the copies next to the open book on the library table in front of me, flipped to the first blank page in the pad, and wrote.

Fires #1 & #2 set in empty stable close to Market Square, between May 1810 & March, 1811. Boy observed at scene of one.
Outcome: fires put out before damage done
Fire #3 set in crockery store near Market Square, March, 1811
Outcome: store destroyed but not surrounding area

Fire #4 set in an old tool shed in the downtown section,
   April 14, 1811
Outcome: fire put out, no damage
Fire #5 set in empty warehouse on Market Square,
   May 9, 1811
Outcome: fire put out, no damage
Fire #6 set in empty stable (same as #1 & #2) close to
   Market Square, May 31, 1811
Outcome: Great Fire of 1811, entire downtown destroyed

All of the fires, except number three, were set in empty
buildings close to Market Square, and all, except number three
again, (and the Great Fire, of course) were extinguished with
no damage done. Other than the first two attempts, the fires
were set approximately every three weeks by "the incendiary"—Samuels assumed it was one person responsible for the
fires. Was it the boy seen at the earlier fire?

Since she was only eight years old in 1811, and because
those events weren't mentioned in the newspapers, my guess
was that, rather than her own recollections, Samuels put forth
the prevailing belief of the time: the fires were all related. In
the wake of the Great Fire, the small fires that preceded it
would have been cast in a new, more menacing light. There
would have been much talk and conjecture.

I read the newspaper accounts on the earlier 1811 fires.
Both were called suspicious, but weren't tied to each other. I
found the copy I'd taken from the newspaper printed several
days after the Great Fire and read it again:

*Whereas there is reason to fear that the great and dis-
tressing conflagration of Friday night last, in this town,
was occasioned by the wicked design of some incendiary, the Selectmen, at the request of some of their Fel-*

low-Citizens, hereby offer a reward of ONE THOUSAND
DOLLARS to be paid to the person or persons who shall
discover and bring to justice the perpetrator.
Signed, Eleazar Rand, Thomas Toole, Merriman Tibbits

It was suspected that the Great Fire was set, yet there was
no published connection to the previous fires. Was it assumed
by everyone that the fires were connected and therefore, the
obvious was not mentioned? What constitutes publishable news
in modern times—for better or worse—differs greatly from
what it did in 1811. Maybe there was evidence to the contrary—
that the fire *hadn't* been set—and either I'd missed it or it
hadn't been published (again, because of common knowledge?).

I skimmed my notes. Succeeding editions of the paper had
not reprinted the city's reward, nor was there further mention
of an "incendiary." The focus was now on rebuilding the town.
Had they given up investigating so soon? I went back to my
list of fires. For the time being I would assume they were all
arson, and all set by the same person(s). So, what was the
motive? The owners would not be suspect as they had no insurance, nothing to gain from destroying their own businesses.
What might someone else gain from the destruction of these
properties?

A stable, a crockery store, a tool shed, a warehouse; I focused
on their commonalities. With the exception of the crockery store,
the sites were uninhabited, indicating that the arsonist chose
empty buildings rather than thriving businesses. All of the fires,
with the exception of the tool shed, were described by their prox-
imity to Market Square; the warehouse had been "on" the square
and the crockery shop and the stable—the sites of four other
fires—were either "near" or "close to" it. Fire number four was
"downtown," which would have been close to Market Square.

I took out a map I'd copied from Mayta's booklet that showed the destroyed area and put marks where the fires had taken place. I put three dots half a block west of the square on the stable, which was already depicted and labeled with "Great Fire began here." Not knowing the exact location of the other fires, I put a dot along one side of the square for the warehouse ("on the square" would have meant that the building bordered the open market area), then randomly placed a dot one street over from the square, both north and south, for the crockery shop and the tool shed.

I looked at the close circle of marks on the map. Accuracy notwithstanding, all fires had been set no more than a city block from Market Square, the business district where farmers sold their produce, citizens assembled to protest or rally, and ships unloaded exotic goods from China and the East. There were other areas of the city where a maximum amount of damage could be done for a minimum of malicious effort, areas that were probably less guarded: the shipyards along the river to the north, the shipbuilding related industries—the sail lofts, rope walks—along the river to the south, even the mix of commercial and residential dwellings tightly packed on either end of town. But Market Square, that triangular area that joined three major roads to the wharves at the waterfront, was the thriving heart of the city. If someone wanted to seriously cripple Newburyport, the target would have been Market Square. Was the arsonist's design from the start to ruin Newburyport?

I went back to the book. Samuels' account of the Great Fire itself differed from the other accounts only in the immediacy that her firsthand knowledge brought to it. I sat looking at the book, my notes, and the photocopies scattered over the library table. They all screamed one thing to me that wasn't said anywhere in actual words: someone had tried repeatedly to destroy a thriving city, had finally succeeded, and then walked away, wiping his hands on his pants, with nobody in pursuit.

Why did the public lose interest in finding the perpetrator of the greatest disaster to strike the city? Outside of one published reward offered for information, and then this book, there was apparently no mention of arson or interest in solving the crime. Since I'd begun this project a number of Newburyporters—Mayta, Gus, Susan, Ginger, and Frank, among them—had told me of the fire's devastation, the resulting architecture and strict fire codes, but none had hinted that the fire was deliberately set. The suspicions had been there; why hadn't they been passed down?

"Did the book help?"

I looked up into Gloria Trainer's friendly freckled face. "Yes, very much. Thanks for finding it for me."

"Well, I thought that you might have overlooked it because of its title, *Miss Samuels Remembers*—it doesn't sound like a serious historical book—and I've heard it has some good information from the time period you're interested in. I'm glad it was a help." She moved away.

"Gloria," I called her back in a hoarse whisper. "You've lived here all your life, haven't you?" She nodded, smiling. "What do you know about the Great Fire?"

"Well, I am kind of a Newburyport history buff," she admitted, bending closer. "I know most of the downtown was destroyed, and when they rebuilt wooden buildings could only be one story, taller buildings had to be brick and had to have fire walls—you can see them on the roofs coming up between each of the connected buildings. That's why the chimneys are so tall, too."

"Do you know how the fire began?" I inserted quickly.

She frowned. "Some kind of an accident, I think."

"Some people, including Miss Samuels, believed it was deliberately set," I said.

"Really?" Her face registered puzzlement. "I didn't know that."

THIRTEEN

I KNEW I'D DELVED far more into the history of Newburyport than my assignment warranted. I'd started with the first settlers because I wanted a full picture of how the First Parish wove itself, strand by strand, into the tapestry of eighteenth century Newburyport. Learning about the people, both as individuals and as a society, helps me understand why they did what they did.

I felt that I'd become acquainted, to an extent, with those early members of the First Parish. I could connect individual names with roles they played in the development of Newbury and later Newburyport, and later yet, the United States. Likewise, I felt that I understood something about them as a society: their character, political leanings, hopes and fears. For example, I could understand why droves of them interpreted local earthquakes, strange lights in the sky, and other unexplained natural phenomena of the 1700s as God's wrath against the sinfulness of the times and, in fits of religious hysteria, had deserted their more liberal churches. It made sense that the response to the Boston Tea Party by these rugged independent seafaring folk was to stage one of their own. And it wasn't out of character for one Newburyport congregation, when a recruiter came to the church door, to rise in unison in the middle of a Sunday service and stamp out to join General Washington's troops.

Historically speaking, we interpret events in light of what

has transpired before, a simple notion until you introduce the human element in the process, namely the historian. For history (*his story*) is nothing more than what someone has chosen to tell about what happened at a given point in time. We tend to trust that what the historian tells us is truthful, accurate, and impartial. I'd never been more aware of the human element in the historical process than I was with this project.

I tried to pinpoint where I'd sensed something missing; when did the reported events not fit with what had gone on before? I thought of the fire. Following on the ruinous heels of the Embargo Act, it was second in a double whammy inflicted upon the city. The accounts of the disaster and the almost palpable anguish it caused were believable; what puzzled me was what came—or rather didn't come—after the outpouring of pain in the written words of the time. The immediate change in focus from agonized loss to hopeful rebuilding left a gap. Where was the anger? Why was there no demanding of answers, resolution, and justice from these outspoken and independent people? It didn't fit with what I'd come to know of them as a society or as individuals. What I expected from Thomas Toole, Merriman Tibbits, Eleazar Rand, even Miss Bettyann Luther of the Women's Alliance Committee, was nothing less than complete concentrated effort on catching the perpetrator of this crime.

Few sources made any mention of a firebug or "incendiary" and none, except Miss Emmaline Samuels, made the connection between the Great Fire and the previous ones. The fact that there had been a reward posted meant, at the very least, that suspicions had been known to the general public. My hunch was that the public did believe—at least for a time—that the Great Fire was premeditated, and that it was most likely perpetrated by one of their own citizens. I figured that public demands for justice were, for some reason, either ignored or squelched and, with the exception of Miss Emmaline Samuels, left unpublished.

I hadn't found any corroborating sources; still I had a gut feeling that Samuels' account was accurate. Even though she'd been elderly and far removed from her childhood experience of the Great Fire when she penned her memoirs (or perhaps *because* she'd written them many years afterwards and was therefore at liberty to relate more openly the suspicions of the times) I believed her.

Meanwhile, I hadn't answered any of my original questions. Besides coming to a dead end concerning the who and the why of the Great Fire, I hadn't uncovered architectural plans for the meeting house in the archives, nor could I find any more references to the missing baker's apprentice. Did he perish in the fire? Meet with foul play? Had he been found and returned to his master by someone seeking a reward, or did he go back on his own, or did he never go back at all?

I couldn't stop thinking about him. The contract between an apprentice and his master was a legal and binding document with serious consequences for failure to comply; if this boy had run away, it wouldn't have been on a whim. Had he found his work intolerable? Was his master abusive? Had he committed a crime? Or was it something as simple as homesickness? Whatever his fate, I probably wouldn't learn it because a missing baker's apprentice hadn't been worthy of much publicity. As for the remote possibility that he was our Mr. Bones up in the steeple, there seemed to be no way to know.

Time was getting short. Although I'd amassed a lot of information for the book, I had more to do, and had yet to begin compiling it all. Every morning Gloria, whose interest had been piqued by my question on the fire which she assumed was the focus of my research, had something new for me—an old scrapbook, an obscure book or pamphlet, a document or article. I'd been spending my kindergarten hours in the library—when I could catch both Gloria in the reference section ready to assist me, and the history room downstairs open—and hadn't met with Ginger and Frank in over a week, so one afternoon I invited them over for coffee.

Ten minutes before the Van Amburgs were expected, I ushered Max and Molly into the house. Shifting into high gear, I jerked the vacuum cleaner back and forth across the center of the living room carpet a few times, then followed a zigzagging path down the hallway into the dining room, the vacuum pinging as it sucked up sand and dirt, making an occasional clunk and whine when it bit into, then digested something heartier, like a small stone or a LEGO.

I put Moose out in the backyard and then, lowering my usual standards concerning movies during the school week, grabbed Disney's *Lion King* off the shelf, thus ensuring me eighty-eight minutes of uninterrupted adult conversation. I'd made a fresh pot of coffee, defrosted a loaf of Mayta's banana bread, and was slicing it when the Van Amburgs arrived.

Once we were seated at the dining room table we quickly brought each other up to date. Frank had already started on a foreword to the book, having finished the research that Ginger was now writing into chapters to fit with Etta Mae Frisch's section. Their part of the book, Ginger figured, would be finished within two weeks.

"As for our side research," Frank said, shrugging, "we didn't come up with anything on how or why somebody could have gotten into the steeple."

"Runaway slave," Ginger prompted. "Remember, dear, we talked about that?"

Frank shook his head. "I don't think so. We had abolitionists in the congregation, but there's nothing to indicate the church helped runaway slaves. Besides, the time period is wrong; if the body has been up there as long as the police think, it was before they had runaways this far north."

"What about you, Andy?" asked Ginger. "Did you find out anything?"

"Maybe." I rested my arms on the table and leaned forward. "I think there's a connection between Mr. Bones and the Great Fire."

"The Fire of 1811?" Frank peered at me over his glasses. "Connected how?"

"Timing, to begin with," I said. "We know that Mr. Bones was put in the steeple sometime after the fire, perhaps immediately afterwards, because that was when the tankard disappeared." I showed them my map with the dots of the fires that preceded the Great Fire. Then I brought out my notes on each fire, and they leaned in to inspect them. Frank frowned thoughtfully as I talked. "Everything leads back to the fire, which leads back to the fact that it wasn't an isolated crime."

"The fire was a crime?" Ginger asked.

"Sorry. I've jumped ahead. Yes, the Great Fire was set deliberately. Most people now don't know that because the fact wasn't passed down. But—well, here, I'll show you—" I was interrupted by a commotion at the front door.

I heard Max exclaim, "Hi, Grandma!"

"We're in the dining room, Mayta!" I called in greeting.

"Well, Ginger, Frank!" Mayta enthused in her gravelly voice, entering the room. "What a surprise!" She gave me a sly look, which let me know she hadn't just been driving by. "Are you people working on your project?"

Frank stood to greet her as I gave her a quick hug.

"Hello, Mayta, dear," said Ginger warmly. "How are you? We were just enjoying some of your delicious banana bread."

Making no apologies for her timely arrival, Mayta went

straight to the table and bent over my spread out notes, squinting. "What's this? 'Fire number one' and 'fire number two'?"

"Andy thinks the Fire of 1811 was deliberately set, and that other attempts were made prior to it." Frank's skeptical expression was mixed with anticipation of Mayta's response.

Mayta took her glasses out of her pocketbook, put them on, then picked up the pad. When she finished reading, I stuck the map under her nose. "This shows where the fires were set. This—" I pointed to the square that said "stable" "—is the site of the first two and also the last one, the Great Fire." She nodded slowly, bunching up her mouth on one side. "This was number three, here. And numbers four and five. Exact locations of fires three and five are guesses but probably close."

"All of them surround Market Square," Mayta observed. Frank leaned over her shoulder to see and Ginger rose from her chair. I began to get excited. I wondered if she would come to the same conclusions I had. But it was Frank who voiced them.

"One, two," Frank said, tapping on the map, "three, four, five," he moved his finger in an arc around the triangular plot that denoted Market Square, "and six." His finger moved back to the stable he'd tapped at first. "A pattern, a plan? Is that what you think, Andy? That there was a plan to burn down Market Square itself?"

"The business district of the city," I said, nodding.

"Let me see," said Ginger. I stepped back, letting the three of them put their heads together over the map.

"Have you ever read the book *Miss Samuels Remembers?*" I asked.

Frank looked up. "Emmaline Samuels? Certainly. Hers is one of the few firsthand accounts of nineteenth century Newburyport."

"Do you remember the part about the fire?" I asked, then

rushed ahead before he could answer. "She said that attempts had been made to burn the town before the Great Fire and that patrols had been beefed up to try to catch the culprit."

"I read that book," Mayta said. "I don't remember anything about an arsonist."

"It's written in such a matter-of-fact way it would be easy to miss unless you were looking specifically for the cause of the fire, which I was."

Frank's brow furrowed. "The book came out in the late eighteen hundreds. Samuels was very young at the time of the fire—"

"Yes, I know," I acknowledged patiently. "Even so, she would have carried with her the attitudes and beliefs of those around her as she grew up. And, years later, she'd be free to tell the story more honestly."

"What do you mean more honestly?" Mayta demanded.

"Let's sit down." I motioned them back to the chairs. "Coffee, Mayta?" She waved the offer aside so I sat down myself and waited for them to do the same.

"What did you mean by that?" repeated Mayta.

From the other room I heard the cub Simba brag that he would someday be king of the lion pride. I took a long slow breath. It wasn't easy to tell three self-professed experts on local history that, way back somewhere, there had been something rotten in Denmark when Denmark was their hometown.

"It's a hunch I have—a feeling, really—that everything wasn't on the up and up after the fire." Silence. I continued. "It just doesn't make sense that the citizens wouldn't have done more to find the person responsible for setting these fires!"

"Do we know for sure they were all set?" Ginger sipped her coffee daintily.

"Yes," I answered. "I checked. They were all arson."

"Who says they were arson?" Mayta wanted to know.

"The newspapers. For each fire Samuels described, I found a corroborating account that it had been set on purpose. They thought it was a firebug."

"They believed the fires were set by the same person?" asked Mayta.

"Only Samuels said it in so many words but the newspapers hinted at it."

"And Samuels is the only one who connects the small fires to the Great Fire," Frank spoke for the first time.

"Right."

"And nowhere else," he continued, "is it stated that the Great Fire was set."

"Wrong. A reward was offered—I have it here." I shuffled through my papers.

"They always offered rewards for information on fires, didn't they?" said Mayta and Frank nodded. "It didn't necessarily mean they thought somebody set it."

"No, they believed that it was set," I said firmly. "It's here somewhere."

"Isn't that interesting?" Ginger refolded her paper napkin and tucked it under the lip of her plate. "I've never heard that the Great Fire was arson."

"Here it is!" I held up the copy of the front page of the *Herald* for June 4, 1811. "Listen: 'Whereas there is reason to fear that the great and distressing conflagration was occasioned by the wicked design of some incendiary ' etcetera, etcetera It's signed by Merriman Tibbits, Eleazar Rand, and Thomas Toole, selectmen of Newburyport." I handed it to Frank and the women leaned in from either side to read.

"'Reason to fear' sounds a shade doubtful," said Ginger.

"No," Mayta said. "That's the way they talked. They believed it was set."

"But why isn't it part of written history?" Ginger asked.

"Maybe it was determined that the fire was an accident after all," said Frank.

"Nope," I said. "These guys—Rand, Toole, and Tibbits believed it was arson. Samuels believed it was arson. Nobody—that I've been able to find anyway—has ever stated otherwise; it's only been *assumed,* after so many years, that it was accidental. If the Great Fire had really been caused by an accident it would be common knowledge today. Everybody knows that the Chicago fire was started by—"

"Mrs. O'Leary's cow," finished Mayta. She cut a hunk of banana bread and slid it onto a napkin. "So, are you saying they just gave up looking for the arsonist?"

"Well, think about it. There are a number of arson attempts, finally one attempt succeeds—the whole downtown is destroyed—and the selectmen post a reward for the perpetrator. They print it only once and then it's dropped. Nothing more."

"But why would anyone want to burn down the town?" asked Ginger.

"Who knows? Maybe someone was angry at something he felt the town had done to him. Maybe he just liked to set fires for the thrill of it."

"Why, if indeed this horrendous crime was purposely caused, wouldn't they continue searching for the arsonist?" Frank hunched over the map again, rubbing the top of his forefinger back and forth under his chin.

"A cover-up," Mayta said bluntly. "Is that what you're getting at, Andy?"

"It's possible," I said, as if it was her idea, not mine.

"A cover-up. That's what it was." Mayta wiped her fingers on her napkin, then started sweeping up crumbs on the tablecloth with the side of her hand.

"But whatever for?" Ginger turned wide eyes on her husband. Frank made a sound in his throat that sounded like a mild protest. "I suppose there could be a cover-up for negligence on the part of some city employee," he said, almost choking on the words. "Or—"

"Nah," Mayta interrupted. "If a lowly city employee goofed up, they'd have run him through the wringer, hung him out to dry, and been done with it."

"Or," Frank cleared his throat and continued, "perhaps they found the responsible party and decided to keep it quiet for some reason."

"But, why..." Ginger looked puzzled.

"Because it was somebody influential," Mayta answered the unfinished question. "Some muckety-muck who could pay people off."

Ginger breathed out a soft "oh" sound. Frank adjusted his glasses. Mayta continued brushing crumbs into a neat pile. I furrowed my brow as if pondering the idea for the first time. I knew we were treading on thin ice. Influential people back then tended to be descendants of founding fathers, and Frank, Ginger, and Mayta—modern day descendants of founding fathers—were clearly worried that their lineage was about to be besmirched. A dyed-in-the-wool Yankee believes he is a composite made up equally of who he is in this life and who his earliest ancestors were. It doesn't matter if an ancestor never did a noteworthy thing as long as he (always *he* not she) was around long enough ago to have his name mentioned in old church records, engraved on a granite marker, or etched on an ancient cemetery stone.

I knew Ginger and Frank—and Mayta and Gus, too, though they never talked much about it—identified, in a way that I would never completely appreciate, with those first family members who set foot in the new land. And I knew at this moment the three before me were thinking about the ramifications of having an ancestor who wittingly or unwittingly took part in the most heinous crime recorded in the annals of Newburyport history.

FOURTEEN

THEY'D BEEN POLITE about my Great Fire theory. Nobody said, "Andy, you're a shovel short in the tool shed." But then nobody said, "Andy, that's brilliant!" either. After the initial flurry of talk everyone got quiet. We set a new deadline for work to be done—the third week of April—and then they scooted out. Frank and Ginger had grocery shopping to do and Mayta had to get to the bank before it closed. So, while the *Lion King* held the kids hostage in the living room with twenty-one minutes left of potentially uninterrupted adult conversation, I sat by myself wondering how three retired people had suddenly gotten so busy. And if I'd been taken seriously.

I didn't have to wonder for long. For the first time since negotiations for the new contract had started, Gus arrived home right after school. Max ducked from his kiss, and Molly flung her arms around him, maneuvering so that she could both give and receive affection without experiencing any viewing obstructions.

"I had a meeting with Ginger and Frank," I explained in answer to Gus's look that questioned a movie on a school day.

"Oh, yeah," he said and gave me a quick kiss. "Mayta told me about it."

"Where did you see Mayta?" I followed him into the kitchen where he deposited his lunch bag, then into the dining room where he laid his sports jacket over the back of a chair, and slid his briefcase into a corner.

"At the bank," he said. "I stopped by there on the way home."

"Oh, right. She said she was going to the bank." I began straightening the papers strewn over the dining room table, stuffing them into their manila folder.

Gus did not go greet Moose, who was whining outside, smearing his nose all over the glass of the back door. He did not pester the kids to turn off the TV, or go upstairs to change, or do any of the usual things he does when he gets home. He just stood there with a look that was a mix of wariness and puzzlement and something else—amusement?—on his face. That's when I knew I'd been taken seriously.

"So," said Gus, "tell me what got my mother all riled up."

"She was riled up?" I asked innocently. Then I pulled the papers back out and went through it all again: the X's on the map, the passages in Samuels' book, the reward in the newspaper. I watched his face for a reaction. There was the polite skepticism of Frank and Ginger, but he spoke with the bluntness of his mother.

"You think somebody burned the town down on purpose?"

"The facts support the theory."

"And that somebody was a prominent person of the time?"

"Well, it fits," I said, hedging. "Why else would it be hushed up?"

"It was hushed up?" Gus looked up quickly.

"If the Great Fire was caused by arson and certain people knew it, why didn't it become general knowledge? Suspicious, don't you think?" In the background there was a click of claws against glass as Moose assaulted the door.

Gus picked up the map with the "X's" and pondered it. That quizzical-tinged-with-amusement expression was back on his face. "So, what does this mean?"

"It means that one of Newburyport's revered and honored

ancestors—perhaps your very own—was a rat. Speaking of which, who *was* your revered ancestor?"

He laughed, tension suddenly dissipated. "During that time period I have no idea, but back in the seventeen hundreds, there was a never-do-well fishmonger named Theophilus Ilsly who liked to go around disrupting religious services by shouting 'pagans' at the congregations. Remind you of anybody in the present generation?"

"Sounds a bit like Mayta."

Gus grinned. "I always thought so, too, though I'd never tell her." He tapped the side of his forefinger on the paper in his hand. "This idea of yours could shake things up among certain circles. It's not going in the book, is it?"

"No. It's just something I came across and pursued out of curiosity." Gus gave an inaudible sigh of relief. I knew he was thinking it would be difficult in this town to be married to an ancestor basher.

"What will you do with it—this theory?"

I shrugged. "I sure would like to know who the arsonist was, though."

Gus puckered his lips and nodded. But his brow was still creased as he went to let in Moose, who was now lying sedately on the welcome mat.

FIFTEEN

FRANK AND GINGER were standing outside on the wide granite step to the church when I pulled up in front of it early the next morning. Frank had called the night before to tell me he'd found some old records I might be interested in. He was going into the church early, he said, and would show them to me if I wanted.

There was a balminess to the air that promised spring was finally on its way. I'd worn my coat out of habit and as I got out of the car, I shrugged it off and threw it in the backseat. It felt good to be unencumbered by an extra layer of clothing.

"Hi, folks," I called to Frank and Ginger, whom I assumed were waiting for me outside in order to enjoy the sun. "What do you say to a climb up into the bell tower? You know, for old time's sake?" I gave a Quasimodo impersonation, rolling one shoulder forward and putting a lurch into my walk.

Ginger smiled weakly. "We can't go in, dear," she said apologetically. "We have to wait for the police."

"The police?" I looked from one to the other. I noticed then that both looked strained. "What's going on?"

Frank lowered his voice. "When we got here about ten minutes ago we found a man passed out in the vestibule."

"Frank called to him—but couldn't rouse him." Ginger wrinkled her nose, pale freckles crowding together across it. "It smells of alcohol in there."

"You know, there was a time when churches were refuges for people that were down and out," mused Frank. "Doors were left unlocked and it wasn't unusual to find a drunk or a bum sleeping in the pews. Things are different these days."

Ginger nodded regretfully. "We just can't afford to be as trusting."

"Still, I felt kind of guilty calling the police."

"Neither Susan or Nancy are in yet," Ginger said to me.

Frank pushed at the bridge of his glasses with his index finger and then rubbed the middle of his forehead. "I wonder how he got in. The door was locked."

"Are you sure?" I asked.

"I locked it myself last night. Susan asked me to check out the sound system—it's been crackling during service. I was careful to lock up when I left."

The wail of an ambulance pierced the early morning quietude, and a moment later the white and orange vehicle stopped in front of the church, lights flashing.

"The police must have called them," Frank said.

We moved out of the way as two attendants hurried toward us. Ginger waved a hand at the middle door. "He's in the vestibule." The great door, crafted by a shipbuilder, was designed as it would have been on board a ship: weighted on the outside edge to close automatically. The clang of the iron latch, which echoed off the interior walls, was cut off when the door fell shut behind the attendants.

An instant later a police car pulled up. "Lew Wenninger," Ginger observed as the sergeant emerged from the car. As he made his way over to us, I checked him out more thoroughly than I had at the police station. He was good looking in a petulant kind of way, his face still handsome though its features had coarsened with middle age and weight gain. He moved purposefully without hurrying, his gait that of an athlete, though he was clearly past his prime. He nodded to Frank, but only glanced at Ginger and me as he continued on without pause and entered the church.

A car door slammed then, and we looked over to see Reverend Tenney hurrying around the front of her blue Buick that she had parked in back of the police car. Impatiently, she tried to tame her skirt billowing out in the mild breeze with one hand while slapping away the scarf that flew up into her face with the other. Frank strode across the wide brick walk and met her halfway. The two conferred for a moment, the tall, thin man bent over the diminutive woman, before joining us.

"Good morning, Andy, Ginger," Susan said distractedly, adjusting her scarf as she split her attention between the church door and us. "I suppose I should go find out what the situation is."

Just then the heavy door swung inward and an attendant called out, "Could somebody hold this? And turn on the lights in here?"

Set in motion, we all rushed to help. I held the door while Frank looked for the granite paving stone that acted as doorstop. Susan flipped on the light switch that was partially hidden by an ornate picture frame that held one of the flower watercolors I'd admired a few days before. The wall lamps didn't add much illumination because they were focused on the paintings along the walls of the vestibule. However, the bright sun streaming in the doorway sufficiently lit up the scene. The attendants knelt on either side of the man and spoke in low tones as they turned him over. My view was obscured so that all I could see were the bottom of tan colored pants that ended in recently polished loafers with worn soles.

It was those shoes that made me uneasy. Even before the attendants' pace slowed I was thinking that this was more than a drunk sleeping where he shouldn't be sleeping. When the attendants sat back on their heels and exchanged looks across the man's midsection, I realized the situation was no longer an emergency.

I leaned forward and got a good look at the man who now lay spread-eagle on his back, his rigid grayish-blue eyes regarding the ceiling through a veil that would never be lifted. Nearing middle age—late thirties, early forties—he had been good looking before death had erased personality from his face, replacing it with a painful grimace. He wasn't dressed as a homeless man. Neither was he dressed in jeans, which was how I'd last seen him. Above the nicely pressed chinos he wore a short sleeved striped shirt that had probably also been neat appearing before something black had stained the entire front of it—blood, I realized. Where had it all come from? A dark crusted trail, like a cooled lava flow, led from his chest around his neck toward the back of his head. Did it originate from his chest or the back of his head or both, I wondered, feeling oddly removed from the situation. From the back of his head, I decided, noting the pool on the floor that fanned out around his head like a black halo. Legs clothed in the somber navy of the police uniform moved into my line of vision then, just beyond the striped shirt, and my gaze was deflected up to meet the stare of Sergeant Wenninger.

It was discomfiting to have Sergeant Wenninger watch me when his attention should have been on the poor man who had died. Wasn't there something he should be doing? All at once I realized that circumstances had changed; the blood meant that something more than death had happened here, that a—it was hard to even think the *word*—murder had taken place. I glanced over at Susan who had frozen, hand at the light switch, and then at Frank who had both arms around Ginger, her face a white blur against the brown of his sweater. Their expressions told me that they, too, had recognized the circumstances. And the victim.

"Body's cool. There's stiffening in the neck," one of the attendants said.

Wenninger squatted beside him. "How long has he been dead?" His voice was almost a whisper, yet in the sudden stillness I could hear his words distinctly.

"At least four hours."

"Cause?"

"Preliminary cause is cardiac arrest." The attendant shrugged and got to his feet. "You'll have to wait for the medical examiner."

Wenninger put on a pair of plastic gloves, then reached across the body and slid a hand carefully into the left front pants pocket. He pulled out a thin black leather wallet and flipping its loose flap open, peered at its contents.

My stomach felt queasy and I averted my eyes, noticing an unstoppered wine bottle lying within a damp circle on the floor a few feet from the polished shoes. A small amount of pale gold-colored wine remained in the bottle, trapped by the curve of the neck. I became aware then that the musty smell of the church, a sensation I usually found pleasant, was laced with another smell besides the wine. Whether real or imagined, it was one I'd never experienced before and I gave it a label: death.

I looked to my friends, this time searching their faces, seeking reason or reassurance. I expected some form of solace from Susan for, as minister, she must have been in similar circumstances before. But she was as horror-struck as I, fingertips pressed to her cheeks as she gazed at the dead man. Ginger's face was buried in her husband's chest, tight within the cocoon of his arms. And finally Frank, the traditionalist, the protector; his mouth was set in a rigid line and his eyes, when they connected with mine, were electric with anger. Then Susan found her voice. "It's, oh my God, it really is him," she blurted out, unnaturally loud.

Wenninger's head snapped toward her. "Okay," he bellowed, "everybody outta here. But wait outside—don't get lost."

As if released from a spell, we moved numbly outside. The door closed behind us because Frank hadn't found the doorstop. This time the attendants left it closed. On the brick walk, the four of us formed a loose assemblage, Susan and I standing apart from Frank who still held Ginger. I folded my arms tightly across my chest and shivered, the warm sun failing to penetrate the cold that encased me. Susan clasped her hands and held them to her lips, her expression a mix of concern and bewilderment. It was the first time I'd ever seen her not completely composed.

Sergeant Wenninger had followed us out but continued on to his cruiser. He reached through the open window and pulled out his mike. Leaning against the car door, he spoke in low tones between periodic squawks from the radio. After he replaced the mike he came over to us.

He slid out a narrow notebook from his back pocket and wrote down our names. "Okay, tell me what happened," he said, looking up. "Who found it?"

"It?" I asked before realizing that Wenninger was referring to the body. "Oh!"

"Frank and I did," said Ginger. She shivered and Frank's arm tightened around her. "We opened the door and walked in and…found him."

"We've been working on a project up in the choir room," Frank explained.

"I was meeting them," I said. "I got here afterwards."

"At first we didn't see him," Ginger continued, "because it was rather dark and our eyes weren't used to it, coming right out of the sun. But then, just as we started up the stairs, I glanced over and saw this man lying there." Ginger's voice caught on the last word.

"I'm sorry, I need to ask these questions," Wenninger said. Then he added in a kinder tone, "It will only take a few more minutes. Did you approach the body?"

Frank took over then, patiently answering Wenninger's questions. No, they hadn't approached the man. Frank had called out— "Excuse me," or something like that—but received no response. Assuming that the man was sleeping—drunk because of the strong smell of alcohol—he and Ginger had exited the building and gone next door to Parish Hall to first call Susan, and then the police. They had not reentered the church. "We had no idea he was," Frank cleared his throat, "dead. He was on his side. We didn't see the blood until they turned him over."

"When was the church last unlocked?"

Susan caught her lower lip with her front teeth then released it. "I'm not sure. There weren't any planned events last night, but so many individuals have keys, they can come and go without my knowledge."

"I stopped by around seven to look at the sound system," Frank said. "I assumed I'd be the last one so I locked up. That was around eight."

"I'll need a list of those who have keys to the church," Wenninger said.

Susan looked doubtful. "I can give you a list, but I'm afraid we don't keep very good records."

"Anyone who is using the Parish Hall on a fairly regular basis now or was using it in the past has a key, from the local theater group to AA to the chairs of all the church committees," explained Frank.

"And having a key to the Parish Hall means they have access to the church as well," said Susan. "The same key is used for both buildings."

Wenninger made a small sound and shook his head as he jotted something in his notebook. "Who locks up at night?"

"Whoever is using the building," Susan answered. "I often stop and double-check in the evening."

Then Wenninger asked the question he should have asked to begin with. "Can you think of any reason this man would have been in the church last night?"

"No. Jason doesn't work at night," said Susan. "And I don't know how he got in because he'd lost his key. He'd been borrowing one and returning it each day."

Wenninger's head snapped up. "Jason?"

"Jason Snoud," whispered Ginger.

"He works here," I explained. "Jason Snoud works—worked—on the steeple."

SIXTEEN

"FINDING BODIES in the church is getting to be a habit." The way Gus put it sounded heartless, but I knew he was trying to keep me from getting hysterical.

I paced the living room. "I'm sorry for interrupting your class. I should've waited until you got home."

"Hey," his voice softened, "you can call me anytime, you know that. God, what a horrible experience, discovering him."

"Yeah, Frank and Ginger were pretty upset once they realized what they'd walked in on. I better call them later. Make sure they're okay."

"Excuse me a minute," Gus said. I heard him give terse instructions to his students. Today the secretary had put me straight through to his room.

"I was okay until I got home and then I just kind of fell apart. Gus, I've never seen anybody dead like that before. I've been to funerals, but this was different."

"I know," he spoke quietly. "I mean, I don't know, but I can imagine it would be. Listen, why don't you go out to Ma's for the afternoon? I'll come home early today. We'll take the kids out—Ma, too—get something to eat."

"Okay, maybe I will," I said, knowing that Mayta would refuse to let us take her out and insist on making dinner for us. "Meet us out there right after school?"

"Promise."

"Okay," I said again, still hanging on. "Love you."

"Me you, too," Gus said, in case he was overheard.

I picked up Molly from kindergarten and took her to lunch at Kmart because I felt the need to be where people were. We whiled away an hour looking at Barbie dolls and children's spring clothes and then went to the Tot Lot downtown where we sat in the sun-warmed sand, Molly chattering about school, her best-most-favorite teacher, and worms among other topics, and me mustering up just enough enthusiasm in my responses to keep her chatter, which was a soothing balm, flowing.

At one point she picked up a blue jay feather, exclaiming in delight, and made me put it in a safe place in my purse. Then I caught hold of her and pulled her to me. She protested a bit, then yielded, and we melded into a single figure. I gave in to my grief then, which was not for Jason Snoud, whom I scarcely knew, but for my safe warm world that was crumbling. I had deluded myself into believing I could order up a storybook life for my family as easily as I might order up a cheese omelet at the Fish Tail Diner: I'll have a quaint seacoast town with a white steepled church and a small old-fashioned school that still has PTO bake sales. No violence, please.

I'd left crime-ridden Detroit only to run smack dab into what I thought I'd left behind. And not once, but twice. Separated by almost two hundred years, but still twice and in the same spot. For, although I'd talked all around it, denying that little voice that spoke inside me, I knew now that the first body we'd found up in the steeple had also been a murder victim.

Molly clasped her grubby little hands around my neck and her head knocked into my nose with eager clumsiness. "I love you, Mommy," she said. And I cried without sound into her hair, which smelled like baby shampoo. I cried for myself, because I had thought that I could keep her safe, that I could control things I couldn't. And I cried for Molly because someday she, too, would realize that bad things happen in life and sometimes there's nothing anybody can do about it.

May 31, 1811
11:00 p.m.

HITTY FLINCHED at the touch on her back.

"Aw, for pity's sake, Hitty, it's only me. How come you jump at everything?"

"Peter? Are you all right?" She looked around in confusion, expecting to find that the fire had reached them, that the roof had fallen in on them, but everything was as before. Even Peter, except for the hair that stuck up around his wound, looked like his old self as he bent over her. "Are you feeling better, Peter?"

"I'm okay," he said shortly, touching the side of his head gingerly.

"Who hurt you? Did you see him? I heard you talking."

Peter shook his head carefully, indicating that either he didn't know or wouldn't tell her. Then he turned, muttering, "I can't wait around for my money."

"Where are you going?" Hitty scrambled to her feet.

"None of your business," he said over his shoulder.

"I ain't going back to the Stockwells either," Hitty informed him, jutting her pointy chin out. "I'm going with you, Peter."

"No you aren't!" He snorted as if the idea were funny. "I'm not getting stuck with a whiny orphan." He strode down the aisle and Hitty hurried after him.

Instead of descending to the vestibule as Hitty expected him to do, Peter darted behind the organ. When Hitty reached the corner of the massive instrument, Peter had already loped up the narrow flight of steps wedged behind it, and was ducking through a small door set in the back wall of the sanctuary.

Hitty slipped off her shoes and scampered up after him. On the other side of the door was a small unfinished room with a high window that let in enough light for her to make out her surroundings. Opposite the small room to her right was a cavernous attic that ran above the sanctuary from where they'd just come. At the far end of the attic light pulsed from behind glass panes of a window, casting a pale orange wash over the slanted ceiling and roughly hewn beams. In front of her was an open staircase that led upwards as far as Hitty could see into the dark. It was in this direction that Peter had gone; she heard him pounding the rungs overhead.

Hitty hitched up her skirt and followed, her bare feet sprinting lightly up the rough splintery treads. She climbed past the attic, past another small room on her left before she figured out that they were ascending the tower to the steeple. She marveled that Peter knew about this place. But then Peter knew about many wonderful hiding places in town, like the secret tunnel he once showed her down at the waterfront through which one of the ship owners smuggled goods to avoid taxes.

The stairs ended at a square opening in the ceiling of the third room. After a slight hesitation, Hitty hoisted herself up through the opening and out onto a floor littered with paint shavings and bird droppings, next to a hulking black shape. She immediately recoiled from the sharp noises and acrid air. She pressed the hem of her skirt over her nose before raising her head to see that she was in the belfry and that the black shape next to her was the church bell.

Eyes tearing, Hitty squinted through the smoky haze. Peter was on the other side of the bell, peered off into the distance, his brow puckered and mouth working as if talking to someone. Hitty couldn't hear his words above the awful cacophony around her: buildings crumpling and crashing, people wailing in anguish, cows lowing in a single terrified pitch, and everywhere, the constant deafening roar of the greedy fire as it coursed up chimneys. Using a brace that held the great bell, Hitty pulled herself up next to Peter. His back to the maelstrom, he was pointing north.

"There," he said calmly. "That's the road that leads to New Hampshire."

But Hitty's eyes would not move away from the scene immediately below her. From the height of the steeple, the fire took on a different perspective. The movements of the people battling it seemed as inconsequential as the scurrying of ants. The fire was a monster who, having devoured Market Square, had moved on, leaving charred bones crumbling in its wake while it ravaged the waterfront, setting alight wharves, ships, and warehouses with the licks of a thousand fiery tongues. Overhead, thick smoke hovered, shrouding the city and intensifying the heat and glare of the flames so that it was as hot and bright as a midday in summer.

Suddenly the bell came to life with a deafening toll of its clapper. Hitty shrieked and Peter grabbed her, pulling her down to the filthy surface of the platform. Crouched between the swaying giant and the edge of the steeple roof, they wrapped their arms over their heads. With each measured clang that resonated through her body, Hitty flinched and squealed. When at last the peals ceased, they cautiously uncovered their ears. Peter crept to the edge and looked over.

"Don't get too close, Peter," Hitty whimpered. "You'll fall off."

"Oh, good Gawd!" he exclaimed, pulling back.

"What is it, Peter? What's the matter?"

"The colonel's down there but I can't go down because he's with other men!"

"We can't stay up here," wailed Hitty. "The meeting house will catch fire!"

"Stop your whining! The fire's going the other way, any idiot can see that."

"He don't know we're up here, Peter, does he?"

"Naw, he'll just leave the money and when he goes I'll get it." Peter fingered the side of his head. "Did we leave blood anywhere?"

"Oh, no, Peter," Hitty reassured him. "I put a rag to your head and then afterwards while you was sleeping I cleaned the wound up right proper with water."

"Did you shut the door?" He looked at her feet. "Where are your shoes?"

Hitty's eyes widened in alarm. "Oooh! I left them by the organ."

"Damn you, Hitty! I should have made you leave before!" Peter raised his hand to strike her, then changed his mind and scrambled across the floor. He dropped down through the opening and Hitty scurried after him. She had to go backwards for the first set of stairs—the steepest section—but when she got to the wider steps, she turned around and moved quickly down the next two flights. Peter had reached the bottom and was standing beside the open door, beckoning impatiently.

"Where did you leave them?" he whispered harshly, his face close to hers.

"Under that first step." Hitty jabbed a finger downward.

Peter sidled down the back of the organ and was back within a few seconds. "Here!" he said, shoving the misshapen shoes at her. "Keep ahold of these if you're not going to wear them." As he pulled the door closed they heard voices in the sanctuary. He flashed a warning look at Hitty and held up a hand, indicating she should stay. Then he stepped beyond the staircase into the attic above the sanctuary. Nimbly, he ran along its wide center beam to the middle where he crouched down, listening. After a few moments, he returned to where Hitty waited and brushed past her, taking the steps two at a time as he bounded back upstairs.

Once more Hitty followed Peter up the interior of the tower and out onto the bell platform. This time, however, Peter crawled to one of the wide corner supports for the upper steeple. He placed his hands, palms up, on the floor and slid his fingers into the space between the wall of the support and the flooring. Amazed, Hitty watched as he pulled and a wide board came free, exposing a black hole. He turned and backed into the hole, then poked his head out and said, "Come on!"

When Hitty had crawled in next to him, Peter carefully fitted the board back into its spot. In the hot, dark closeness they listened to each others' shallow rapid breathing, a layering of sound that mercifully muffled the hellish sounds of a city writhing in agony. "Who made this hidey hole?" Hitty asked him.

"I did," Peter said proudly. "I cut out a place under the board, scraped out the glue, and then pried it open. Now, shut up."

After a while Hitty realized that other refugees from the fire had also claimed this place. Tiny unseen feet scratched in the corners and twice she'd felt the whisper of fur against her bare toes. Now and then she kicked a foot out or made a shooing sound "hsss!" to keep them away. She sat hugging her knees tight to her chest in the stifling space that smelled of smoke, damp wood, and the stale odors of their own bodies for what seemed like hours. Peter fell asleep, his head lay heavily against her shoulder, his breathing uneven and labored. When she couldn't stay there another moment, she bumped him with her shoulder and said, "Peter! Wake up!" Her breath hung hot and moist in the air.

She pushed him away and leaned forward onto her knees, groping for the wall amid the frantic skittering and outraged squeals of disturbed rodents. Peter swore, and swiped his hands over himself as Hitty pushed on the panel and it clattered onto the floor outside. They squeezed out side by side, breathing in smoky air that sent them into jags of coughing. Peter clambered on all fours around the bell to the trapdoor, flung it back, and jumped through in almost one motion.

But Hitty hesitated. She covered her nose and mouth with her hem and glanced earthward. Through bleary eyes she took in the fact that while the fire had progressed, the firefighters' attempts had not. The eastern part of the city was ablaze for as far as she could see. She turned back to their hiding place, reached in and grabbed up her shoes. Her chin tucked into her chest, she scrunched her eyes tight and crawled blindly across the rough dirty boards. At the opening she stretched a bare leg behind her down into it, feeling for the first rung, and then de- scended into the tower where Peter waited, listening, at the door behind the organ.

Just as Hitty reached him, Peter darted through the door and sidestepped down the steep staircase, which was too narrow for his large feet, and edged cautiously around the organ. After a stealthy peek over the gallery wall he loped downstairs to the vestibule. Hitty slipped on her shoes and hurried after, catching up to him as he entered the sanctuary. She followed him up the middle aisle, the soles of her shoes slapping the smooth wood, and wondered anxiously what Peter was up to now. Here he was, running around the meeting house, unconcerned, as if he were playing a game of hide and seek while the whole city was burning because of what he had done. Oh, Peter, she asked him silently for the hundredth time in the past couple of hours, why have you done this?

He stopped at a pew on the right, close to the front, twisted the little brass fastener, and pulled open the half-door. He dropped to his hands and knees, lifted the lid of a narrow built- in box on the floor that ran the length of the pew, and crawled alongside, sweeping his hand inside from side to side. Hitty could see that the only thing the box held was a brass spittoon, flecks of dried tobacco splattered on its wide brim, but Peter stuck his head inside, peering into the corners. Finally, with a cry of "Damnation!" he slammed down the lid.

"Peter," Hitty reached out a tentative hand.

"You just shut up!" Peter whirled on her. "I told you before I don't want you here. Now get out!" She backed a few steps down the aisle as he advanced toward her, shaking his fist in the air.

"I did my job and I wasn't paid," Peter yelled. "I will be paid!" He turned and lifted his gaze to the pulpit. Hitty watched uneasily as Peter strode with purpose to the front. She wondered if Peter had gone crazy from the blow to his head like Gilly Hamner's horse had when it got hit with the blunt end of a hatchet that flew off its handle, and always afterwards ran around the field shaking its head, not letting anyone near until Gilly finally had to put it out of its misery.

Movement overhead caught Hitty's attention. Up in Reverend Mr. Andrews' pulpit, which was mounted as high as the galleries on either side, Peter straightened himself to his full height and looked out over the sanctuary. For a moment he stood perfectly still, the sounding board suspended from the ceiling above his head like a huge halo. Hitty knew that he was claiming something for himself. She'd seen him do it at the bakery when Mr. Stockwell left the room; he'd throw out his chest and order Hitty around, grab a freshly baked loaf of bread and break off a piece. She'd seen him do it other places also: Mrs. Stockwell's house, the shops they delivered to when the owners were in the storeroom. Peter owned what others left unguarded, and Hitty worried now as she watched him in Mr. Andrews' pulpit.

As quickly as he had appeared, Peter was gone. Then he was back down, hugging something to his chest. "What do you have?" Hitty's whisper wafted in the air like a thin stream of smoke, dissipating immediately in the vaulted expanse of the sanctuary. She repeated the words, stronger this time, "Peter! What do you have?" But he shoved past, ignoring her. Hitty grabbed his arm. He shrugged free, but not before she caught a glint of silver under the sleeve of his shirt.

"Peter—" she was interrupted by the echo of the door latch in the vestibule. They darted into pews, she in the colonel's, and he in one further down the aisle. Hitty ducked down, kneeling close to the door, blanketed by its shadow. Her heart pounded equally with fear of being found and with anger at Peter for his crimes. Peter had gone beyond all bounds when he'd set this fire. The worst of it was that he didn't seem at all repentant and was now stealing sacred silver from the church. At that instant Hitty almost wished Peter would be caught with the silver in his arms. Maybe then he would be stopped from his wrongdoing.

A set of heavy steps accompanied by a sharp rap—the tip of a cane—proceeded up the middle aisle, then paused halfway to the pulpit. "Well! Look what I've found!" a voice matching its weighty tread called out. Immediately, Hitty was sorry for her wish. She did not want Peter to be caught. Please, dear God, she prayed for the first time in her life, let him escape this time.

"It's a boy! Stand up you ruffian," the gruff voice demanded and the cane rapped the floor three times. "What are you doing here? Explain yourself!"

She would not let Peter be taken away alone so she made ready to stand, but then froze in mid-rise as a high, thin voice that did not belong to Peter answered, "I been hiding from the fire." Hitty lowered herself to the floor again, bewildered.

"Speak up, boy!" Another strike of cane, this time against the edge of the pew.

"I got scared, sir," the boy's voice wavered. "The fire, it was all around and Ma and Pa were gone. I didn't know what to do so I came here to Mr. Andrews' meeting house." Hitty held her breath; if this boy had been hiding in the sanctuary, he must have heard Peter and her talking.

"I know you," a new voice, Hitty recognized as the Reverend Mr. Andrews himself, spoke with calm distinction. "You're Neb Howser's boy."

"Yes, sir. Ma and Pa went to Aunt Irene's for the day because she's ill. They left me to take care of the house and the shop and I don't know what to do," the boy said, his words rising into a whine. "The shop's caught fire! The flames—"

"There, there, son. There's nothing you could have done." Reverend Andrews sighed. "There's little any of us can do; it's in the Lord's hands, now. But you can't stay here. Is there someone you can go to in the north or west of town?"

"I guess I could stay with the Fergusons."

"Yes, good. The Fergusons will take care of you until your parents come back. You must go at once, though. We've got work to do here."

A pew door slapped the outside wall of the box after it was opened too hastily and swung freely on well-oiled hinges. "Sorry, sir," the boy mumbled. Hitty heard the door being fitted back and a tiny sound of metal on metal as the latch was turned, then the close steps of a small person moving reluctantly up the aisle.

Hitty expelled her breath slowly, wondering why the boy had said nothing about Peter and her to Reverend Andrews. Had he seen Peter up in the pulpit? Had he seen the silver Peter carried? And what had he heard? Hitty thought back on what had been said and relaxed some. The boy probably thought they were just hiding from the fire like he was. She concentrated now on the voices in the aisle which had grown in number within the last few moments, for more men had joined Reverend Andrews and the man with the heavy step and the cane.

"If we can keep the sparks off the roof we might stand a chance of saving it," one of the men was saying. "But we better remove the valuables just to be safe."

"What should we take?" asked another.

"Reverend Andrews, sir!" The shrill voice from the back of the sanctuary pierced the adult voices. Hitty sucked in her breath again. "Reverend Andrews," the boy said with a high pitched nasal intonation, "I think I should tell you—"

"Son, it isn't safe for you to be here." Reverend Andrews sounded impatient. His voice took on a commanding quality. "You must leave now."

"Yes, sir, but—"

"Now. Immediately."

"Yes, sir." Hitty could barely make out the response. But this time she listened until she heard the door open and the clink of the latch as it swung shut.

"We must take church plate, of course, and the Act of Parliament clock," Andrews said. "It'll take two to remove the clock. Jeremiah, you and Eleazar go up to the gallery. You can haul it up over the wall. Merriman, help me with the silver."

Merriman. Of course! The man with the heavy step and cane was Colonel Merriman Tibbits. She fit a picture in her mind to the gruff voice. Like all the leading men in the community, Colonel Tibbits wore his white hair in a long queue down his back and had large silver buckles on his knee breeches and his shoes. But Colonel Tibbits was distinguishable from the others in two ways: one, having attained fame during the Revolutionary War, he still wore the colonial three-cornered hat, and two, he carried a carved cane with a brass fitting around its tip which he used more to wave around and strike with than to assist with his walking. Could he be Peter's colonel? As quickly as she considered it, Hitty dismissed the idea. A man as important as Colonel Tibbits would have nothing to do with a baker's apprentice. Peter's colonel must be somebody who just called himself by that title.

"Where is the church plate kept?" Colonel Merriman Tibbits asked.

"In the robing room," said Reverend Andrews. "Except for two tankards in the pulpit which I used in my sermon on Sunday. I'll get those."

Hitty inched under the bench of the pew, tucked herself into a tight ball, and scrunched her eyes tight, waiting for what she knew must follow. There was a dull scraping from above as the clock was hauled up over the gallery wall and the great door in the vestibule opened and closed twice before the call that she expected came.

"Why, where are they?" cried out Andrews. "I can't find the tankards!"

"Are you sure that's where they were?" Tibbits called down from the gallery.

"Yes, I'm certain."

"They have to be there, then," assured a third voice.

"But they are gone, I tell you," came the reverend's anguished voice. "Oh, I should have come back immediately to lock them up!"

"We'll look around," the third person said. "They've just been misplaced."

"No!" thundered Colonel Tibbits, thumping his cane on the floor for emphasis. "A thief has stolen them! And he could still be here. Check the pews!"

"Perhaps the boy—" the voice was timid.

"No, you fool!" There was more furious thumping of the cane. "He had nothing on him, anyone could see that! Search the pews!"

Hitty bit her lip to keep from whimpering and opened her eyes, her head still tucked down. She stared at the cloth of her dress that was an inch from her nose, concentrating on the faded and weakened threads that were stretched taut over her knees. It was done now. They would be caught and Peter would be found out. What would they do to someone who stole church silver? Hitty's experience didn't include this knowledge. But she did know that setting a fire was a hanging offense, Peter had said so. "Please, dear God," she began again but let the prayer linger.

Tramping feet hastened along the sides of the galleries overhead, up the outside aisles of the sanctuary and down the middle. A shadow passed over Hitty's pew, but didn't hesitate. It would take a closer inspection to see her tucked under the seat, but Peter wasn't as small and would be found by a glance into his pew. Hitty's back ached from the strain of her position as she waited for a cry of discovery.

"Fire on the roof!" A voice rang out from the back of the sanctuary. "Grab your buckets!" There was commotion as the men rushed for the door. And in an instant, the miracle Hitty hadn't dared pray for happened; the sanctuary was empty.

Her fingers fumbled with the latch as they nervously twisted it. "Peter!" she whispered hoarsely, bumping the door open with her hip. "They've gone!"

Peter bobbed up from several pews behind her, his eyes large and dark in a wan face. Shoving a tankard inside each flap of his jacket, he made his way quickly on feather-soft tread down the aisle and through the vestibule to the left side door where he pushed down the thumb latch and eased it open. He pressed an eye to the crack for an instant and then pushed the door shut again, lifting the latch with his fingers so there was no sound.

"They're hauling water up to the roof," he whispered to Hitty who had followed. "We're going to have to wait until they leave."

"Is there another door?" she whispered back.

"The one in the robing room but that's where the fire wagons are."

"What about the windows on the side away from the fire?"

Peter whirled around and raced back into the sanctuary. He flung open the door to a side pew and stepped up into it, carefully placing the tankards on the floor. Hitty saw them clearly for the first time and, although she knew nothing about silver, she could tell they were valuable from the fancy work on their handles and hinged lids. "You shouldn'ta took those goblets," she said.

Peter was standing on the bench, pulling on the sash. "Oh, shut up, for cripes sakes, and help me!" She climbed onto the bench and tugged alongside him but the swollen window wouldn't budge. They tried three more windows, able to open only one more than a few inches.

"It's just as well, anyway," panted Peter as he wiped his upper lip with his sleeve. "In a few hours it'll be pitch dark and I can sneak out."

"You should put those back before it's too late," Hitty said. "It's stealing."

"Listen here, I got to live, don't I?" Peter whirled on her. "The colonel didn't pay me after I did a job for him. That's stealing, isn't it? He stole my payment from me! So now I have to leave and I need money. I only took two of their stupid cups. You heard them—they got lots more locked up somewhere."

"It's not right," mumbled Hitty.

"You keep quiet! And get away from me." He waved at her like shooing a fly. "Go back to Stockwell or run away, I don't care. When I'm gone I don't ever want to see you or anyone else from this damned town again."

"But I got to go with you! Don't leave me," Hitty pleaded, touching his arm.

Peter grabbed her wrist and pulled her close to him. Between clenched teeth he said, "You are not going with me. Do you understand?" He flung away her hand. "And don't follow me!"

Hitty watched him disappear into the vestibule, probably to go upstairs to some other secret place that only Peter would know about. She settled onto a bench with a soft cushion in a back corner pew that had a window offering a partial view of the street. Resting her chin on her arm, Hitty watched the men run back and forth with buckets that were hauled on long ropes up out of her sight to the roof above. She would listen and watch for Peter to leave and then follow him. Once they were away from here, she would reveal herself. Peter would let her stay with him because he always had before. Despite his words, he knew they belonged together.

SEVENTEEN

A GOOD DOSE of Mayta was exactly what I needed. After I picked up Max from school I drove out to Plum Island. Mayta took one look at my face and shooed the kids out the back door onto the beach, supplied with fistfuls of cookies and a bucket of sand toys. She said nothing until she'd poured us each a cup of coffee, sliced a lemon poppy seed loaf cake, and set it on the table. Then she sat down, wrapped her gnarled fingers around her mug and said, "What's up?"

Without preliminaries I told her about Jason Snoud's death. Then I backtracked and told the details: how the Van Amburgs at first thought he was a sleeping alcoholic, how the police and ambulance came, and we realized that it was Snoud and he'd been murdered. I told her about the rest of my day, even how I'd turned into a sobbing mess at the Tot Lot.

"You know," I said, "what bothers me the most—this is going to sound pretty selfish—is that it had to happen here, where we—the kids, Gus, you, me—live."

Mayta nodded. "That's a natural reaction, I think."

"But murder isn't supposed to happen here! Detroit, yes, but not Newburyport!" The instant the words were out I knew how Mayta would react.

"Ha!" She grinned wryly. "You think we're different out here."

"I didn't mean—"

"Oh, we are in some ways," she assured me. "But all the vices and hatred and prejudice that you lived with in Detroit—

well, they're in every big city and small town, be it north, south, east, or west. Even here in Newburyport."

"I know that," I said, unconvinced.

"Look," Mayta said, "in all your historical research, didn't you ever come across some of Newburyport's more heinous crimes? The robbery that took place about ten years ago at a floral shop down on Merrimack Street—it's that small business equipment store now—where the owner was shot dead?" When I shook my head she went on. "Well, the ones who did it were local kids. Probably went to that quaint little grammar school your own kids attend. And what about our beautiful colonial courthouse that was bombed back during the early seventies by those hippie outlaws? You had to have heard about that."

"Yeah, but—"

"And back in the sixties the synagogue in town here was painted with swastikas and hate words. And when the ministers of all the churches in town got together to protest and invite speakers to come talk against hate groups, the leader of the American Nazi Party announced he was coming to Newburyport to speak."

I gave her a skeptical look.

"This is true!" Her silver curls quivered as she nodded emphatically. "The grand leader of the American Nazi Party! Thankfully, the jerk was stopped by the police at the New Hampshire border and arrested on some minor charge. But you figure it out; how'd he get that far—how'd he even know what was going on to begin with—if there hadn't been a faction of Nazis in the area?" She paused a moment to let it sink in. "Do you hear what I'm saying? Even though some of us like to believe it, Newburyport isn't sealed in a Mason jar. Whatever hateful thought, belief, or act there is, it can be found here as well. Only difference is that being a small town means it doesn't happen here as often as it does in big cities."

She was right. Ever since I'd come to Newburyport I'd been acting as if I'd found a Mecca populated by a rarefied breed of human being. I felt a bit embarrassed, having her call me on it.

"But having said all that, I still believe that Newburyport is a great place to bring up kids." Mayta smiled sympathetically, lecture over. "I didn't live my whole life here just because my family had always been here. I chose to stay."

We talked about Jason Snoud then. Mayta had known his family but not Jason, himself. "His father was quite a craftsman," she remarked, "well known for his restoration work on historic homes around town as well as steeples. Jason must have taken over the business while I lived away those few years."

"But who would have killed him? And why do it in the church?"

Mayta shrugged. "Maybe he was killed elsewhere and just put there."

"This sounds like the conversation we had about the skeleton: 'Where did he die? Was he put in the steeple before or after he died?'"

"Are you suggesting you think the two deaths are related?"

I hesitated. "I don't know, Mayta. Maybe. Do you think it's a crazy thought?"

She shook her head slowly. "No. It doesn't seem likely they'd be related but then it's odd finding the second body right after finding that first one who'd been up there for who-knows-how-long. And both of them in a church, of all places."

I took a gulp of coffee. "Well, I think I'm over my shell shock because now I want to do something. The police will find out who killed Jason Snoud, but nobody cares about Mr. Bones. I'm more determined than ever to find out about him."

"That a girl! Let me know how I can help."

I bit into my slice of lemon poppy seed cake. "Mayta, you are the best cook!"

"Aw, come off it, Andy. I'm not perfect, either. You think I spend every day baking? That cake came from the farm stand."

GUS WAS TRUE to his word. He left school promptly at the close of the day. No meetings, paperwork, or chats with the principal. The three of us rehashed the events of the day, sitting around Mayta's table accompanied by the lilting voices of Max and Molly as they played in the sand just beyond the screen door.

Other than where they were found, there was no obvious connection between the two deaths, but my intuition linked Jason's murder with that of the unidentified person we'd found in the steeple. For my peace of mind, I had to know who Mr. Bones was, why he was killed, and if his death was related to the Great Fire. Although I couldn't begin to tell how, I was sure the answers to these questions would shed light on Jason's murder. And for some unexplainable reason, Mayta and Gus were with me on this. Maybe Jason's murder brought reality to that old death. Whatever it was, it had galvanized us into making a plan for action.

I formed some questions about specific town forefathers to ask Frieda and Herb Cole when I had tea with them on Wednesday. In the meantime, I would find out who had owned pew number 77 back around the time of the fire. I would also try to get hold of a town directory for 1811, which would give me some addresses to go with some names. Gus said he'd call an old friend that was connected to the state police lab to see if he could get information on Mr. Bones. Mayta kept mum about what she was planning, but from the determined look in her eye I knew she had something up her sleeve.

EIGHTEEN

"MY DEAR, wasn't it just terrible about poor Mr. Snoud!" Frieda Cole lamented as if to herself. To intone it as a question would have made her seem curious, which would have smacked of tactlessness. As it was, I'd been given a tour of her stately three story Federal home and its accompanying perennial gardens laid out in original Victorian fashion with stone pathways, trellised arbors, and boxwood borders, and then settled with a cup of tea on the brick patio before Snoud's name had been brought up.

It had been five days since we'd found Snoud's body, and his murder—they were calling it that now—had been the lead story in the *Daily News* for three of those days. The empty wine bottle found with him had led to speculation among the general population: Snoud had been drinking with somebody who killed him; he'd been drinking alone and surprised somebody who came in; he hadn't been drinking, the killer tried to make it look that way. Of course, my name, along with Frank's and Ginger's, had been mentioned in at least two of the newspaper accounts, so we were getting our share of attention at the grocery store, pharmacy, and on the street.

Dressed in baggy brown pants and a faded plaid shirt, Herb joined Frieda and me on the patio. There was dried mud on his shoes and dirt under his fingernails, and he brushed off the seat of his pants before settling into one of the wrought iron chairs. "I've been thinning out seedlings," he explained, waving off his wife's offer of tea. "I have four flats of—"

"Herb," Frieda interrupted gently, "I was just remarking on what a terrible thing it was about Mr. Snoud." They turned expectant eyes on me, and before I knew it, I was giving an account of the Van Amburgs' finding Snoud, my arrival on the scene, the police, the ambulance and, finally, the body—which I knew they wanted to hear even though they winced at the indelicacy of it.

"Oh, the poor man!" Frieda refreshed my cup with a splash of tea from a china teapot painted with blue forget-me-nots. "Who would have done such a thing! And in the church of all places! I remember him as a child," she went on. "His father did some work for us once and brought little Jason. He was so cute, following around with his own little hammer."

"That's right," Herb said. "Snoud repaired the lookout on the roof didn't he?"

"Are they an old family?" I asked.

"They're descended from a shipwright family—Caleb Brown," said Frieda.

"I read about Caleb Brown," I said in surprise. "He was one of the craftsmen who built the church. I wonder if Jason ever saw the original plans for the steeple."

"Oh, I don't think so," said Herb. "Nobody's ever found the building plans for the church."

"Frieda tells me you're responsible for these beautiful gardens," I said, changing the subject. "I didn't realize there was so much land behind the houses up here."

He smiled modestly. "People don't expect High Street properties to be so deep because the houses are close together. There used to be wonderful gardens behind all of these homes. I've tried to keep ours as close as possible to the original Victorian layout."

"The estate has been in my family for four generations." Frieda held out a small tray with creamer and sugar bowl. I plopped two lumps of sugar into my cup purely for the experience of using the cute little silver tongs. "My great-grandfather, Eleazar Rand II, built the house in 1807," she continued, her chin lifting a little, "and the property was passed down through my grandfather and father to me."

"Frieda has lived here all of her life," Herb said. "She was an only child."

"Mother would have garden teas." Frieda smiled reminiscently. "The ladies of High Street would come dressed in their fine dresses, wearing hats and gloves. The tables were covered in white damask, and set with the family silver. The servants passed around the trays but Mother always poured. I loved watching Mother pour from the silver tea service." As Frieda took a dainty sip from her cup, its fragile handle held by thumb and forefinger, I had a sudden glimpse of a little girl at a formal table, feet dangling beneath her long white dress, sipping her tea, proud to be included in her mother's social event.

"Frieda and I have no children," Herb said matter-of-factly, breaking into his wife's reverie, "so the property will eventually go to the Historical Society." Frieda gave him a sharp look. "It's the best way to preserve the family history," he continued. "We couldn't bear for the house to be turned into condos and the gardens torn up. The Society has promised to keep it intact."

"How can they promise that?" Frieda pressed her lips into a tight line and looked out over the three landscaped tiers that graduated down from the patio to the back of the expansive lot. "They can't afford the upkeep."

"Now, Frieda, they've said—"

"This is not the time to discuss it." Frieda's tone ended the topic. She offered me a plate daintily stacked with triangular cut sandwiches.

"Thank you," I said, thinking that the decision to bequeath the Rand estate was far from final.

After Herb, seemingly unconcerned about his wife's reprimand, took three sandwiches, Frieda put the plate on the low table in front of us without taking one for herself. "Now, dear, I see you have your notebook with you," she said. "You would like information on the Rands for your research."

"Oh, yes." I wiped my fingers on my napkin and picked up the steno pad I had set on the ground at my feet.

"Don't rush the girl. Let her eat," Herb chided his wife. But he set down his plate, rose, and entered the back door of the house. A few minutes later, he returned with a cardboard box filled with file folders and loose papers and placed it on the patio in front of Frieda. She brought out the top folder and opened it.

"This is the family tree," she said, holding up a photocopy of a stylized "tree" that fanned out into tiny branches filled in with names and corresponding birth and death dates, written in the varying script styles of different generations of recorders.

"The original page is in our Bible, of course," said Frieda. "I use this copy to save the wear and tear on the Bible. It's so old."

"I'm interested in the Rand who would have been around in 1811," I said.

"Why 1811, particularly?"

"Well, my research is the period between 1800 and 1850, and I thought I'd start with the first big event of that time period, which was the Great Fire. The church was so close to the fire," I said, improvising, "that the congregation had to have been affected by the devastation and also, involved in the rebuilding."

"I think that would have been Eleazar Rand II, but we'll find out as we go along." Frieda pointed to the trunk of the tree. "Now, my first ancestor to reach the shores here was Amos Rand back in 1630," she began. I took another sandwich. There would be no leaping ahead; we would get to 1811 by climbing twig by twig up the Rand family tree.

We continued through the generations. I listened patiently until we finally reached a branch in the midsection of the tree, where the birth and death dates ranged from the late 1700s to the early 1800s. "A tankard was given to the church to honor the birth of Eleazar Rand II." Frieda paused, her finger on his name. "I think this is the Rand you're interested in. He's the one who had this house built."

I leaned in to read the minuscule lettering. Eleazar Rand II had been born one year before the American Revolution, in 1775. He married a Sarah Sweet in 1807 and they had a single child, John, in 1810. Eleazar died in 1814, three years after the Great Fire. "He was still in his thirties when he died," I observed.

"Hmmm, yes—of consumption," said Frieda, regret in her voice. "Had he lived longer he would have done much for New-buryport. At the time of his death he was already a prominent banker and a selectman of the city and was successful enough to be able to build a fine house for his wife and young son." Her finger twitched on the page. "His son, John, was my grandfather."

Of course. Eleazar Rand was one of the city selectmen who had signed the notice in the newspaper of 1811 asking for information on the fire. "What else can you tell me about him?" I asked quickly before we shimmied up higher on the tree.

Frieda shuffled through the folder and pulled out a sheet with Eleazar Rand II typed across the top. "I hope to have someone type all of this onto a..."

"Word processor," Herb supplied.

"Yes, a word processor, and then have it put together in a book." She handed me the paper and I scanned what was mostly a list of Eleazar Rand II's accomplishments. He must have been on almost every board and committee in town, including the Committee of Proprietors of the First Parish House of Worship.

"He was quite active in the church," I noted.

"Oh my, yes. He was a deacon, you know." She pointed at the page I held.

"I'll bet his notes and minutes describing the workings of the city were very interesting." Since Frieda lived in her ancestor's home I figured it was possible that such papers still existed in attic corners.

"Oh, I wouldn't know," she said. "If he kept any they disappeared away years ago. Of course, formal minutes of meetings would still be in church or city records."

"Of course," I said. "I just thought that since your great-grandfather lived at a time of dramatic change in town—the Embargo, the fire—" Frieda and Herb nodded in unison, "that he might have kept a journal or personal notes."

"If he did," said Frieda, ruefully, "they haven't survived. He did keep close records of his accounts in the blank pages in the back of the family Bible."

Accounts. It was something, anyway. "Would it be possible to see those?" I thought of the earlier comment about saving wear and tear on the Bible.

Frieda pressed her lips together but Herb spoke up. "We have copies of those as well, don't we? They're quite boring. Just house expenses, that sort of thing."

"I would like to see them," I spoke quickly, "if you don't mind."

Frieda shuffled through her folder again and came up with a sheaf of papers held together with a large paper clip. I skimmed through pages filled with tall looping penmanship and slanting oversized numerals, not sure what I was looking for. Then, while Herb straightened papers in the box, and Frieda tidied the table, I read page by page, determined to find a clue to the man himself.

"On this page, what does this mean: 'September 10, 1812, to Davison $35.00 for M.P., clothes, expenses'?" I asked.

"Davison was Eleazar's younger brother," Herb said.

Frieda frowned. "Davison Rand was a successful farmer in West Newbury. I can't think why Eleazar would have given him money for clothes and expenses."

"Here it is again, three months later: 'To Davison, $20.00 for M.P., expenses.'" I flipped through the pages. "There are three more after that, in March, June, and September of 1813—all entries for twenty dollars—then no more."

"Let me see." Herb craned forward and I tilted the paper for him. "That's curious. I wonder who M.P. was."

"Probably a servant who bought things for the household," Frieda said dismissively.

"Whose household?" I asked. "Eleazar's or Davison's?"

Frieda shrugged. "There are some references that we aren't going to be able to figure out. Now John, who was Eleazar's only son and my grandfather, kept meticulous household records. I can show you those." She leaned over the box.

"It wouldn't have been a servant," said Herb. "A servant wouldn't have been given that much money." Frieda straightened and gave her husband a sharp look.

"What about Davison's farm records?" I asked. "Would you have those?"

"No," Frieda said shortly. "They would have gone to his ancestors and at this point in time I don't even know who those people are."

Herb nodded in agreement. "The last of that side moved away long ago."

Frieda bent back to her task. "Ah! Here he is," she said with exuberance. "John Rand, born 1810, died 1883." She set a bulging file folder on the table and I resigned myself to moving on up the Rand family tree.

Frieda cleared her throat and began, "My grandfather, John Rand, was very influential in the China trade."

NINETEEN

CARL MCBRIDE, Gus's old friend, had been away on vacation to Martha's Vineyard so it was nearly a week before he got the message Gus had left at his place of employment—the state lab in Salem where Mr. Bones had been taken. I was in the kitchen trying to put together something for dinner when Carl called back on Friday afternoon. Having pulled out half a dozen boxes with about ten pieces of pasta rattling in each, I was rummaging in the pantry for a jar of something tomatoey to use for sauce when I realized it was Carl that Gus was talking to. I emerged from the pantry and stood at the door to the dining room, listening to one side of the dialog. I waited through the so-what-the-heck-have-you-been-up-to part of the conversation, the family update, and the old friends update (they'd graduated high school together) before Gus finally lapsed into one syllable responses meaning, I hoped, that Carl was supplying the information we'd been waiting for.

"Uh huh. Uh huh. Wait a minute, let me get something to write with." Gus waved at me and I grabbed a colored pencil from the pile in front of Molly, who was drawing at the counter, and handed it to him. I followed him over to the dining room table and peered over his shoulder as he jotted down on the back of an envelope, "170-200 yrs, 13-19 yrs old." Then he paused.

"You could?" said Gus. "Great! Hey, why don't you come for dinner?"

Horror-stricken, I moved into Gus's line of vision, shaking my head and jiggling an empty rotini box at him. "Oh, you have a meeting." His voice fell. "How about afterwards, then? Come by for a beer?" Another pause. "Great! See you then."

"Carl's stopping by around eight on his way home," Gus announced.

"I thought he lived in Boston."

"He did. But he moved back to the area—West Newbury— a couple of years ago. Funny how you lose touch with people. Too bad, I mean."

I took the envelope from his hand. "One hundred and seventy years plus. So, we were right. Mr. Bones is old enough to have been around in 1811."

"Who's Mr. Bones?" asked Molly.

"Thirteen to nineteen years old? Can't they narrow it down more than that?"

Gus shrugged. "I guess not."

"Male or female?" I handed back the envelope and turned to stir the boiling noodles.

"I didn't ask," Gus said. "We'll find out when he gets here. He can't bring the report itself, but he can explain the findings."

"Who-is-Mis-ter-Bones?" Molly jabbed her pencil into the paper with each syllable.

"Don't do that," I admonished Molly as Gus took her paper and pencil away. With raised eyebrows, he held up the picture for me to see. It was an obvious depiction of a skeleton.

"Nice picture, Molly, dolly." Gus handed it back to her. "Are you going to put some clothes on your person?"

"He's not a person. He's Mr. Bones," Molly said.

"Okay. Time to wash hands and get ready for dinner," I said firmly.

Dinner was mediocre by adult standards, but elicited a fair amount of excitement on the part of the younger half of the family who were intrigued by the four different varieties of pasta in the main course. I was finishing up in the kitchen and Gus was tucking the kids into bed when Carl arrived.

I had met Carl only once and couldn't place him until I opened my front door and saw him standing on the porch. He wore a rumpled trench coat with half of its collar stuck in and baggy khaki pants that drooped over paint-spattered Nikes. Wiry black hair bushed out from beneath a Red Sox baseball cap. I remembered him instantly because he was dressed about the same way he had been the first time we'd met: at his and Gus's five year reunion, a semi-formal affair.

By eight o'clock we had the social preliminaries out of the way and were settled in the living room with beers for them and a glass of Chardonnay for me.

"First of all," Carl said, "I had a textile expert look at the clothing to help us fix a time period." He set a beat-up vinyl briefcase on the coffee table, clicked open the one fastener that wasn't broken, and took out a fat file folder with corners of papers sticking out around the edges. "Her findings corresponded with ours. Our subject died in the late seventeen or early eighteen hundreds—say between 1790 and 1820."

"So, what can you tell us about him—or her?" I asked.

"Well, what we have here is an individual of European descent," he began as he sifted through a clutter of loose papers. "The recessive cheekbones, narrow nasal aperture, and overbite are Caucasoid characteristics."

"What about age?" I asked. "You said it was thirteen to nineteen years old?"

"Yes, probably closer to thirteen or fourteen, given the size. I'm looking for the—here it is, the stats on the epiphyses." He pulled out a page. "You see, the teeth and the length of the long bones tell us the individual was in his or her teens. We know this because the epiphyses—the bony caps on the ends of the arms and legs—hadn't united. That's usually happened by age twenty."

"You say his or her," Gus said. "You haven't determined the sex?"

"Well, not unequivocally," Carl hedged. "In most cases it's easy to determine sex in adults because a woman's pelvis is usually broader than a man's. However, many times the pelvis is not fully developed until early adulthood. Our subject here, could be a female whose pelvis was not yet defined. But," he added, sensing our disappointment, "there are other factors that help us make a determination."

"Like?" I prompted.

"Females usually have smaller skulls because their structures tend to be smaller overall. This individual has a large skull for his size."

"So it's a male?" Gus asked.

"It could be a small male," acknowledged Carl. "But without other substantiating characteristics, skull size isn't enough to determine gender."

"What other characteristics do you look at?" I asked.

"Teeth," he announced. "Males tend to be one or two years slower in overall physical development than females, except in dental maturation, so comparing skeletal and teeth development can oftentimes identify gender."

"You mean that if the bones say it's someone older and the teeth say it's someone younger it's a male," I said. "If not, it's a female."

"It's not quite that simple, but yes, basically, that's it," Carl said.

"So, which is it?" I persisted. "Male or female?"

"We can't be completely sure. Some of the teeth are missing. They might have been lost before death, or fell out after death or they may have never developed. We'd need to do further testing to find out these things. That's why I stress that this is a preliminary report."

"Okay," I said, bluntly, "but you can make some educated guesses, can't you?"

Gus's knee nudged mine in warning but Carl grinned for the first time since he'd arrived. He took a hearty gulp of beer, wiped his mouth with the back of his hand and said, "Dr. Fitzpatrick would have my hide but I'm going to go out on a limb. I think there's enough to put together a pretty accurate picture of this person."

We waited while Carl rearranged his notes in front of him. "I believe," he said, "that the remains are those of a male Caucasoid. Besides the other indicators I mentioned, the remnants of clothing on the subject indicate male attire for that era. Our subject was somewhat malnourished, which would account for his small size and poor teeth. His living stature was about four feet, ten inches, and he was probably thirteen or fourteen years old. From a thatch we found nearby, we know that he had straight blond hair, some of it about four inches in length. He was left-handed. He wasn't old enough to have worked long, if he worked at all, and therefore had no identifying wearing patterns that would denote a means of livelihood."

"You can tell all of that from the bones?" I said, impressed.

"I could've told you much of that from a single bone," Carl boasted. "With just a thigh bone I could tell you a subject's diet and rough age. Using a mathematical equation, I could determine within a few centimeters his height in life."

Gus and I exchanged looks.

"Now, as to the condition of the bones, we have a complete and—except for the skull which fell off—undisturbed skeleton." To me he added, "Because the skull is the heaviest part of the body and is supported by one of the most fragile parts—the vertebrae—it's inevitable that it will eventually fall off if the skeleton is left in an upright position. After all, heads will roll." He chuckled at his macabre joke. Gus and I laughed weakly.

"Rarely do we get such a preserved specimen," Carl continued with enthusiasm, "especially this old. We tend to get bodies from shallow graves in wooded areas where wild animals and dogs scavenge, chewing on and scattering bones."

"What about the cause of death?" Gus asked.

"Ah, that's interesting." Carl pulled out a paper with sketches and notations. "There are indications of trauma to the head."

"Trauma?" I said.

"Yes, if I had the pictures, I could show you better. But look at this." He drew an outline of a skull with holes for eyes, nose, and mouth. "On one side there's a partial circular imprint about an inch long," he drew a small moon shape above where the ear would have been, "with fracture lines that extend from the imprint up to the lower edge of the right eye socket." He made several wavy lines connecting the moon shape to the eye hole.

Enthralled, Gus and I hunched over the crude drawing. "Any idea what happened?" I asked.

"He either fell onto or was struck with something heavy that would leave a half circle pattern."

"Like the end of an iron bar?" Gus said.

"Yes, like that, but the circle is a basic shape. The rounded corner of a box or piece of furniture would make a partial circular imprint, as would many tools."

"Somebody bashed him on the side of the head with something like an iron bar and hid him in the steeple," I surmised, a picture forming in my mind.

"That may or may not have been the cause of death," Carl said. "Even though the lack of healing indicates the trauma took place either shortly before or at the time of death, we can't rule out the possibility that the victim died of other causes."

"You mean he could have lived with that kind of injury?" Gus said.

"Not for long, but yes, he could have lived afterwards."

"But did you find any other 'trauma' or clues to his death?" I asked.

"No, nothing else."

"Then can you make an educated guess that he died of head injuries?" I said.

Carl grinned for the second time that night. "Yes, we probably could do that."

As he put away his papers the talk turned to social banter. Over a second beer apiece, Gus and Carl caught each other up on news of old friends and classmates. Then, on his way to the door Carl stopped. "Oh! I just remembered something. I got sidetracked when we were talking about the fabric and forgot to mention that traces of grain and opium were found on the clothes."

"Opium?" Gus and I said together.

"Numerous medicines of the time contained opium," Carl explained. "Anybody—even a child—could obtain them over the counter. Our subject here was probably self-dosing himself for some malady. We didn't find a trace in either bones or hair, so if he ingested it, it was short term. Perhaps he took it after his head injury to dull the pain."

"What about the grain you said you found?" Gus asked.

"Wheat. There were traces of ground wheat grain found on the front of the linen shirt the boy was wearing."

TWENTY

WHEAT GRAIN on the front of the shirt. Could our Mr. Bones be the baker's apprentice, Peter Chambers, who was missing at the time of the Great Fire? Our skeleton was a male, came from the correct era, was the same age as the missing apprentice, and was littered with grain that somehow survived nearly two centuries. It seemed too easy to go looking for a person who had disappeared in 1811 and promptly find him in the newspaper's period equivalent of the want ads, but there it was. Gus thought I was being contrary. One piece of the puzzle—who Mr. Bones was—had been solved, he said. Accept it.

Saturday was warm and blustery. Gus, the kids, and I spent it with Mayta, enjoying spring as it seeped visibly onto Plum Island, tingeing the marsh grasses pastel greens and golds. The wind was more playful than harsh, and the sand shared its warmth with us as we ran barefoot above the tide line playing Frisbee and Nerf football, and then sat wrapped in blankets and ate sandwiches.

At twilight we walked along the beach which extends as far as you can see in either direction from Mayta's little cedar-shake cottage. The tiny twinkling lights of Gloucester were just becoming visible in the fading light on the southern horizon.

"An end to a glorious day," Mayta remarked, stooping to pick up a shell.

"Hmmm," Gus agreed. "May weather in March."

"April," I corrected him. "Today's the first day of April, April Fool's day."

"Molly! Max!" Mayta called out. "Collect some big clam shells for me. I need new ones for my garden border."

Molly held up a shell. "Like this, Grandma?"

"Yes, but even bigger if you can find them. Look up along the tide line."

They ran ahead, following the jagged line of litter the tide had made, stopping here and there to choose treasures that they put in Molly's jacket pockets or Max's sweatshirt which he had taken off and gathered up into a sack.

We had filled Mayta in on Carl McBride's information earlier and now she suddenly said, "I wonder if that apprentice had anything to do with the Great Fire."

Until then I hadn't gotten beyond the excitement of identifying Mr. Bones—Peter Chambers as I was learning to think of him. Carl's information had fleshed him out with height and probable weight, with hair color and texture, features, even clothing, so that now I had a picture in my mind of a real person. All of which made the idea that he met his end in a lonely hiding place more tragic. About the only thing Carl hadn't been able to tell us (besides who killed him) was whether Peter Chambers had anything to do with the fire. Mayta's remark started me thinking again—with justification now that he'd been identified—about a possible connection.

"Chambers had the silver tankard when he was found," I answered, "and we know it disappeared on the night of the fire, which means that he stole it or…"

"Somebody else stole it," said Gus, "killed him, and put it with him in the steeple support." He kicked a foot across the sand sending a light spray into the air.

"Which doesn't make sense," said Mayta.

"Maybe whoever killed him didn't know he had the tankard," suggested Gus.

"It was too big to hide in clothes," I said. "Maybe it was an accident."

"No," objected Gus. "If his injury was an accident, say a fall, he couldn't have gotten himself up into the steeple, pulled open a board, fit it back, and then died."

"Listen. Maybe somebody killed him accidentally—hit him too hard—and then had to hide the body. Maybe this somebody felt guilty and left the tankard with him as an apology or something." Gus and Mayta gave me skeptical looks. "Okay, forget the part about the tankard. It could explain why he was in the steeple, though."

"Why did this happen on the night of the fire?" asked Mayta, getting back to her original question. "Did the theft and murder have anything to do with the fire?"

"You mean was he killed because he knew who set the fire?" Gus said.

"Maybe he set the fire himself," I said. "A boy was seen running from one of the previous fires, remember?"

"Who killed him, then?" asked Gus. "Somebody he was working with?"

"Wait a minute." I halted, remembering something. "Seventy-seven."

"What?" Gus said, stopping also.

"That was the number on the scrap of paper in the tankard," I said excitedly. "I had this thought in church a few weeks ago that seventy-seven might refer to a pew. Then I forgot to look in the record book to see who owned that pew in 1811. It could be a clue to who else was involved in the fire. I'll look it up tonight."

On the way back into town I thought about the deaths of Peter Chambers and Jason Snoud. In addition to their being killed in the church, one within a few weeks of the discovery of the other, there was now one more coincidence: both had died as a result of a blow to the head. Come on, I chided myself, next you'll be thinking it was the same killer with the same weapon. Still, I found it hard to ignore a niggling feeling that the two murders were connected in some way.

I UNWRAPPED THE DEEDS BOOK from its protective tissue paper, and laid it on the coffee table. About nine by fourteen inches in size, the leather cover was worn, its corners rounded and made feathery soft by two centuries of thumbs and forefingers opening it. A label, pasted in the center, identified the contents as "Deeds to Pews 1801 to 1830." On the inside cover two columns listed the pew numbers, divided into five classes, and their corresponding prices—from one hundred to two hundred thirty dollars. Generally speaking, the pews at the front and along the sides of the sanctuary commanded the largest sums. However, there appeared to be no hard fast system of pricing because some members paid larger sums for pews that were further back.

I proceeded to read the first handwritten entry: "Know all men by these present, that we Thomas Toole, Eleazar Rand, and Merriman Tibbits, all of Newburyport in the County of Essex and Commonwealth of Massachusetts, a Committee of Proprietors of the House of Public Worship of the First Parish of Newburyport, by virtue of the power and authority given us by said proprietors…" The eighteenth century legalese continued for half the page, eventually recording the pew number purchased, the purchaser, and the price: "In consideration of two hundred and thirty dollars paid us by John Settle we convey to John and his heirs and assigns forever one pew on the lower floor of the new house of public worship, number 32…" with both purchaser and justice of the peace signed below the date, August 23, 1801, and the Committee of Proprietors—Toole, Rand, and Tibbits—signed as witnesses to the sale.

Toole, Rand, and Tibbits, again. As it had when I read the

tax books, Merriman Tibbits' bold and showy signature
prompted the picture of a pompous old retired colonel, stubbornly wearing his Revolutionary tri-corner hat like a war
medal twenty years after the war had ended. I hadn't yet
pictured Toole or Rand but I now knew a bit about them.
Eleazar Rand, Frieda's ancestor, was a banker who paid support
to his brother for some reason (for MP). Thomas Toole, whose
family line would die out with his great-granddaughter
Jeannine (Ginger's lady of the clashing hats), was a powerful
ship owner like Tibbits. What struck me about these men was
that I kept coming across their names together. They were city
selectmen and members of the Committee of Proprietors for
the church. What else did they control?

I read the first few entries of the deeds book and then flipped
through the rest of it. The wording on each page was exactly
the same. The only changes were the amount paid, the purchaser's name, and the signatures at the bottom. The vast
majority of sales were in the first few years of the building of
the meeting hall. After that, sales were sporadic; on occasion
a box would again be sold when the owners died, leaving no
heirs who either wanted or needed a pew, or when a family left
the church. As the years progressed, the original members of
the Committee of Proprietors were replaced, one by one, until
on October 10, 1830—the last entry—the names Toole, Rand,
and Tibbits had disappeared altogether from the list of signatures.

Because the records were ordered according to the date the
pews were sold, not according to the pew number, I started
again at the beginning and proceeded page by page. I hadn't
gone far before I found what I was looking for: Number
seventy-seven was sold on August 25, 1801, to Merriman
Tibbits.

The name wasn't a surprise; by now I'd expected the owner

to be one of three names—Toole, Rand, Tibbits—that kept popping up. So, what did it mean? What relationship would a poor young apprentice have had with a pompous wealthy ship owner? Did Chambers have Tibbits' box pew number in his pocket because he was supposed to deliver or pick up something? Meet someone there? Do something to the box? I discounted the last two; it was unlikely that a baker's apprentice would be hired to make cushion seats or build a bread board for a church box. Nor did it seem practical to use a pew as a meeting place. The only plausible reason for Peter Chambers to have Merriman Tibbits' pew number was that he planned to either put something in or take something from it. And that something, I was willing to bet, had to do with the Great Fire.

Pew number 77 was simple, adorned only by a hymnal rack—a modern addition—and an arm rest, which may or may not have been part of the original design. The bench was built into the paneled walls and the floor, carpeted now, but it would have been bare back in 1811. The only place in which to conceal anything was the narrow lidded box on the floor, constructed to hide the messy spittoons sea captains used during the long Sunday services. Besides a spittoon or two, there was enough room for an article of clothing or a medium-sized bag. Or a silver tankard. Had Chambers found the tankard in Tibbits' pew? Did Tibbits himself put it there?

I set the book aside and dug out my notes. Besides their positions as city selectmen and church leaders in 1811 Newburyport, Thomas Toole, Eleazar Rand, and Merriman Tibbits had other things in common. All were descendants of the original settlers and were, along with their ancestors, the primary benefactors of the silver owned by the church up to present day. Thomas Toole's great grandfather had given the two great flagons after a vow made at sea. Eleazar Rand had donated one tankard, and Merriman Tibbits two—in honor of the Declaration of Independence, I recalled—the same two that had been stolen. Which answered one of my questions: Tibbits wouldn't have taken a tankard he himself had donated.

I left the puzzle of the silver tankard for the moment and thought about the Great Fire. If there was a connection between Tibbits and Peter Chambers, was there a connection between Tibbits and the fire? If he set it, why? For gain? For revenge?

Was there a larger picture? Did the men of the Committee of Proprietors conspire to set the fire? I dismissed the idea immediately. Even if I could accept that on a given church committee three such evil and like-thinking men could be found working together, what possible purpose would be served by them destroying the town upon which they depended for their livelihoods? Besides, it made me sweat to even think about maligning all of the town fathers in one breath; if I ever dared whisper a conspiracy theory I'd be tarred and feathered and run out of town on a rail with my own mother-in-law leading the parade.

Unless—I couldn't stop myself from persisting in the same vein—it was by accident. What if Tibbits or all of the Committee of Proprietors intentionally set the fire for some reason, thinking that it could be contained to that one stable or row of buildings? Perhaps the target was one of the neighboring buildings and, because of the wind that night, the fire got out of hand. Suppose there was a cover-up because of the prominence of the individuals involved. That would account for the downplay of suspicions in the newspapers. It might also account for Peter Chambers' death; perhaps he was killed because he knew who started the fire.

It was mostly conjecture, but for the first time I could string together a plausible explanation for what happened on the night of the Great Fire. The scrap of paper with Tibbits' pew number found on Chambers linked this unlikely pair to each other and, because of the timeliness of Chambers' death, to the fire that devastated Newburyport. Were other town leaders involved? If so, they would be ancestors of some prominent citizens today, including the present mayoral candidate of Newburyport, Ben Barrett. Was the murder in the past connected to the murder in the present? Was it possible that somebody today—say, a descendant—didn't want the past to be known? Might he or she be willing to kill to keep it secret? The thought sent an involuntary shiver down my spine. Would Ben Barrett kill to ensure his election? Would prim little Frieda Cole, proud descendant of Eleazar Rand, steeped in her genealogy and her husband's plans to bequeath the family home to the Historical Society, kill to keep her ancestry unsullied?

I needed to find out more about Ben Barrett and Frieda Cole and also Thomas Toole, despite Ginger's assurance that Jeannine Toole of the clashing hats was the last in the family line. Then I remembered something else: Jason Snoud's ancestor had been a builder of the church. Was this another piece in the puzzle?

Suddenly I felt tired. I closed the old book carefully. The kids were asleep and Gus had gone upstairs to read in bed, leaving me to lock up. Moose lay stretched out on the floor by my feet, his head under the coffee table. The house was quiet. A block down Merrimack Street, its traffic usually humming on a Saturday night, was quiet. It seemed that all of Newburyport was still while a racket of thoughts jostled around inside my head, and something that felt like unleavened dough sat in my stomach. That was when I recalled one other little thing that brought the past into the present, an incident that hadn't fully registered as significant before. What if someone had rifled through the historical papers in the sea chest, not out of idle curiosity as Ginger and I had reassured each other, but because he was looking for something. Perhaps information from the past that would reflect badly on him in the present?

A sudden whoof from Moose set my heart hopping in my rib cage like a trapped rabbit. He bumped his head on the underside of the coffee table, tilting it while scrambling to free himself from the table legs. I grabbed for the deeds book as it slid toward the edge. "Damn it, Moose," I reprimanded, "do you have to go nuts every time a four-legged creature passes the house?"

But it wasn't the front bay window that Moose was interested in. He lunged for the side window that looks out on the driveway. A regiment of prickles converged at the base of my neck, marched out across my shoulders and down my arms. There were bushes outside that window, an unlikely place for a dog to be passing by. Raccoons were rare in our neighborhood, squirrels weren't worthy of his attention, and Moose wasn't attuned to cats unless he actually saw them.

He was barking full force now, front paws on the sill, nose stuck through the split in the sheer curtains. Fur stood at attention along the ridge of his spine and tail, and a regiment of prickles followed suit down my back. I stood rooted between coffee table and couch, the deeds book in my hands. Had someone been watching me? Was he watching me still? I set down the book and made myself move. First to the front door to make sure it was locked and to flip on the porch light, then down the hallway to the kitchen, which was lit faintly by the lamp just outside the back door. I checked the lock and peeked out. All was still within the halo of the lamp but at the edge of the circle of light, at the bottom of the porch steps, there was an indentation in the dirt where the grass was worn away. A footprint? The rabbit in my chest began leaping again. Was someone out there prowling around?

I flattened myself against the wall beside the door the way they do in police shows, expecting…what? A barrage of shots through the window? When nothing happened after a few moments and the strong urge to pee presented itself, I began to feel foolish. It was probably Gus's footprint; he goes out to the garage at least a half dozen times everyday. Still. I shivered. What if it wasn't Gus?

I realized then that Moose was next to me, and that he'd stopped barking. Whatever or whoever had been out there was gone. "What do you think, old boy?" I whispered. "Is it safe?" He nudged his nose against my leg. "No way," I said a little louder, a little bolder. "You can just cross your furry little legs. I'm not opening that door tonight."

TWENTY-ONE

IN THE MORNING we found footprints around the window outside. Gus called the police to make a report, but since the house hadn't been broken into, there wasn't anything they could do. "Yes. Well, thank you," said Gus, his voice tight.

I followed him back outside. "They're sneakers," I pointed out. "Kind of big."

Gus put his foot next to one of the prints. "Not so big. About a size ten." He mumbled something and plopped down on the middle step of the back porch.

"So, what do you think?" I sat next to him. "A peeping Tom or somebody casing the joint?"

He shook his head. "It's related to your snooping," Gus said. "You've ruffled a few feathers in town. Doing the research for the book was one thing, but poking into the fire and making comments about the founding fathers is another."

"Damn it, Gus," I protested, "I haven't been going around accusing the precious founding fathers of Newburyport of setting the fire."

"I know," he said in a tired voice. "But sometimes even the smallest comment can rattle cages. You know that."

"Whose cage am I rattling?" I demanded.

He rested his elbows on the step behind him and leaned back, stretching his legs out so that the heels of his shoes made grooves in the wet dirt. "Ginger thinks maybe you should let it alone."

"Oh, Gus! She's just spooked because of finding Jason. It

was a shock and then there was all the attention we got. Frank is as anxious to figure out things as I am."

"No, Andy." He looked at me sideways. "They want to find out about the skeleton but they aren't interested in coming up with an answer to the Great Fire or in starting up an independent investigation into Snoud's death."

"They told you this?"

"No. It's just an impression I got talking to Frank yesterday. I think he and Ginger feel you're going too far with this whole thing." Gus looked off in the direction of our neighbor's yard, which, even in its early spring brown-and-battered-down state, looked well-tended. "But there are others."

"Like who?" I demanded again. "Who are these 'others'?"

Gus shifted his attention back to our yard, littered with last summer's sand toys, a few weather-whitened papers—candy wrappers or mail flyers—and the occasional decomposing doggie pile—"Moose mines"—which had been missed in the last pick-up. "All right," he said, finally. "Lew Wenninger, for one. That was him on the phone. He made it clear that he thinks you're interfering."

"Oh, pooh!"

"Then there are the Coles. They acted kind of cool to me when I ran into them at the hardware store. And the other day," Gus pulled in his legs and sat forward on the step, "I was in the church office to drop off an announcement for the newsletter and Nancy—the secretary, what's her name?"

"Freeman," I supplied.

"Yeah, Nancy Freeman. Anyhow, she said something. I can't remember her exact words, and she said it jokingly, but the message was that she felt you were getting carried away blaming the Great Fire on historical leaders."

"How do these people even know I'm interested in the fire? I've only talked about it with you and Mayta and Ginger and

Frank—" I stopped. "Gloria at the library. She's friends with Nancy; I've seen them having coffee together at Bergson's. I'll bet Gloria told Nancy and Nancy, who sees everybody because she's in the church office all day, has been talking to the Coles and others. The whole town is probably abuzz with the news that Andy Gammon is slandering the town fathers."

Gus put his arm around my shoulders and pulled me into his side. "I wouldn't worry about it. If you let it alone, the talk will die down after a few weeks."

I pulled away. "But I can't let it alone, Gus. Don't you see? This is more than a few ruffled feathers. If someone felt threatened enough to search through the papers at church and then to spy on me in my house—maybe even break in, if Moose hadn't been there—it proves that the past is connected to the present. It means that either Chambers' death or the Great Fire is connected with somebody around today. Maybe even Jason Snoud's murderer."

"Oh, come on!"

"I'm serious," I said. "Just think about it for a moment. Why would anybody care what happened in the past, unless it could hurt them now?"

"I don't know, Andy," he said skeptically. "It seems farfetched."

"We know that Jason's murderer is most likely somebody from the church—"

"Wait a minute, how do we know that?"

"Jason didn't have his key, so it had to be a member who let him in."

"Unless the door was left unlocked," Gus pointed out.

"Jason wouldn't have come to the church expecting the door to be unlocked."

"Maybe he was meeting someone."

"It's possible," I conceded, "but why *there* if that someone wasn't a member?"

"Who knows?" Gus sounded exasperated. "Listen, Andy, I can't explain what happened to Jason Snoud. All I know is this is my hometown and I've known these people all my life and things like you're describing—" he faltered, "well, they just don't happen here."

"Whoa, there!" I turned to look straight at Gus. "What kind of things don't happen here? Things like murder? Like a boy being bludgeoned to death and stuffed in a picturesque steeple? Or a workman getting beaten over the head inside the quaint church which supports the aforementioned steeple?"

"I mean—"

"Or do you mean that the common motives that prompt people to kill—greed, jealousy, anger, covering up something damaging in the past—don't happen here?" Mayta would've been proud of me, spouting off her lesson almost verbatim.

But Gus was shaking his head. "I just can't buy it. Not when we're talking about the Coles or the Barretts."

I sucked in my breath and held it a few seconds before letting it out. "Okay," I said equably, "let's forget about the people you've known all your life, the obvious descendants of the city's forefathers like Ben Barrett and Frieda Cole. Who else has a staked interest in preserving the reputations of Newburyport's forefathers?"

"I don't know," he said. "I guess it would be somebody who stood to lose something, like prestige or money or something he or she believed strongly in."

I nodded, encouragingly. "Like who, for instance?"

Gus leaned forward and rested his arms on his knees, letting his hands dangle in front of him. "Well, you'd think it'd be the old families that were the most anxious to preserve the past," he said, warming up to his idea. "But, some of the strongest preservationists of local history are from elsewhere. They move here, adopt Newburyport because of its history, and then fight tooth and nail to keep it the way they think it always has been and always ought to be—quaint and charming."

"Kind of like me, huh? Thinking I've found life preserved in amber."

"Naw, you're not that bad." He rocked sideways, bumping me playfully. "You accept our past, warts and all. Also, you recognize that change can be good."

"You mean like Mark Levenson, then."

"Yeah, like Mark. He comes to town—what, three, four years ago? —from some place out west and appoints himself chief historical preservationist of the First Parish and of Newburyport in general. He sits on every historical committee and board in town and has a say in every historical decision. The guy bugs me."

"He bugs me, too," I said, thinking about Mark's officious attitude in Susan's office and at the service when the silver was on display. "Do you think he'd get ticked off enough at not being consulted or included in our research to spy on me?"

Gus screwed up his face. "It doesn't seem like his style."

"Wait a minute! Mark's writing a book on the early founders of Newbury. What if he thought somebody was re-scripting Newburyport's past? Would that anger him enough to commit murder?"

"Are you talking about Jason Snoud?"

"Yeah. Suppose that while he was fixing those supports in the steeple, Jason found something—something that would really screw up Mark's work, like proof that long-ago members of the church were responsible for the Great Fire, or for killing the baker's apprentice and stuffing him into the steeple. Then suppose he showed Mark what he found, told him he was going to take it to the newspapers or something, and Mark murdered him in order to preserve the past as he feels it ought to be preserved." In the pause I heard the muffled ring of the telephone from inside the house. "What do you think?"

Gus gave a short laugh. "Pretty farfetched."

"Yeah, I guess it is." The kitchen door opened and Max leaned out. "Mom, Grandma's on the phone."

"LOOK AT THE North Weekly section," Mayta demanded. "Read the first page and call me back."

Gus had followed me in and was pouring another cup of coffee. "What's up?"

"She wants me to read something in today's paper." I shrugged acquiescently and went to find the *Boston Globe*. Even before I had completely separated out the North Weekly section from the rest of the cumbersome bundle, a headline smacked me in the face: SUSPECT SOUGHT IN NEWBURY-PORT MURDER.

"Listen to this!" I called out as I skimmed the article. When Gus joined me, I read aloud, "'Police in Newburyport are looking for information in the murder of Jason Snoud, a stee-plejack who was found bludgeoned to death on March 24 inside the church where he'd been working... The murder weapon, which police believe was a heavy object with a sharp edge, has not yet been found'—wait a minute...here, listen to this— 'Snoud left his house at eight p.m., the night of March 23, after telling his wife that he was meeting friends at the Grog, a popular local bar. Snoud was not seen at the Grog and the friends he named say that he had made no plans to meet them that night. Police are looking into leads that he may have been—'"

"'Involved with a woman,'" Gus finished reading over my shoulder. He gave a low whistle. "The *Newburyport News* didn't say anything about that."

"Maybe the police didn't want it known and somebody leaked it to the *Globe*. If there is a woman involved, that would present another motive," I said. "One which would have nothing to do with the past."

"Ah, yes," Gus said. *"Cherchez la femme."*

"Cherchez la femme with a heavy sharp-edged weapon," I amended.

"It's well known that Jason Snoud liked the ladies," Mayta informed me when I called her back. "I've been checking around."

"So the way he acted wasn't just a macho put-on, huh?"

"Nope. Apparently he's worked his way through a half-dozen or so women in town. Some eligible and some not-so-eligible, like himself."

"Which means there's a host of possible suspects: disgruntled girlfriends, disgruntled husbands, his own disgruntled wife—what about her? How did she handle his indiscretions?"

"She tossed him out a few times but always took him back again."

"How do you know all this stuff?"

"His wife goes to my hair salon, so I listened to the scuttlebutt among the younger women and asked a few questions."

"Oh," I said, impressed with the source. Rumors passed around at the Clip 'n' Color were usually the gospel truth. "Any names mentioned?"

"None I recognized. But I'll keep working on it."

"By the way, I meant to tell you yesterday that I liked your hair," I said diplomatically. "A different shade, isn't it?"

"Dorothy put a toner on but I don't know." I could see her on the other end of the line patting curls that resembled polished silver coins. "It's still pretty bright."

"Oh! By the way, I've got an appointment to see Ben Barrett on Tuesday. To talk to him about his ancestors—you know, for the church history—but, also, I'd like to ask him a few questions. I was wondering if you'd go with me."

"Aw, Andy, I don't know. I don't think so."

"Come on, Mayta," I pleaded. "You don't have to do

anything but sit there. He'll tell me more if you're there because he knows you."

She grumbled a bit longer but, in the end, agreed like I knew she would.

TWENTY-TWO

IT WASN'T THE BEST of starts. Mayta arrived at the house ten minutes later than we'd planned. In all fairness, however, I have to say that I wouldn't have been ready on time myself. Just as he was set to walk out the door, Max had got a call from his pal, J.T., who wanted to ride bikes to school, so there ensued an energetic scramble to root out Max's helmet and bike lock from the basement where they'd been tossed back in the fall sometime. Then we sorted through the various keys on the hooks by the door, trying each in the lock before finding the right one. Lastly, I pulled the car out of the garage and moved various lawn implements to clear the path to Max's bike. By the time I'd waved Max down the street, Mayta was pulling into the driveway.

I ran back to close up the garage. While I was kicking aside the brick I'd used to prop open the side door to the garage, I had a sudden thought. The church's doorstop—a heavy granite paving stone with sharp edges—hadn't been there on the day of Jason Snoud's murder. We'd held the door open ourselves. Where had it been? Was it still missing? Could it be the murder weapon? Mayta tooted her horn and I waved at her as I darted back across the lawn to the house to make a call.

"Hi, Nancy! It's Andy. How are you?"

"I'm fine. How are you?" the chipper voice at the other end returned the greeting. "I haven't seen you lately. Not since—"

"Jason's murder," I finished for her. "That was so awful, wasn't it?"

"Yes," she replied soberly, "it was."

"His death must be hard for you. I know how friendly you were."

"We were?" Nancy asked, then sighed. "Oh, yes. After all these years it will be strange not having him around working on the steeple."

"Is Susan in?"

"No, she's at the clergy association meeting. Can I take a message?"

"Please have her call me after two this afternoon. I need to tell her something I just remembered. It has to do with Jason."

"Will do," Nancy chirped.

Mayta insisted on driving. We took off—more precisely, crept off—in her blue Buick, with me tensely clutching the folder in my lap because I hate to be late for anything, and Mayta acting like we were taking a Sunday drive.

"We're going to be late," I muttered, looking pointedly at my watch.

"So? It's not like he's a big shot or anything." She decelerated midway down Pleasant Street, considered a parking spot then, for whatever reason, crept on past it.

"Well, actually, he is a big shot," I said, getting perturbed. "He's a two-time former mayor and could very well be mayor again. But that doesn't matter. It's rude to be late for an appointment. There! What about there?" I waggled a finger at a parking spot at the end of the block with plenty of maneuverability in front of it.

"Too near the intersection," she said. "Somebody cutting the corner could bash me."

I clenched my teeth, thinking that if she didn't park soon *I* was going to bash her.

"I think I'll try the parking lot." Mayta made a slow wide arc into the public lot and began a systematic cruise up and down the aisles. Finally, she pulled into a space that met with her approval. I grabbed up her purse along with my own and jumped out of the car, starting off in the direction of the brick row building that housed Barrett's law offices. Mayta finally found high gear and caught up to me before I reached the brick walk.

In the waiting room of Barrett and Sagamore, Attorneys at Law, we were met by a young secretary who singsonged, "Right this way!" We followed in her energetic wake down a short hallway to Barrett's office where she announced our names and offered us coffee in the same breath. We declined.

Ben Barrett was seated at his desk, his back to a couple of nine-over-nine paned windows that looked out on the historical section of State Street with its brick walks and gas-styled lamps. The wall of the room to our right as we entered was decorated with Barrett's diplomas, including one for Harvard Law School, and one for the Massachusetts Bar, along with a smattering of pictures that featured the ever-smiling Barrett (dead center) with various groupings of people. Mayta gave the pictures the once-over, undoubtedly recognizing many of the people and even some of the events or circumstances that brought the groupings together, although she didn't let on like she did.

Bestowing upon us his trademark 100-watt smile, Barrett rose from his highly polished mahogany desk, the splendor and size of which would have overshadowed many men but fit him perfectly. He introduced himself to me and leaned across the desk to shake our hands. Mayta gave a tight smile and said, "Hi, Benjy."

Barrett waved off my apology for arriving late. "Great to meet you, Andy," he said expansively. "I have nothing but the highest regard for your husband. Used to watch young Gus play football up at Newburyport High—did us proud. Good student, too. Now he's back up there teaching, I hear. History, isn't it?"

"English," I corrected him.

"Ah, yes, English." He nodded slowly as if digesting some important fact, then turned to Mayta. "And it's lovely to see you, Mayta, dear. What are you doing these days? You were missing in action for a few years after Augie died."

"Oh, this and that," Mayta said airily. "Spent some time out in California with my sister, traveled in Europe a bit. Came home."

"But you're not in town, anymore, are you?"

"I'm out on the island. Gus and Andy have the house."

"We were at school together," Barrett said to me, amusement plucking at the corners of his mouth. "Mayta was a cheerleader when Augie and I played football."

I made a show of raising eyebrows at Mayta, to which she responded dryly, "There are probably a couple other things in my life you don't know about, too."

"Dear Mayta!" Barrett chuckled. "You always were so witty! How did Augie win you out from under my nose?"

"Ha!" Her exclamation was part snort, part guffaw, which had the effect of fanning Barrett's chuckle into laughter. Mayta's mouth twitched and then she burst into laughter also. When the two of them finished they were grinning at each other, sharing something from the past, I supposed, and that's when I realized that, for all her harsh words about him, Mayta was not impervious to Barrett's charm. Moreover, she didn't dislike him at all.

"Excuse us, Andy," Barrett said, drawing me back into the circle of conversation. A couple of involuntary chuckles escaped before he stifled them completely. "Now, then," he said, all seriousness, "what brings the two of you here today?"

"Andy, here, is putting together the church history for the Tricentennial of the First Parish," Mayta explained, her tongue now loosened. "That's her background, historical research. She and Gus met at college out in Michigan and taught in Detroit for a while before they came back east. Or rather, Gus came back east; the East is new for Andy—she's from Detroit. Anyway, she's doing research into the early members of the church which will be published into a book."

"That's wonderful!" Barrett exclaimed. "I heard there was some kind of project in the works but I didn't realize there was going to be a book written."

"Actually, a history of the parish is already written," I said "We—Frank and Ginger Van Amburg and myself—are updating the book that came out in the nineteen thirties. My part begins with 1800. May I ask you a few questions?"

"Certainly," Barrett said.

I consulted my notes. "Could you tell me about your ancestor, Merriman Tibbits? He was involved in the church when the new meeting house was built."

"Yes, he was." Barrett put his elbows on the arms of his chair and leaned forward. "My family has been active in the First Parish of Newburyport since its inception, when it split from the original parish. Even before that, as a matter of fact. Merriman's great-grandfather, William Tibbits, was one of the colonists who came from England to establish the first settlement on the Parker River." I arranged the expression on my face to register mild surprise. Thus encouraged, Barrett continued. Mayta, having done her job of priming Barrett (if indeed he had needed priming), sat back and listened along with me.

"You must be proud of your heritage," I said when I could get a word in.

"I am," Barrett said, soberly. "But you can't live on the laurels of your ancestors. Each generation has to make its own contribution to society." He paused for a moment during which I nodded and drew a star burst in a corner of my paper, waiting for the political plug. "Which is why I'm running for mayor, again. I want to make a difference."

"Like you did before," I said in a perfectly even tone. Mayta darted a look at me.

"I'm proud of my record as a leader in this community," he said. "Back in the eighties I fought to bring the train back to town. When service was finally restored, it was like a shot in the arm for Newburyport. Various groups became interested in preserving the city's history and the downtown was revitalized." Unspoken was the taint of the misspent funds and the fall from grace of his preservationist group.

"What can you tell me about your ancestor, Merriman Tibbits?" I asked, drawing him back to the original subject. "I've read he was quite the character."

"Oh, that he was!" Barrett exclaimed. "When I was a child there was a trunk in our attic that had old clothing and belongings of ancestors from way back—some of it had probably belonged to Tibbits because his household records were in there as well. Anyway, my brother and I used to dress up and play at being seventeenth century gentlemen. We'd put on these ruffly shirts and velvet pants and clump around with sticks." He chuckled at the memory.

I smiled, sharing his amusement. "Did you find any tri-cornered hats?"

Barrett gave me an appraising eye. "Ah, so you have done your homework! That story about old Merriman wearing his Revolutionary hat decades past the Revolution may or may not be true. I'd like to think it was because it makes him more of a character. However, I never came across a tri-cornered hat. Maybe he was buried wearing it." He chuckled again. "Yes, sir. Richie and I were sure disappointed when my father carted off that trunk to the Historical Society."

"The Historical Society has Tibbits' belongings?"

"Well, we don't know for sure exactly whose they are so they aren't labeled in the clothing display. But the society does have his household records."

"I don't remember seeing any records on display."

"Oh, they're not on display. There are boxes of records and papers that haven't been cataloged yet. Not enough volunteers to do it."

I wrote "visit Hist Soc" on the slender notebook in my lap and underlined it three times. "Tibbits was a ship owner, wasn't he?" I prompted.

"Yes, he owned a number of ships throughout his life. Newburyport was a maritime town in those days and promising young men began their careers by working in ships' counting rooms on the wharves or by going to sea, which was how Merriman Tibbits began." Barrett gazed off over our heads seeing not, I suspected, the straw matted wallpaper adorned with the physical evidence of a twentieth century lawyer's accomplished career, but a prosperous waterfront of more than two hundred years ago, vigorous with its preparations for ships' arrivals and departures.

"He began as a cabin boy and worked his way up. By age twenty he was a captain. Less than five years later, he had his first ship built in the Currier shipyard."

"Quite an accomplishment," I said. "That was when ships still put in port here, wasn't it?"

"Yes. Later in the century, when the trend moved to larger vessels, ships were towed out of the harbor, empty and on a high tide. Once loaded, they drew too much water to cross back over the sandbar at the mouth of the river, so ship owners used deeper ports like New York. But back in the early eighteen hundreds, during Tibbits' time, ships could still navigate the Merrimack and goods were brought home to Newburyport."

"It must have been quite an event when a ship returned," I remarked.

"I've often tried to picture it." Barrett rested his elbows on the desk, the fingertips of each hand meeting in front of his face. "The excitement on the wharves as wives and children met husbands and fathers who had been away for a year or more. Just the fact that they returned alive was reason enough to celebrate. But the goods!" Below Barrett's pensive gaze his fingertips galloped in unison against each other. "Fabulous treasures from India, the Philippines, and China: casks of exotic foods, bolts of muslins, silks, and velvets, embroidery such as nobody on this side of the world could begin to duplicate. We can't imagine today what that must have been like; our world is so much smaller and more homogeneous." Just before his eyes refocused on the twentieth century with Mayta and I sitting in the curved leatherette and chrome chairs in front of him, a fleeting expression of almost painful yearning passed over his face.

"But, already in the early eighteen hundreds the decline of mercantilism had begun," I said.

"Yes," he said almost sadly, "the decline began with the Embargo Act of 1807." He glanced down at the notebook in my lap to see if I was taking notes and I dutifully formed three loop de loops on the first line. "President Jefferson forbade American vessels to dock at foreign ports because English ships were harassing us at sea. The Embargo Act hurt commerce terribly; our ships lay idle for two years."

"Of course, there were ships that continued to trade even though it was illegal to do so," I commented.

"It was their livelihood," Barrett said in a defensive tone. "Many had to."

"Did Merriman Tibbits continue trade during the Embargo?"

"I presume so, although records from that year are, under-standably, sketchy."

"But he did continue to thrive during those lean years?" I asked. "Even after the Embargo, when British ships still made it risky to be at sea?"

"I don't know if he 'thrived,'" Barrett's voice put quotations around my word, "but he managed to survive the Embargo intact."

"Until the Great Fire."

"Yes, until the Great Fire." Barrett sighed as if talking about an immediate relative, not a relation five or six generations removed. "After his wharf was burned and his docked ships damaged beyond repair, he was a lost man. He never recovered financially or emotionally. He died a year or two after the fire."

"But Tibbits was still active as a selectman of the city," I said matter-of-factly. "His name was signed on a newspaper notice asking for help in finding the perpetrators of the fire."

"The what?" Barrett's eyes narrowed.

"The perpetrators. Notices were put in the newspapers offering a reward for information on the person or persons responsible for setting the fire."

"The Great Fire wasn't set deliberately."

"That's what the notices implied," I said. "And Merriman Tibbits' name was among those at the bottom of each notice."

Barrett's face relaxed. "Oh, that," he said. "As selectmen, his name would've automatically been included. The truth is he was in such a state of depression after the fire he never left his bed until he died."

"So, you don't think he believed the fire was deliberately started?"

"I don't think anybody really believed the Great Fire was deliberately started. It was customary to put out reward notices to reassure the population that every possible cause was being investigated." I looked skeptical and he continued patiently, "Look, fires were a constant threat in those days of lighting with oil and heating with wood. These towns were like tinder-boxes with their old wooden buildings, wharves, and ships. For every colonial town there's a story about a great fire that destroyed some section of it."

"And sometimes those fires were intentionally set."

"Ye-es," Barrett said, drawing out the word into two syllables, "that's probably true, but it didn't happen often. Arson was such an abhorrent crime, given the utter devastation it caused."

I nodded. "A fire setter back then would have been considered with the same intense fear and hatred as, say, a mass murderer. But, despite public abhorrence, there are mass murderers today just as there were arsonists in the eighteenth century. And reasons for arson back then, I'm sure, were much the same as today: revenge or to hide something."

"To hide something?" Barrett looked amused again. Mayta, meanwhile, made a show of indifference, holding her purse in her lap with both hands, and looking with idle interest at the pictures on the wall.

"Yes, you know," I shrugged nonchalantly, "like smuggling."

He gave a short loud laugh.

"Those tunnels that led underground from the waterfront up to the ship owners' homes on the ridge weren't just for convenience," I continued. "You know the history of the times; a lot of untaxed goods came in."

Barrett's amused expression was beginning to gel.

"Let's say a ship owner had a very lucrative smuggling operation," I said, deciding to push a bit more. "Now, let's suppose that ship owner was in danger of being found out or, perhaps he had an exceptionally large shipment coming in. A fire away from the waterfront would be a perfect distraction."

Barrett sat up in his chair. "How did you come up with this idea?"

I shrugged again. "Oh, through research and putting things together."

"Will you put this hypothesis in the church history?"

"Oh, no," I reassured him. "It's just to satisfy my own curiosity." I watched him visibly relax before adding a white lie, "Of course, the state police would very much like to solve the murder."

"Murder?"

"Yes, the baker's apprentice in the steeple was killed the night of the fire so they're obviously related." I thought I heard Mayta stifle a chortle.

"But how can you know that? Besides, that was ages ago."

It was my turn to adopt a patronizing tone. "Just because almost two hundred years have passed since the crime was committed, it doesn't mean there won't be an investigation. In fact, I was talking to the state forensic doctor just the other day and there are several clues that could connect that ancient crime to a recent one—Jason Snoud's murder." I couldn't help adding that last part. What's that expression: in for a penny, in for a pound? Anyway, Mayta kicked me in the ankle and I knew I'd gone far enough.

Barrett was a little distracted as I graciously thanked him. On our way to the door he and Mayta exchanged banter. Then I asked him something that had bugged me since we'd entered his office.

"Why, when you have windows that look out over the most scenic part of the historical district, do you have your desk so that your back is to the view?"

He raised his eyebrows in surprise but answered readily. "So I don't get distracted thinking about the past."

TWENTY-THREE

"So, HOW MUCH of that was hogwash?" Mayta wanted to know the minute we left the building.

"Some of it."

"On your part or his?"

I grinned sideways at her. "A bit of both, I'd say."

"The smuggling through the tunnels, that's true enough," Mayta said. "Every dozen years or so a road crew or somebody putting in a foundation for an addition breaks into one of those old tunnels. But would Merriman Tibbits—you were talking about him, weren't you—start a fire just to cover up his smuggling?"

"That was a guess," I admitted. We'd reached the car and I talked over the roof as she unlocked the door on the driver's side. "But it's plausible. If his operation was large enough and he felt threatened, Tibbits might have set a small fire to divert suspicion away from what he was doing, thinking that it would be a controlled situation, not intending to destroy the town."

I slid across the seat as Mayta turned the key and the Buick came to life under us with a muffled but hearty rumble of the V-8 engine. "I suppose it's possible," she acknowledged. "What about that stuff Ben said about them always putting a reward in the paper even when they weren't suspicious of arson?"

"That, I think, is hogwash."

"Yep," she said, inching the car out of the parking space, "I thought so, too."

"By the way, what was all that chummy business back there? I thought you didn't like the man and here you guys were yukking it up like old pals."

Mayta shot me a surprised look. "I might've said I trusted Ben as far as I could throw him but I *never* said I didn't like him." She threw the automatic lever into first, stepped on the gas, and we shot forward.

"ANDY, IT'S SUSAN. Nancy said you called."

"Hi, Susan. Thanks for calling back." I paused to get my breath. I'd heard the phone ringing from the driveway and had run to catch it. "I just had a question, really. I was wondering if you ever found the doorstop."

"The doorstop?"

"That granite paving block that's used for the church door. Remember? We couldn't find it to hold the door open the day we found Jason Snoud."

"Oh! No, it's still missing. I don't know what happened to it."

"Do you remember if it was there the day before we found Jason?"

"Well, I'm not sure." Susan's voice became more thoughtful. "I thought it was gone before that, but now that I consider it, I'm not sure." I heard the rattle of paper. "Let me look at the calendar to refresh my memory. March 23, a Thursday. No deliveries or meetings noted. Let me ask Nancy. Sometimes she remembers things I don't." She called out and I heard a muffled reply.

"Nancy can't remember either. But, you know, I think maybe you have something. I'm going to call Sergeant Wenninger and tell him about the doorstop."

"There's something else I've been meaning to ask you," I said quickly before she could hang up. "Did you know that Jason was descended from one of the builders of the church— a Caleb Brown?"

"No, I didn't know that," Susan said politely, not getting my point.

"I was wondering if Jason might have known why that support was built with a hiding place in it."

"But I think you asked him if he knew and he said he didn't."

"Yes, that's what he said."

I PULLED THE BELL on the side door. This time I was expected at the Historical Society; I'd called ahead and made an appointment to go through the papers in the library. The volunteer who had given me a tour the first time I'd come, Mary, welcomed me.

"Good morning," I said cheerfully, handing her my application for membership.

"How nice. I'll see this gets processed." She gave me a reserved but friendly smile, and led me up to the library. "Sheila's in a meeting but she left out the papers you requested. If you need help she'll be available in a half hour or so."

"Great!" I said. "Thank you." Despite the built-in bookshelves that lined the two interior walls, the room still felt like the bedroom it had originally been with a marble-mantled fireplace, and faded floral wallpaper that could be caught in glimpses above the bookshelves. An oval mahogany dining table at full extension with four leaves in place took up most of the interior space in the room. Two lidded boxes sat on the table, each labeled with a series of names and corresponding dates from the 1700s through 1800s. This was better than I'd hoped; the papers might be uncataloged but they appeared to be sorted.

"You mentioned the Tibbits family," Mary said, pointing out a line halfway down the list on the second box. "Tibbits, 1750–1812," she read. She lifted the lid and fingered through the tightly packed file folders. "Here it is." She pulled out a fat folder and handed it to me. "If you need anything, give a call. I'll be downstairs."

Left on my own, I opened the other box and breathed in the musty perfume of old documents that arose from both cartons. Here lay the lives of a couple dozen families—more than a century's worth—condensed to paper, I thought. Most likely condensed to numbers on papers. There might be a few letters and personal notes, once in a great while a diary, but I knew that what generally survived were mere numbers: birth, death, and marriage dates recorded in family bibles; financial accounts written in ledgers or daily logs; financial summaries and disbursement in wills. A tally of how many years a person spent on Earth, a sum of what he managed to gather in that lifetime and how much he left behind. Numbers were the bones, the remains after a lifetime of correspondence, of ideas and emotions jotted down, of doodling in margins.

I was confident I would find what I wanted because, for once, what I was looking for were the bones. Down to business, Andy-girl, I told myself, and pulled a Queen Anne side chair up to the table. The first page I picked up was slick and sharp-edged. I fingered through the entire packet with the realization that the musty smell of the boxes had come from other folders; all of the papers in Tibbits' file were photocopies. Either the originals were stored elsewhere or Ben Barrett was wrong and his father had kept them, after all.

I began with Merriman Tibbits' financial statements of 1800. Each month until 1807 Merriman Tibbits had meticulously recorded his income along with detailed household and business expenses. For the years of the Embargo Act there were no entries of income, yet expenditures continued to be recorded ("Repair of the forecastle bridge on the Brig Flora, $70.00"). It wasn't surprising that Tibbits was obviously bringing in money he didn't wish to acknowledge in print;

Barrett had hinted that his ancestor continued to trade during the Embargo.

What *was* interesting was that after the lifting of the Embargo in 1809, when it became legal again to trade, there were still no entries for income. Was Tibbits worried that his records would show he was bringing in more goods than he was paying taxes on? If so, why hadn't he merely put down a deflated figure? Given his meticulous methods, it was funny that he wouldn't have recorded an income somewhere.

I read through the expenditures which Tibbits had continued to itemize with careful and steady hand—despite the illness Barrett had claimed Tibbits had after the Great Fire. The accounts ended abruptly with his death in September of 1812.

I went back and read over the accounts carefully. His household expenses were the usual for the well-to-do of the time; besides food, servants, and upkeep of house and gardens, there were donations to the orphanage, to the "pest house" out on Plum Island for diseased folk, and to the church. One entry listed under "Charity" for June, 1811, caught my eye: "Paid to D. Rand of W. Newbury, $20.00." I recalled that Frieda Cole's ancestor, Eleazar Rand II had a brother, Davison Rand.

I flipped through my notebook to the notes I'd taken at Frieda's house. I had remembered correctly: Eleazar Rand's brother was Davison, a farmer in West Newbury and, like Tibbits, Eleazar had made payments to Davison Rand. But he hadn't identified them as charity; they were "for M.P., clothing and expenditures." I compared dates. Eleazar's payments to his brother were made in September and December of 1812 and in March and June of 1813. There were no more after that.

I referred back to Tibbits' records. After June, there were five more payments to D. Rand: one each for September and December of 1811 and for March and June of 1812, the final one made in the month of Tibbits' death. Each one was desig-

nated for "charity" and nowhere was there mention of "M.P."
In a column, I wrote down the months and years of Tibbits'
payments to D. Rand followed by Eleazar Rand's.

Looking at all the dates together, several things struck me.
They were consecutive; the first of Rand's payments began
three months after Tibbits' had ended. They were regular—one
payment every three months for a period of two years and each
payment (after Tibbits' initial one of $35.00) was in the amount
of $20.00. And finally, or maybe it should have been first of
all, the payments had commenced the month after the Great
Fire.

I chose to ignore the possibility that there were logical
reasons why two men should pay a third man "charity" or
money "for clothes, expenses, etc." Instead, I ruminated again
on the connections between Eleazar Rand and Merriman
Tibbits. Both were direct descendants of Newbury's founding
fathers. Both had been city selectmen, as well as members of
the Committee of Proprietors of the First Parish, at the time of
the fire. Both had been influential men in the community:
Rand, a prominent banker and Tibbits, a wealthy ship owner.

Then I thought of the third man who fit into the same slots:
Thomas Toole, another wealthy ship owner. The Historical
Society had his portrait; I'd seen it on my last visit. Maybe they
also had the family's records since the last of the Tooles,
Jeannine, died in the 1930s. I pushed the stack of papers to one
side and leaned across the table, pulling the first box toward
me. I ran a finger down the list of contents written on the side.
I reached for the second box and saw it instantly at the bottom
of the list: "Toole Family 1805-1930."

My hands trembled with excitement as I pulled the file out
and laid it in front of me. I felt sure that I was about to find the
missing element. I turned pages almost too swiftly to register
their contents; my fingers and eyes working with greater acuity

than my brain. Then stopping suddenly, a finger underscoring a date and two names that took a moment to comprehend: "1813, December 13, $20.00 to Davison Rand for Mehetabah Prince."

A name! M.P. was Mehetabah Prince. I must have whooped because Mary poked in her head a moment later and asked if I needed any help.

"No, thanks. I'm almost finished here," I said, smiling at her. When she left I checked out my column of dates. December, 1813, fit at the bottom, exactly three months after Rand's last payment. Unlike the others, however, Toole made only three payments to D. Rand: the December one and two more, in March and in June of 1814. The March payment was for the usual amount, $20.00, but the June one was more specific in amount and purpose: "$11.50, to D. Rand, burial of M. Prince."

On my way out, I stopped by the office. "Excuse me," I said as Mary looked up from her work. "Can you tell me if Merriman Tibbits' original records are stored elsewhere? The ones in the file are photocopies."

"We used to have those documents," she said, nodding, "but Ben Barrett, who is Tibbits' descendant, took them back."

"Can donors do that?"

"Yes. Like many items in the museum, they're on loan." She hesitated then added, "It's not usual for donors to want something back, especially old documents, but Ben needed them for genealogy work, which is understandable, and he graciously made copies for the files before he took them."

Yes, he would have done that graciously, I thought, perhaps choosing which information not to make copies of. Aloud, I said, "Did this happen recently?"

"A couple of weeks ago. In fact, I think it was the last time you were here."

"Oh yes, I recall passing him on my way out." So, when Barrett told me at our meeting that Tibbits' records had been donated to the society, why didn't he mention he'd taken them back? Something in the middle of my chest sunk in disappointment. If there had been information in those documents that might have shed further light on Tibbits' actions and motives during the years preceding the fire—information that was omitted in the copying—I was betting that I'd never see it. "What do you know about the Prince family?" I asked.

Mary frowned. "The name doesn't sound familiar. I could ask Sheila when she gets out of her meeting."

"I'd appreciate that. One final question: where might the graves of the Rand family be?"

She thought a moment. "The Rands are an old family. The earliest plot would be down in Newbury where the first settlement was, but there's probably a newer one up in the Old Hill Cemetery. Frieda Cole would know; she's a direct descendant. Do you know Frieda? I could give you her number."

"I know Frieda," I said. "Thanks for your help, Mary."

TWENTY-FOUR

THE STEEPLE WAS white-brilliant against the black sky. I was in my body, yet out of it at the same time, my point of view changing between looking up at the scene from below, to looking down on the scene from above.

There was a girl and a boy in the steeple. From the edge of the bell platform, the girl cried urgently, elongated skinny arms, like bleached gnarled sticks, reaching out of loose torn sleeves into the black space. Behind her, the boy rode the wildly swaying church bell like a rearing horse, paying no attention to the girl, intent only on keeping his seat on the curved rim. I could hear none of it, her voice or the bell.

Then a luminous flash in the inky sky behind the steeple and everything was rimmed in orange light: the white of the spire, the black of the bell, the boy, the girl. For a moment it looked like a black and white picture a child had outlined in neon marker. Then the orange light washed over it all.

I could hear the fire now. And I could feel the heat of it as it melted the flesh off the bell rider and the girl with outreached arms. I strained to hear her words as her stretched lips melted back away from her teeth like wax from a wick. In a moment they were both skeletal, he still riding, and she still calling mutely, the only sound the crackling of the fire. And the glass breaking. Instantly I was awake.

Gus was already up. "Damn! The shed's on fire!" He ran out into the hallway. I heard him punch the buttons for 911 and speak tersely over the telephone as I fought with a sheet that had twisted itself ivy-like around my body. Tumbling onto the floor, I grabbed for the glasses I'd worn the night before after I'd taken out my contacts, and knocked over the alarm clock and three books. In the flickering yellow light that played off the walls, I found rubber sandals. I shoved my feet into them and ran out of the room wearing only an oversized T-shirt over underpants.

"Get Molly!" Gus commanded as he raced toward Max's room.

In one scoop, I gathered up a sleeping Molly along with her stuffed bear and favorite baby quilt. Gus and I met back in the hallway, holding our squirming and protesting bundles, and descended the staircase with Moose whining and sidling against our legs, threatening to trip us. Out on the tarmac of the driveway, I looked at the blaze for the first time. Sheets of fire tore up the front wall of the shed and shot angrily into the sky as they devoured the age-dried cedar shakes. One flame licked at the back porch overhang, singeing a branch of our neighbor's oak tree that reached over the fence. A pane in one of the shed's side windows tinkled as it broke.

Even at this distance, the heat was intense. I shielded Molly's face with my hand and Gus tugged on my elbow, pulling me further back until we were in the street. Above Max's soft brown wavy hair, Gus's face was white and stern in the yellow light. He was barefoot, wearing a T shirt and boxer shorts.

We huddled, Moose trembling at our feet. I murmured soothingly to Molly who whimpered. Max asked a dozen questions, some of which mirrored my own: "What happened, Daddy? How did it start? Will my pool burn up? Will our house burn up, too?"

The fire engine arrived then, an instant after the first police car pulled up. After that, the order of events is mixed up in my memory. What I remember most were the faces. There was the smooth faced young policeman I'd talked to the night we'd found the skeleton; I remember reassuring him that nobody was in the shed. There were the concerned or grim looks of our neighbors, some with fingertips to their mouths. There were the openly curious expressions of children and finally, the faces of three teen-agers—eager, flushed, eyes alight, chattering in high voices—as they came running down the street to catch the entertainment.

Fire is a spectator's event. Within the arena of the now cordoned-off city block, a few neighbors approached us to express concern and offer comfort. Most, however, watched from afar, moving around the periphery of a stage brightly lit by emergency vehicle beams, where firemen and policemen moved back and forth, conferring with each other and dragging giant water hoses that crisscrossed the space. Within minutes the fire was reduced to billows of gray-black smoke. Watching it all I felt I would wake up again, for this dream had all the qualities of the first one. And it seemed no more real.

IT DIDN'T TAKE the fire chief long to determine what Gus and I—given the intense burning—had figured out right away: the fire had been set.

There'd been nothing of value inside the shed, only gardening tools and a few summer toys. Even the shed itself was no great loss; dilapidated, it had been slated for demolition at some point in the near future. And yet, we suffered a great loss: our sense of security. Though neither of us said it, we knew that given altered circumstances, it could have been our house. Perhaps even our lives.

The accelerant had been gasoline. Someone had doused the front of the shed and set a match to it. It was that simple. Even after all the reading I'd done on fires, I'd never thought how utterly simple it was to set one. Like starting a charcoal grill: squirt lighter fluid on the briquettes, drop a match onto them, and poof! Flames. You can do the same thing to a building; all it takes is ambition. Throughout history people living in communities of old wooden buildings have been aware of this. In colonial times Newburyport citizens had curfews, night watchmen roaming the streets, and fire buckets hanging over their doors. Even today, with advances in space travel, weather predictions, and disease prevention and cures, we have firemen at the ready in case some person inadvertently—or purposely— causes flame to come in contact with flammable. Arson can't be predicted or prevented or cured.

Our nighttime visitor of a few nights earlier took on a new, more ominous light. Spying through the window was one thing; setting fire to our property was another thing altogether. The day after the fire, when Wenninger came by, we showed him where we'd found the footprints. But the activity of the firemen the night before and the stray streams of water from the hoses had obliterated them.

"They were a man's footprints," I told him. "Gus figured about size ten." But the words were nothing without the prints themselves.

We answered Wenninger's questions. There was nobody we could think of who would want to hurt us. My recent work had raised a few eyebrows, but to the point that someone would set a fire on our property? He grumbled that it was unlikely, but took notes on the nature of my research anyway. Then he left.

The fire marshal came. He asked a few questions, told us the preliminary results of his investigation—the gasoline— then instructed us to leave the fire area alone until the investigation was completed, and left. Mayta took the kids for the day so that Gus and I could begin cleaning up debris in the yard. It was mid-afternoon before we walked into the center of the yard with rakes and looked around.

"It gives me the heebie-jeebies being out here," I said, pulling on gardening gloves. "It doesn't feel like my backyard anymore. It's different, somehow."

Gus picked up a charred wood fragment and threw it with force into the plastic trash container. His face was set in severe lines. "We'll feel better after we get this cleaned up," he said tersely.

Sudden tears pricked at my eyes. "Oh, Gus," I began but the rest of the words, "who could have done this?" stuck in my throat. Wordlessly, I swept an arm above the mess. He came to me then and took me in his arms. There weren't any comforting words to be said at that moment, but it helped to be held. After a while he released me and we continued working in silence, skirting the yellow police tape strung around the charred hull of the shed. I was sure that Gus was thinking the same thing I was: the fire wasn't a random malicious act. It was a personal attack.

"Do you think I angered someone who doesn't want something in the past to come out?" I asked. "There's a parallel; I've been looking into the Fire of 1811 and a fire is set to our shed. Perhaps to warn me off?"

"That's silly," Gus said gruffly. A few days ago he'd believed that I had upset someone with my work but now he was back-pedaling. Maybe it was denial; he couldn't accept that a member from a good old Newburyport family could be so vicious. I tended to agree; it was hard to picture the Coles with their proper tea manners running around our yard with gasoline cans. Nor did it seem likely that Ben Barrett (headline: Mayoral Candidate Torches Backyard Shed) could be responsible. In fact, it seemed ludicrous to think that *anybody* could get that upset over the contents of some old musty papers. But I felt sure someone had.

TWENTY-FIVE

"COME ON, IT'LL BE FUN." I shifted the gears on my handlebar, trying to ignore the griping and whining behind me.

"Mommy, you're going too fast." From the youngest.

"It's too cold for a bike trip." From the oldest.

"Maybe we should wait until Molly gets past training wheels before we do an excursion like this." From the husband.

I'd had to get us away from the house. For two days I'd cowered whenever I looked out at the hulking black mess in the backyard, which was often because Max and Molly were conducting tours on a regular basis and I'd have to yell out the window when they and their friends were hanging too far over the yellow tape. But Gus's reaction had been the hardest to deal with; since the debris in the backyard had been cleaned up, he refused to go back there. He entered and exited the house by the front door. If I said anything about the fire, he'd cut me off, saying that he didn't want to talk about it just then. So I forced this bike trip on us, figuring that we needed to get away from the house for a while. Besides, I wanted to do a little fieldwork. I had a theory that if I could find Davison Rand's burial plot, I would also find the burial plot of one Mehetabah Prince.

I circled around and came up beside Molly. "I'll ride next to you for a while."

"But why do we have to go to an old cemetery?" Max whined. "Why can't we go to the park?"

"Aw, come on, you guys. It's only eight blocks away," I said, then added again lamely, "It'll be fun."

"But we're not going to eat our lunch there, are we? On top of dead people?"

"They're not dead people anymore," I said. "They're just bones. Now ride!"

It was one of those crisp early spring days when the sun is bright but not quite warm enough to take the bite out of the air. Gus had a pack strapped on the back of his bike that contained egg salad sandwiches, chips, juice containers, and a red wool blanket. At the top of our street we turned onto High Street and rode on the wide uneven brick walk. Molly huffed and puffed, her chubby little legs pumping the pedals as she navigated around dips and tree roots in the walk. I slowed down along-side her, admiring my favorite stretch of old ship owners' and captains' houses rising grandly tall and white, each with its own charming feature: an ornate wrought iron fence, a glassed entry, a mansard roof, a "widow's walk."

We crossed High Street at Molly's and Max's school, The Kelley, and made a mandatory stop at the playground, situated on one corner of the old commons, the "Mall"—locals pronounce it the old English way, rhyming it with pal—which was where inhabitants used to graze livestock, train for the Revolutionary militia, and lay out the miles of lines used on sailing ships. On and abutting the Mall's grounds at various times in history were built a windmill and a powder house for storing gunpowder (both gone), various schools (only The Kelley, built in 1873, remains), the County Court House (designed by Bullfinch and still in use today) and a granite jail (now privately owned), and the oldest burying ground in town—our destination.

Gus and I sat on the railroad ties surrounding the sand filled area where Max and Molly climbed on bars and took turns on a tire swing. "Why don't you just call Frieda and ask where the plot is?" Gus suggested for about the fourth time. "I'm sure, with all her family research, she would know where Davison Rand is buried."

"I don't want everybody in town knowing what I'm doing right now," I said with deliberate vagueness.

Gus started to make a comment, then stopped himself. I knew he was struggling with divided loyalties. More and more, there seemed to be two distinct sides: the side that included his family and ancestors, and longtime family friends and *their* ancestors who had been chummy with his ancestors, and then there was the side that was me. Deep down he felt like I did, that my digging into the past had riled somebody, but admitting it would mean that that somebody (who was on the other side) was responsible for burning down our shed.

At that moment I felt alone—really alone—in this place, this city. I'd often joked about never being accepted as a true New-buryporter but I hadn't realized the full truth of it until now. There was a common bond between all those who had been born here—especially strong in those whose family had been here for generations—and I felt that bond would never extend to me. There would always be a relationship with this place that, as close as I might be to them, Gus and Mayta would hold apart from me, probably without even realizing it themselves.

"Andy, I think you should just forget about this whole project," Gus said.

"I can't let Ginger and Frank down." I scooped up a handful of sand and let it sift through my fingers. "Besides, we're almost finished."

"Then what are we doing at the cemetery?"

"I want to find the grave of a woman—a Mehetabah Prince—whose name I found in the Rand and Toole family records. I think she's related to the Fire of 1811 and possibly to Peter Chambers, which might give me a clue to his death."

"There we go again—the fire! It isn't the research you're doing for the church history that's angering people. It's these side issues you're snooping into—the fire, old family records." He shook his head. "I don't know, Andy, maybe family secrets should stay buried for everyone's sake, past and present."

"Well, I don't agree," I shot back. "Finding out how a person's life ended is important regardless of how much time has passed."

"Listen, Andy, write up what you have for the Tricentennial book and call it quits. Forget about these other things."

I scooped up another handful of sand and ran a finger through it, inspecting the perfection of the individual crystals. I thought about the boy who died a lonely death hidden away in a steeple and knew I couldn't just leave it. The story of his life and death had to be known, if only to one person—me. "I'll be careful," I said.

"I know you'll be careful," he said. "But what about Molly and Max?"

"The fire wasn't an attack on them," I protested.

"The next time it could be."

We sat watching the kids with unsaid things hanging in the air between us. I wanted to deny Gus's words but could he be right? Was I endangering my family by continuing to investigate the Great Fire and the death of Peter Chambers? After a few minutes Gus stood and called to the kids. Back on bikes again, he led us along the paved walk toward the old cemetery. I took it as his tacit acceptance that I would continue my "snooping." Silently, I promised him that as soon as I found out what had happened to Peter, I'd be a model of reserve, inquiring into nothing more than in what aisle marinated artichoke hearts could be found at the supermarket.

We crossed the narrow road and entered the cemetery single-file through a narrow break in the stone wall. Where the Mall is hollowed out in the middle, the Old Hill Burying Ground is mounded high, as if some giant scooped a bowlful of mud out of the middle of one and upended it onto the other. The sides of the hill are strewn with weathered slate gravestones stuck crookedly all over, some about to give in to gravity and topple downhill. There must have been an order at one time, but hundreds of years of earth heaving during freezing and thawing have produced curious random patterns that will have a man's footstone three feet from his headstone and over onto his neighbor's grave, giving an absurd picture of a dwarf having been buried on his side with legs stuck out perpendicular to his body.

"Now, remember," I said to Max and Molly as we leaned our bikes against the wall, "we're looking for Rand. R-A-N-D."

Of course they immediately forgot what they were supposed to be looking for and were chasing up and down between the gravestones and around brush which overgrew whole areas of the hill. Gus helped out, halfheartedly at first, then with more enthusiasm as we went along. We searched methodically one side and then the other, which was a bit of a challenge because few of the stones were lined up. Zigzagging back and forth made it easy to lose track of which ones you'd read already and which you hadn't. Around the back of the hill, next to a dense area of low bushes, I found some Rands but not a Davison Rand.

Nevertheless, I met with success. Next to one Jed Rand, a child who died at age six, I found a small stone bearing the name Prince. No willow carving or skull with wings decorated it. No ethereal epitaph. Etched in crude lettering was simply, "Here lyes Mehetabah 'Hitty' Prince, orphan girl. Dyed June 15, 1814. Aged 16 yrs."

It hadn't occurred to me that she'd be so young. Only sixteen at the time of her death, thirteen at the time of the fire. The girl in my dream calling from the steeple had been young. Had it been Mehetabah appearing to warn me about the fire? Perhaps, even, to warn me of something else?

I didn't immediately call to Gus who was up further on the same side of the hill. Kneeling in the long grass next to the humble slate stone, I wondered about the importance of Mehetabah Prince—Hitty, the name she must have gone by. What was her relationship? A ward, a servant? Why would three community leaders pay for the upkeep of an orphan? And why divide up the meager financial responsibility when any one of these affluent men could have easily afforded the entire amount?

I considered what I knew about these men and decided that the key was responsibility. Just as they had shared leadership of the city and of the church, they shared responsibility in caring for an orphan girl. But why? Had Tibbits, Rand, and Toole entered into some kind of pact to protect one of them? All of them?

"Why were you so important to those men, Hitty?" I whispered. "What did you know?"

TWENTY-SIX

ON OUR WAY BACK from the cemetery we passed by the Coles' house, its impressive facade rising up on solid granite blocks, and I decided I needed to talk to Frieda again. Forty-five minutes later I was ushered into the Coles' living room. I sat on a Victorian-era velvet couch and Frieda took a slouchy cushioned wing back chair that had been pulled up. Between us, on an oval mahogany coffee table, stood the silver tea service with a plate of oatmeal cookies. Frieda poured tea and offered it to me, the flower-sprigged cup rattling on its saucer as her frail age-spotted hand trembled. The ridiculous picture of her toting a gasoline can again came to mind.

"Thank you for inviting me right over, Frieda."

Frieda smiled. She reminded me of a polite child as she sat—back straight, her hands clasped in her lap, her feet side by side on the floor—in the large chair whose wings looked ready to wrap around and engulf her small body. "Herb is off doing errands," she said. "He'll join us if he returns in time."

"Oh, that's all right, Frieda," I assured her. "I really wanted to talk to you."

Her smile took on a strained tinge but remained gracious. "Cream, sugar?" At my acceptance of the first she poured two dollops into my cup.

"I wanted to ask about those financial records," I said, jumping right in.

Frieda set the cream pitcher onto the tray, carefully aligning it with the sugar bowl, then took a visible but inaudible deep breath. "I didn't tell you everything when you were here before," she said quietly. "I did know about Mehetabah Prince."

"Eleazar Rand was supporting her," I prompted.

She looked up quickly. "Yes. He and a few others provided for her support."

"Who was she?"

"An orphan." She brushed something imaginary off the edge of the table. "There was an orphanage back then filled with children whose fathers had been lost at sea, whose mothers had died of disease, or whose families just couldn't afford to keep them. From what I've read, it was a fairly respectable orphanage, with decent people who cared for the children."

I nodded encouragement. What Frieda had to impart would be embedded in a history lesson.

"When a child reached a certain age, say ten or older, she or he could be bound out to a family or a business who, in return for services, would care for the child until adulthood. The situation could be beneficial to the child: a boy learned a trade; a girl learned skills that would help her attain a husband. Or," Frieda hesitated a beat, "the arrangement could turn out to resemble slavery." She noticed the cookie plate then, picked it up. "Cookie?"

I took one and murmured a quick thank you.

"Mehetabah Prince was unfortunate to have been bound out to a cruel master who worked her too hard, didn't feed her well, probably even beat her at times."

"How do you know this?"

"When I first started researching my ancestors' papers I found Merriman Tibbits' name in connection to this M. Prince so I went to Ben Barrett, who I knew was also working on family genealogy. Sure enough, Ben had found a reference to an M. Prince, too. In one of his daily logs, Merriman Tibbits had described Mehetabah's situation and the circumstances by which the selectmen became involved."

"And how was that—the circumstances by which they became involved?" I found myself inching forward on the stiff couch cushion which was probably stuffed with eighteenth century straw.

"In the aftermath of the Fire of 1811, this orphan was found hiding in the church. When they discovered her living conditions, the members of the Committee of Proprietors decided to care for her themselves, rather than let her be returned to her master." Frieda's hands escaped from her lap where she had been clenching them, fluttered a moment in midair as if attempting flight, and then lighted on the tea server. She held it in the air, a mute offer at which I shook my head.

"Eleazar arranged to have Mehetabah Prince stay on his brother's farm in West Newbury. There, she helped around the house and with the animals until her death during an influenza epidemic." Frieda looked up again, her eyes meeting mine. Her story was done, but I felt there was more she wasn't telling me.

"What was this orphan doing in the church the night of the fire?"

"She'd become disoriented and frightened and had sought refuge."

"How could they just take her from her master—who was he, by the way?"

"I don't know."

"Why didn't he try to get her back?" I asked. "She was legally bound to him."

"Maybe he didn't want it known that he'd been a negligent master."

"Why did the three of them—Toole, also, for I saw his

records—share the expense? All were wealthy; any one could have footed the bill without burden."

"I don't know."

I softened my tone. "Why didn't you tell me about Mehetabah Prince before?"

"It slipped my mind. It wasn't until afterwards that I remembered about her." Frieda looked at me directly. She was trying to be convincing and she almost was.

SERGEANT WENNINGER CALLED to ask about the granite paving block. With the excitement of the fire, I'd forgotten about the call I'd made to Susan. "Oh, yes!" I said. "I was thinking back and I remembered that the door was propped open with the doorstop that Monday before Jason Snoud was killed. One of the parishioners was putting up an art display and she wanted natural light to see by."

"So it disappeared sometime between Monday and Friday morning. Is that what you're saying?"

"Yes, I think so."

"Do you know of anyone who was using the church during that week?"

"Other than Nancy and Susan and Jason, there's the parishioner with the art. Oh, and Betsy Watson—she's in and out all the time with choir practice."

"Betsy Watson, yeah. I got her name here. Anyone else?"

"No, I can't think of anyone."

"Well, thanks."

"That article in the *Globe*," I put in quickly, "was the information true?"

"Damned reporters," he muttered. "I don't know who told them that stuff."

"*Are* you looking for a woman?" I pressed. "Somebody who was involved with Snoud?"

"Why? Do you know anybody?"

"No, but you might want to talk to the women down at the Clip 'n' Color," I suggested.

"Oh, yeah?" His deadpan voice raised a note. "Why would I want to do that?"

"That's where Jason's wife gets her hair done. My mother-in-law, Mayta Gammon, goes there, too, and she's heard some talk."

TWENTY-SEVEN

I CALLED BEN BARRETT and asked him point blank about Mehetabah Prince. I told him I'd been to see Frieda and that I was thinking about doing research on orphanages in the nineteenth century. I don't know if he bought it, but he was willing to talk to me.

"Yes. I remember her," Barrett said expansively. I could see him leaning back in his leather chair, ready for a chat. You had to give him that—as busy as the man was with his practice and running for office, he always gave the impression of having all the time in the world for whoever wanted it. "I found several references to her," he said. "She hid in the church during the fire."

"Can you tell me anything else about her?"

"Not a whole lot. One of the church members found her and figured that she'd run away because afterwards she didn't want to return to the baker."

"The baker?" Frieda had said she didn't know who Hitty Prince's master was so I'd assumed Barrett didn't know—or wouldn't admit to knowing—either.

"She was apprenticed to a baker in town," he said easily. "He wasn't a good master—starved her, worked her too hard. There was mention of beatings. On the whole, it sounded like a pretty sorry life. So Thomas Toole, Merriman Tibbits, and Eleazar Rand kind of adopted her rather than return her to a deplorable situation."

"Do you know the name of this baker?" I tried to keep my voice light.

"I don't have my papers here," he said, "but I might remember it. It started with an S, I believe—not one of the old names." He paused to ponder. "It'll come to me. Anything else you wanted to know?"

"Why was it that these particular men took on the responsibility of her upkeep? And why did all three adopt her, rather than just one?"

"My understanding is that she was taken on as a church charity. As members of the Committee of Proprietors, they represented the church in the affair."

"But, why—"

"I've got it! The baker's name was Stockly or Stockton, something like that."

"Wait a minute." I shuffled through the papers in front of me. "Stockwell. Could it have been Stockwell?" I held my breath.

"Yes! I believe that was it. How did you know?"

"I found the name in my notes," I said vaguely and, before Barrett could turn the tables and question me, I ended our conversation by thanking him for his help. Barrett promised to make copies of the references he'd found on M. Prince and recommended some sources for information on orphanages.

I sat at the kitchen counter for a moment, the receiver still in my hand. Frieda had appeared to be hiding something when she talked about Hitty Prince but Barrett had seemed forthright. He wouldn't have told me about Stockwell if he'd been hiding something because this was the first clue that directly connected Hitty Prince to Peter Chambers and therefore—at least in my figuring—to the Fire of 1811.

The fact that Hitty and Peter had the same master told me they had known each other and it had been no coincidence both were in the church on the same night. And that brought to mind a host of new questions: had they been merely seeking shelter or were they hiding, perhaps running away together? Had *both* been involved in setting the fire? Did Hitty see Peter's killer? Was her "adoption" an innocent charitable deed performed by Tibbits, Toole, and Rand on behalf of the church? Or was Hitty bought off, offered a comfortable life on an isolated West Newbury farm in return for her silence concerning the fire and Peter's death?

MAYTA CALLED to invite us to dinner and I accepted eagerly. Then, not five minutes later, Frank called to see if I could meet Ginger and him at the church to straighten out the papers and then quickly go over our material before we each began writing final drafts. He'd found out from Nancy that the only night the rest of this week the choir room wasn't going to be used—for youth or adult choir practice—was that night. So, even though it meant taking two cars out to Plum Island and shortening my visit with Mayta, I said okay.

After a scrumptious dinner of roasted chicken, mashed potatoes and corn on the cob with herbed butter, we carried our coffee and dessert out to the porch. There's almost always a sea breeze during the early spring that keeps the coast ten degrees cooler than inland. One kicked up now so Mayta brought out a pile of afghans and blankets and we wrapped up. The water was almost black in the waning light, and deceptively calm, its powerful, undulating surge barely perceptible from a distance. Except for the occasional clink of silverware on china, we were silent as we ate. I found myself wishing I didn't have to leave, that I could stay safe and warm in my cocoon of blankets, an innocent believer that dangerous forces could be held at bay by something as simple as a strip of sand.

"You must be almost done with your project," Mayta commented.

"Tonight we're going over it all to make sure the parts fit together and nothing's been left out. Then we write up the final drafts."

"Does that mean it'll go to the publisher soon?"

"Next month if we're lucky," I said.

Gus had dug out his tide chart that is kept, in order of importance, next to his driver's license in his wallet. "Two hours before high tide," he announced. "I think a little cod fishing is in order."

Max jumped up. "I want to go, too."

"Then your job is to get the rods from the side porch."

"Okay!" Max leaped off the steps in one bound and was around the corner of the cottage in another.

"How about you, Mollikins?" Gus said. "Want to go?"

Molly shook her head. "Grandma's going to teach me how to sew."

"Storm coming," Mayta said. We looked out at the horizon where, in the moments we hadn't been paying attention, tenebrous clouds had begun to amass.

Unperturbed, Gus turned back to his bucket. "We won't stay out long."

"Don't be running with those," Mayta admonished Max who was back, panting, holding a fishing rod in each hand. "You'll fall and get a hook in you."

"Gus, it's coming in fast. Maybe you shouldn't go," I said. Already the black water swelled ominously, waves spilling further up onto the beach with each surge.

"We'll just make a few casts." Gus picked up the bucket, took his rod from Max, and father and son headed out over the sand toward the turbulent surf.

I wanted to protest again. Instead, I called out after them, "Be careful!"

While Mayta settled Molly down in the living room with

needle, thread, and a scrap of cloth for Molly's first sewing project, I cleared dishes from the table, started water running in both sides of the sink, and got out the dish rack.

Mayta came in and plunged her hands into the sudsy water. "I'll wash," she said. "You dry."

I checked the wall clock and realized I'd have to leave soon for my meeting. Quickly, I told Mayta what I'd learned about Hitty Prince. "What do you think? Am I off base to be suspecting two kids of burning down the town?"

She swished a plate in the rinse water before answering noncommittally, "Those newspaper articles you found proved somebody did it. Could've just as easily been a couple of kids as a couple of adults, I guess."

"Yeah, well, I'm sure now that Peter Chambers was killed because of his connection to the Great Fire." I fished three plates out of the rinse water and stacked them in the dish rack. "I believe he set that fire and all the little ones before it. One news account mentioned a boy running from the scene of an earlier fire and I think Peter was that boy. I also think that he was working for someone—Tibbits, perhaps, because Peter had his pew number on him—although I can't figure out a motive. Why would Tibbits want to burn down the town?"

"How does the girl—what was her name—fit into it?"

"Hitty. I'm confused about that, too. If we assume Peter started the fire, then he was in the meeting house between nine o'clock, when the fire was started, and about ten o'clock when the tankards were discovered missing. And if Hitty was seeking refuge as Frieda and Ben claim, she was in the building at the same time, just after the start of the fire. She wouldn't have come in later because that whole area was in the path of the fire and nobody would have sought refuge there."

"Maybe they were running away together." Mayta swirled a wine glass in the rinse water and handed it to me. "They could have met at the church, saw the silver, and stole it to sell later."

"Or when she got there, it was too late: she found him dead. Or didn't find him because he'd have already been stuck up in the steeple." I opened the corner cupboard door and slid the wine glass onto the upper shelf in line with the rest. "Maybe Hitty was still waiting for Peter when the members of the church came in," I said thoughtfully, "and never even found out what happened to him. Maybe she witnessed his murder and was paid off with an escape from her horrible life—a comfy position on a country farm."

"Are you saying one of the church members killed Peter?"

"Well, think about it," I hedged. "Why didn't these men return her to her master like they should have legally done? Running off from an apprenticeship was a serious offense. The baker would have demanded her return. Granted, Tibbits, Toole, and Rand were influential, but they wouldn't have gone above the law unless the stakes were pretty high or unless they had something on this baker."

Mayta turned on the tap and held a handful of silverware under the running water, as if weighing the collective pieces along with my words. "But if one of them killed the boy, why didn't he kill the girl, too? And would all three be in on it?"

"Two of them could have been covering up for the other," I said. "If any of these scenarios are close, Hitty had to have at least known who set the fire."

"Which would've put her in a curious, perhaps dangerous position to begin with," Mayta commented as she pulled out the stopper and drained the sink.

"Exactly. Mayta, do you think I'm crazy, like Gus does, for trying to figure out what happened nearly two hundred years ago?"

"No," she said unconvincingly. "It is kinda funny, though,

us pondering that murder and forgetting about Jason who was killed here a few weeks ago."

"I haven't forgotten him. It's just that the police are working on it. They aren't working on Peter Chambers' murder because it was so long ago and that's something I can do."

"Yeah," Mayta said, "you're good at that kind of thing— finding out stuff from the past. As for Gus, he's just worried."

"He says I'm putting the kids in danger by continuing this whole thing."

"That shed fire's got him spooked 'cause somebody meant to do you harm and he can't figure out who." She eased herself into a chair at the table, rubbing the joint of her little finger with the other hand. "Look, if you want my two cents worth, I say find Jason's current girlfriend and you'll find his killer. Also, when the police find the person who set your shed on fire it'll be some nut who has nothin' to do with any of this. You might've ruffled some feathers snooping, but any logical person can separate himself from his ancestors."

"Then you wouldn't feel threatened if it turned out to be your ancestor who lit the match?" I glanced at the clock and began collecting my things.

"Ha!" She flung back her head as she uttered the single loud syllable. "Don't forget that it's your family now, too. But to answer your question: I don't see that it has much to do with me, so no, I wouldn't feel threatened." She chuckled at the thought. "It might make the family history a bit more interesting."

"What about Frieda," I said at the door. "Does *she* separate herself from her ancestors?"

"Frieda's not always logical, but she wouldn't compromise her position in society by doing anything foolish." She chuckled again. "She might tell white lies to cover up dirt in the past, but she wouldn't burn down your shed."

I gave Mayta a quick hug. "Thanks for dinner. Everything was delicious as usual. Don't let those guys stay out there long."

Mayta shooed me out. "You go on to your meeting and stop fretting. It's gonna start pouring any minute now and they'll be back in a heartbeat."

"Bye, Mommy!" Molly called out. She was settled into the corner of the old sofa under the orangey glow of the floor lamp, concentrating on her square of cloth.

"Bye, sweetie, see you back at home." I blew her a kiss.

TWENTY-EIGHT

THERE WERE NO LIGHTS on at the church when I got there. Having left my key at home, I waited for Frank and Ginger on the outside granite step. A few moments later, an overhead bolt of lightning, immediately followed by an ear-splitting crack of thunder, prompted me to try the latch. I was surprised, after the recent security vigilance, to find the door unlocked. I entered the dark vestibule the same instant a deluge of rain splattered the brick walk behind me. I hoped Gus had been prudent and had gotten himself and Max back to the cottage before the storm hit.

The great door swung slowly shut, and the metallic echo of the thumb lever hitting the cross piece and then falling back to its resting place reverberated off the walls. I turned on the vestibule ceiling lamps. Their meager light stretched just far enough up the stairs to get me to the light switch on the wall outside the choir room door. I flicked it on and entered the room. The air was still and cold, heavy with a pungent musty smell of old wood brought out by the damp weather.

Figuring that Frank and Ginger must be waiting out the downpour somewhere, I decided to go ahead and begin sorting through the records in the sea chest, organizing them the way Frank and I had talked about doing. I turned on the small brass lamp on top of the pump organ. Its yellow light was strong enough for my purposes, but it cast the rest of the room in shadows. I knelt on the worn Oriental rug, a mantle of cold settling on me, and opened the chest.

I worked to the accompaniment of rain pummeling the roof, punctuated by an occasional rumble of thunder. The wind kicked up, rattling loose sashes. Outside a high window, the bare angular branches of a churchyard tree swayed wildly, eerily silhouetted against background flashes of lightning. Once, between rolls of thunder, I thought I heard the click of the thumb latch on the downstairs door. I paused, listening for footfalls on the stairs. When they didn't materialize, I went back to my task, admonishing myself for being jumpy, for hearing things.

I had roughly a quarter of the chest's contents out on the table, sorted into three piles, and was kneeling to look at the next layer when the lights went off. During the ensuing moments, when I expected the electricity to come back on and it didn't, I cursed my luck for being caught in a blackout in the same place twice within a month. The difference this time was that I was here alone. Frank and Ginger had obviously had the sense to cancel out. In all likelihood there was a message to that effect on my answering machine at home.

"Okay," I said aloud to the powers that be. "I give up." I stacked each pile back into the chest, hoping that pages weren't getting bent in the dark. The lid didn't close all the way so, rather than risk damage, I left it open, figuring I'd be back in the morning, anyway. The light of street lamps filtering through the window helped me find my pocketbook. I looped the strap over my head so that my arms were free to hold the folders, and got to my feet. Then it occurred to me that the last time the lights went out—the night we found the skeleton—the entire block had lost power. I stood on tiptoes and looked out a window; besides the street lamps, light came from businesses on the street. Why would just the church lose power?

I took advantage of a lightning flash to pick my way toward the door. Once there I stopped, hoping for another to light my way through the choir loft and down the stairs. I was in luck, but when the white flash illuminated the path I wanted to take, I stood rooted to the spot, my body instinctively refusing to cross the threshold.

I had seen nothing, but I knew just as surely as if I had, that someone was outside the choir room door, next to the light switch. "Hel—" the rest of the whisper, "lo," died in my throat and the dark absorbed the initial syllable, ate it up immediately so that no sound remained in the space between me and whoever was a few feet away. A chill pricked along my spine.

After an eternity my brain regained control of my body. I backed up, bumping into a music stand that tottered before I caught and steadied it. A rustle of loose fabric—a coat? A skirt?—sent me dashing for the other door that led to the opposite side of the gallery. This time I didn't pause to catch the music stands that fell at a mere grazing, tipping on their three legs, crashing to the floor with tinny sounds. I gained the door and realized my pursuer was not behind me. Had he anticipated my movements and run around the organ in the loft to catch me at my destination?

I retraced my steps, miraculously avoiding the skeletal-like debris of stands scattered about the floor. Back at the first door, I took stock of my options: I could run for the stairs which would be chancy, not knowing where my pursuer was; I could duck into a gallery pew which would put me further from the only way out—the staircase down to the vestibule; or I could hide somewhere close-by so I could run for the stairs when I had the chance. I decided upon the last.

I slipped out into the choir loft and darted up the stairs behind the organ, crouching down, the folders gripped tightly in my hands. From my vantage point, pressing the side of my head against the wall, I could see—if you could call distinguishing shades of black seeing—for a radius of only about forty-five degrees. I'd have to know where my pursuer was before I dared make a run for the staircase. As I huddled there, trying to control my heavy breathing and thundering heartbeats, my thoughts whirled with questions: who was chasing me? Why? Was this related to my research? If so, what secret was so important to go to such lengths to protect it?

I thought of the shed fire. Could it be one of the descendants of the Committee of Proprietors of 1811, trying to keep quiet the true story of the Great Fire and whatever part the orphan girl Hitty Prince played in it? Was it Ben Barrett, whose campaign slogan, "Newburyport's son," traded on his ancestry to win votes in his bid for mayor? Was it Freida or Herb Cole, whose integrity and reputations, indeed lives, had been built upon the foundation of Freida's illustrious ancestry?

Or was it someone with a different motive for keeping the past unknown? Was it Mark Levenson, antique dealer and self-appointed church historian, whose interest in his adopted home of Newburyport had become overly possessive?

There was a flutter at the choir room door below me. A silent flash of light colored cloth—a skirt? Instinctively, I backed up a step. I was now almost at the small door that led to the steeple. The woman—I was sure it was a woman now—had moved back into the choir room. I heard her searching, making no effort at stealth. In fact, she was talking, not loud enough for me to identify her, but clear enough to recognize her voice as that of a younger woman. Not Frieda Cole.

Grabbing my chance, I crept back down and got ready to run for the staircase. Lightning had ceased, thunder was a mere rumble in the distance, and the rain was a gentle thrumming overhead. I remembered Ginger and Frank. Since the storm was abating, maybe they'd come after all. A feeling of hope was immediately followed by a flutter of panic as I thought of them walking into this situation.

"Where are you?" The whispered words came from only a

few feet away. I drew myself close to the organ's paneling and kept still, watching the figure at the choir room door. Even in the dark, in gradients of gray and black instead of the vivid hues by daylight, I recognized the abstract pattern of her skirt. It was the one I'd admired several weeks ago, the one she'd told me she'd bought at Marshall's. At once I understood that I had it all wrong; I was being stalked not because of tampering in the past, but because of some threat I posed in the present.

"I know you're here because you didn't go downstairs," the low voice continued reasonably, the way I'd often heard it over the past few years, giving information, taking messages. "If you'd just come out we could talk."

I was tempted to do as she bid, for she had always been reasonable—if you discounted her present behavior, of course. She had been a reasonable person in an orderly office under reasonable circumstances. When had she changed? When had circumstances tilted, sending her flying out of control? Or, I wondered, thinking of Susan's reticence that day I'd complimented her in Susan's office, had her private life always been in disarray? Was she somebody who over-achieved in one area to compensate for inadequacies in another? Had there been a point when she began coping with disorder in her private life on a different plane? A point when coping included murder?

Then I knew why she'd come after me. She believed that I suspected her of murdering Jason Snoud—which I hadn't until that instant. This was more than just a chase in the dark; Nancy Freeman meant to kill me.

I ceased worrying about Frank and Ginger. I was sure Nancy had called Frank and delivered a message—like the good secretary she was—that my plans had changed and couldn't meet tonight. She'd assumed she'd have the upper hand, arranging it so that I'd be alone and in the dark—for I was also sure that she'd flipped the switches on the circuit breaker. The instant she moved back into the choir room or out into the gallery, though, the situation could be used to my advantage. Under cover of darkness I'd fly down the stairs and be outside screaming bloody murder before she saw I was gone.

I almost had my chance to run when Nancy took a step toward the gallery. But then, for some reason she suddenly turned back, switched on a flashlight and shined it in my direction just as I involuntarily moved my foot.

"Oh, there you are, Andy." She greeted me pleasantly, as if she'd been sent by Susan to set up a meeting time for the Religious Education Committee.

"Hi, Nancy," I said awkwardly. Had this been a joke? Above her flashlight Nancy looked as she always did, eyeliner perfectly drawn, each lash stroked with mascara, lipstick moist on her lips. "I think the storm and the power outage has us spooked." My chuckle sounded more like phlegm being cleared in my throat.

She switched the flashlight from one hand to the other and her skirt rustled again as she withdrew something from a pocket. I think the first thing I noticed was her manicure: fingernails fashionably squared off and polished clear with just the long tips painted white. The second thing that registered was the gun.

It was small and toy-like, reminding me of a model in colorful plastic that was lying on Max's bedroom floor. But when Nancy raised it the comparison faded. Facing the blank stare of a gun, regardless of its size, was unnerving. She switched off the flashlight then and set it on a step.

"This isn't about my research, is it?" I said, needing to utter something.

"No." She gave a tinkling laugh that had probably first attracted Jason Snoud.

"Well," I said, trying to think of something to say to stall whatever was about to happen and give me time to think of a way out, "you had me fooled with that business of messing up the records in the trunk."

Nancy cocked her head in amusement. "That was Jason. I wouldn't have messed up the records." Certainly not. Lure someone to an empty church, stalk her in the dark, threaten her with a gun, yes. But not mess up the church papers.

"Why did Jason go through the trunk?"

"He was looking for something to tell him where the other tankard was."

"Why was he interested in the other tankard?"

She sighed impatiently. "From some old family papers he had, Jason thought that the silver cups were hidden in the steeple somewhere and he figured that he'd find them someday—no hurry. But then you guys came in and found one and screwed things up so he had to find the other one quick before somebody else did."

"Why did he want to find them?"

She sighed again. "Do you realize how much they're worth? There's a web site that buys and sells church artifacts, top dollar, no questions asked."

"Wait a minute," I said, recalling something. "When the restoration committee looked into having the weathercock restored it was you who looked up its worth. That's how you found out the value of the silver."

"Yes," she said tersely. "I looked it up, but I couldn't care less about the stupid silver. I was only helping Jason."

"Then why are you here, doing this?"

"It was your remark," she said. "You said that you knew Jason and I were lovers—'friendly' was the word you used."

I remembered the comment, made without any knowledge of an amorous relationship between Jason Snoud and Nancy. "But I didn't—"

"And when you started asking about the doorstop, I knew that you knew."

"Knew what?" I tried to sound demanding, but my voice wobbled. "I don't know anything. So why don't we just leave it at that? It's late and we both want to go home…" My voice trailed off in a whine as I set down the folders and rose from the step cautiously.

"Stay where you are!" She jiggled her well-manicured hand to draw attention to the weapon.

"Okay, okay." I froze in mid-rise and, influenced no doubt by TV, stupidly showed the palms of both hands. "Do you want me to sit again?"

She pursed her lips. "No. You can stand."

I straightened up and lowered my hands. "Don't you want to tell me about it?" I could think of no other plan than to get her talking. "Did you love Jason?"

"Yes. I did," she said, willing to talk. "And I thought he shared the feeling, but he was just using me. He only wanted my help in getting that stupid silver so he and his—his *other* girlfriend could run away." Her voice shook in anger as did her hand that held the gun.

"He was like your ex-husband, wasn't he?" I ventured.

She drew a shaky breath. "I thought he was different. We'd meet at the church where we wouldn't run into anybody we knew. I had the keys and knew when it would be free. We'd go up to the top of the steeple and drink wine and look out over the city." She paused, remembering. "Jason made me feel attractive and desirable again," she said. "Until I found out he was seeing another woman."

I didn't think she meant his wife. "What did you do?"

"We met at the church as usual." Her voice was quiet, composed. "I confronted him with what I knew, still believing that he loved me. I was going to forgive him, accept him back if he'd promise to be true, and to begin divorce proceedings."

"But he wouldn't," I guessed.

"He laughed at me," she said bitterly. "He said I should know better than to expect loyalty from a man who cheated on his wife."

I could see Snoud delivering the line—an oft-used one I was sure—with boyish charm, not realizing it would be the last time he used it.

"He said that I shouldn't ruin the good thing we had. That what we had was an 'untethered love'—those were his words. Love!" she spit out the word. "Jason didn't know the first thing about love." A lock of hair had fallen onto her forehead and unconsciously she pushed it back with the top of the gun's barrel.

"Be careful!" I said instinctively, then bit my tongue when Nancy's attention was drawn back to the present. She looked at her hand as if surprised to see a gun in it, then pointed it at me again and took a determined stance. I noticed her feet: large for a woman's and clad in running sneakers.

"You," I whispered. "It was you at my window. You burned down my shed." Nancy watching me, sneaking into my back yard, pouring gasoline on my shed and setting a match to it. The picture was vivid and for some crazy reason chilled me more than my immediate predicament.

Nancy followed my look to her feet. "I tried to scare you off. But you kept asking questions and talking to the police." Her voice had turned stern like a mother who was done with foolishness and meant business. "Now, I have to ask you to go up those stairs behind you," she said. "We're going up into the steeple."

"Why?" I asked stupidly, my heart beginning to hammer in my chest.

"I'm sorry. I wish there was another way, but there isn't."

Every atom in my body reacted against going up into the steeple with Nancy behind me. I stood rooted, my thoughts tumbling over each other. Would she shoot the gun, knowing it might be heard by somebody in one of the apartments above the stores across the street? Maybe she didn't care if anyone heard. Then, why make me go up into the steeple? Suddenly the entire midsection of my body froze. Was she going to push me off the bell platform?

In my childhood nightmares of free falling into a vast black space, I never reached bottom. I would awaken screaming, wringing wet from sweat. Was I finally to achieve the ending of the nightmare—the churchyard on Pleasant Street?

"Nancy, we don't need to do this," I said, trying to control the panic in my voice. "Let's just leave. I promise never to tell anybody, okay?"

"I'm sorry, Andy. I like you but I don't have a choice."

"Look," I said urgently, "people will understand about Jason. He betrayed you. But they won't understand you hurting me—a friend."

"He deserved to die and you don't," she agreed. She pursed her lips as if considering, then shook her head. Her show of reasonableness was beginning to grate on my nerves. "But there's no other way. If I do this right, nobody will know I was here with you tonight. And you're the only one who connected Jason and me."

"Listen, Nancy—" She cut me off with an impatient jiggle of her weapon.

"I'm sorry, Andy," she repeated primly, waving me upward with the nose of the gun. "Now move." Ultimately, I obeyed the authority of that few ounces of steel. But I also obeyed something in Nancy I'd never seen before, something diamond hard under the politeness that assured me she'd shoot if provoked, and inept as she might be with the gun, it would be impossible to miss in such close quarters. I started up the steps but kept my head to the side so I could see behind as well as ahead.

"Tell me what happened," I said, hoping to distract her by conversation again.

"You were right, Andy, when you said Jason was just like my ex-husband," she said, willing to talk again now that we were moving. "When I hit Jason I thought of Keith and I got angrier and angrier at the injustice of it all. I thought of all the women the Jasons and Keiths of this world hurt."

"I know what you mean," I said, matching her tone. "Some men are creeps." Too late, I sensed this was the wrong tack.

"How would you know?" she demanded, her voice harsh. The barrel of the gun grazed my back and I leaped up the next step. "Gus is one of the good guys. You have two lovely children. You have everything, the perfect life. I can't ever tell the good guys from the bad until it's too late."

Desperately, I wracked my brain for a way out. "My children—"

"I can't think of that," Nancy cut me off. "Go on through there." We had reached the door to the steeple. As I twisted the knob and pushed the door inward, an idea came to me. I stepped in quickly, and started up the first set of stairs before Nancy could remember that there was only one window and that she'd left her flashlight below. "Not too fast!" she said sharply.

"So you hit him," I prompted over my shoulder, midway up the stairs.

"Yes, I dropped my keys and pretended I couldn't find them," Nancy said. "Gee, I'd forgotten how dark it is in here."

"There are windows up a little ways," I lied, hoping she didn't know better.

"Don't try anything, Andy," she warned. "I can see well enough to shoot."

"You were telling me how you hit Jason," I reminded her. I reached the first landing and moved quickly to the second set of stairs. Surprising how one can overcome fear of heights when one's life depended on it. If I recalled the layout correctly, my chance for escape would come on the next landing, before the last narrow ladder that led to the bell platform. It would have to be then because I vowed I would not go out onto the bell platform.

"So, when Jason knelt to look for my keys that I'd dropped," Nancy said as if it were conversation over coffee, "I picked up the granite block that holds the door open on warm days and hit him on the head with it." She gave a wry laugh. "All those workouts with weights at the gym paid off."

The stairway had gradually become darker as we ascended, which I had counted on. But it had become steeper as well, which I didn't like.

"He fell and I thought of all the other women who'd been hurt like me and I hit him again." She paused, considering. "I think I hit him four times altogether."

A vivid memory of Snoud lying in a pool of blood came back and I suddenly felt dizzy. In spite of myself I looked down. A web-like zigzag of staircases disappeared into a black abyss. All that protected me from falling into it were meager treads attached to stringers with no risers, and a single two by four nailed between posts for a rail. I closed my eyes at once but it was too late. That old feeling that I was being pulled over the edge swept over me and I swayed.

"Keep going!" Nancy had caught up to me. She poked me with the gun.

"I can't," I said. "I'm scared." I clung to the ladder, eyes squeezed shut, body paralyzed with fright.

TWENTY-NINE

IT TOOK AN ETERNITY but my right foot moved, pulling dead weight onto the next tread, then my left foot moved. My hands slid along the rough rail. I heard Nancy as if she were background music on a radio tuned low. "I had to do something with the doorstop," she was saying matter-of-fact, "so I wrapped it in my sweater and put it in my car. I drove down to the pier and dropped it in the water."

I made an effort to subjugate the wild beating of my heart, to concentrate on her words. A splinter stabbed my palm and I flinched but kept my hand on the rail.

We'd reached the last landing but I had let the fear in, allowed it to delay me, and now Nancy was too close for me to try my escape plan. With panic fogging my brain, I tried to think of another way out. Could I dart suddenly to the left or to the right?

"At low tide you can see it among the other rocks," Nancy said, more to herself than to me. "I went down the other day. It looks like it belongs there."

I didn't respond, didn't interrupt her. I felt her breath on my back—or maybe I just imagined it—as we moved in tandem across the floor to the final ladder-like steps to the belfry. If I stopped abruptly, would she bump into me and drop the gun?

"You wouldn't know it hadn't always been there," she said almost in reverie.

Every plan I thought of was too risky. An unexpected

movement could get me shot. And if I managed to get away from her up there, where could I go? It was clear that my best chance was to gain advantage before we got through the trapdoor.

The last set of steps was almost vertical. I recalled how Frank, Ginger, and I had had to go one at a time, each waiting until the person ahead had climbed above head height before starting up. Then I had an idea that might work if I could summon enough courage. Nancy continued to talk but I tuned her out; it would take all my concentration to do what I had to do. Giving an air of defeat, of reluctance, I pulled myself up onto the first step. Nancy waited until I climbed above her, the way I had waited for Ginger that first time. If I were dreaming, I thought, this would be when, as a last recourse, I sprouted wings and took off over her head. But there would be no ethereal solution to this situation; if I were able to escape, it would be physical.

I felt her weight on the ladder. Because of the pitch, she would be holding on to both rails now. I glanced down, taking care this time not to look into the space beyond. Her right hand gripped the rail, holding the side of the gun handle against it, barrel facing out. She was saying something about Jason dropping the wine bottle and how nobody could connect it to her. Then she took another step and I did too, watching out of the corner of my eye to keep my knee even with, or just below her head. We were halfway up the ladder. If I was going to act it would have to be now.

Now! I screamed inside my head. I raised my right knee and kicked backward forcefully, ramming the heel of my foot into her neck. Caught by surprise, she uttered a grunt. I kicked at her again and felt the ladder lurch as her right side broke loose of the rail. The gun hit the floor below and skittered across it but Nancy managed to hold on. She regained her balance and grabbed at my feet, missing widely as I raced up the remaining steps. I reached the trapdoor and pushed up hard against it with both hands, forgetting about the latch that secured it.

Below me, Nancy shook the rails in anger and although the ladder, securely attached at top and bottom, swayed only slightly, the movement was enough to knock me off balance. I grabbed hold of the rail with one hand while the other scrabbled along the edge of the trapdoor where I remembered the hook to be. Blindly, I swept my hand back and forth across the area, hitting a piece of cold metal once in mid-swipe, finding it again on the return swipe. Then, like an iron cuff, Nancy's hand clamped on to my right ankle, jerked it off the tread, and I lost contact with the hook. My knee came down hard on the step below, rays of pain shooting up through my leg. I kicked futilely with my right foot, then gave up. With great effort I hauled myself back up onto the next step, dragging Nancy's weight along with my own. Holding on tightly with one hand I reached overhead and hit at the hook again, this time striking it right the first time. The hook flew out of its eye.

Nancy yanked down on my ankle but my foot was planted firmly on the tread. I reached down and clawed at her hand. "Let go," I said between gritted teeth. She expelled a low rasping sound, able to do nothing but endure my vicious scratching as she held on to the rail with one hand and my ankle with the other. She butted my arm with her head but I grabbed her forefinger and bent it back as far as I could, feeling a surge of confidence. Without the gun, the odds had been evened; I felt ready to match Nancy in both wits and brute strength. With a sharp cry she broke her hold and I lunged at the trapdoor, pushing on it with all my force. The door rose up into the night, came almost to a standstill at ninety degrees and then, as if making a sudden decision, fell away out of sight. I hoisted myself onto the edge of the opening, but before I could bring my legs up, Nancy got hold of my ankle again. I twisted around and kicked her square in the forehead with my free foot.

"Bitch!" It was a muffled scream for she had shrunk back into herself for a moment, head bowed into the crook of her arm which curled up in front of her face, fist pressed tightly to the top of her head. Losing no time, I scrambled backwards onto the bell platform and got to my knees. Fear forgotten, adrenaline fueled me now. Although I had only a fuzzy plan, each response presented itself to me clearly the instant it was needed. I crawled around to the other side of the trapdoor and was about to slam it onto Nancy's head that appeared in the opening, when I changed my mind. Instead, I waited while she climbed up onto the platform, eyes squinting in the sudden glare of a corner spotlight, and started after me. I darted around the side of the bell, my feet sloshing through small puddles left from the rain and slipping on wet places where the gravelly surface had worn away from the tar-paper floor covering. I kept close to the hulking mass of the bell, away from the edge of the platform that was no more than four feet away and tried not to think how high up I was (three stories) or how flimsy the enclosure was (loosely attached chicken wire).

As I moved, I dug into my purse, still strapped across my chest. I pulled out a little metal car and flung it at Nancy. It glanced off her arm as she rounded the bell toward me. I found another one, Max's tiny fire engine with plastic ladders, and threw that, too. She yelped as it dinged her on the side of the head. Then I fired off my change purse, credit card wallet, key ring, comb, and moist towelette container.

My purpose was not to hurt her, obviously, but to agitate and confuse her and to keep her from figuring out that I was trying to get her away from the trapdoor. I was succeeding on the agitation part, at least; Nancy shouted and swore every time a missile hit its mark, and then lunged at me with increased determination.

Keeping the bell between us by jockeying back and forth, I dug deeper into my arsenal. Before I ran out of hard objects, I had fired off three marbles, two McDonald's Happy Meals figures, a tube of lip balm, and an array of pens, pencils, and crayons.

Desperately, I raked through the soft stuff on the bottom of the purse—empty gum wrappers, store coupons, bird feathers, a plastic bag—balloons! I squeezed finger and thumb into a torn hole of the bag and pulled out one. Hooking it over my thumb, I stretched the rubber back as far as it would go and let it fly. It fluttered past Nancy's ear, creating no stir, except that she didn't know what it was and slapped her hand at the air beside her head. Then, with a fierce "raughh" sound, she leapt after me. I fired off another balloon and sprinted a couple more feet, completing full circle around the bell. But before I could jump down the hatch, Nancy caught hold of the purse strap across my back and pulled me up short.

I flailed helplessly as she swung me in an arc toward the edge of the platform. I dropped to the floor, dead weight. Nancy kicked at me from behind, pulling the strap taut so that I couldn't turn. When she failed to budge me, she let go of the strap and shoved. I fell forward and for a scant moment lay flat on the wet flooring, two inches from the edge, peering through the octagonal frame of a segment of chicken wire into black space. Then I scrambled to my knees and twisted away as she lunged for me again. I ripped the nearly empty purse over my head and flung it at her.

In the instant it took for her to flinch, I gained the hatch hole and slid down into it, landing on a step. I reached out, seized the handle of the trapdoor, and pulled on it. Nancy caught a corner and we engaged in a tug of war with the door in midair. She dropped down onto her rear end and kicked at me through the opening. I dodged her foot the first time but it got me in the chest the second time. I lost my footing for a moment, and hung free from the trapdoor handle. My full weight won the tug of war; the door crashed down on Nancy's leg. She screamed and pulled her leg out as I regained my footing. The door slammed down again, this time bonking my head when I didn't duck fast enough. While Nancy pounded with fists overhead, shouting curses, I fumbled sightless until I found the big hook and its corresponding eye, hooked the door, and then scrambled downstairs.

IT TOOK THE WEIGHT of my whole body on the rope to produce that peal high above, after which I surrendered power, letting the great bell's sway pull me back up with the rope so that my feet almost left the floor. Pull, release, pull, release. I rang the bell for all I was worth, like people had done for two centuries: to summon, celebrate, mourn, alarm. As the streets resonated with the tolling, I felt an odd connection to the past, to the emotions that had prompted others through the ages to pull on the bell rope: joy, grief, terror. Especially terror. The idea that an everyday kind of person like Nancy Freeman could be a murderer in a picture perfect town like Newburyport was terrifying. Mayta's words finally hit home; the vices, hatred, and prejudice I thought I'd left behind in Detroit could be found anywhere. Even here.

They found me after what seemed like hours but which was, in actuality, only two and a half minutes. Sergeant Wenninger came up from behind and gently, but firmly, put his hands on my arms, stopping them in mid-pull. Then Susan was there, her nightgown peeking out from under her rain slicker, and afterwards, Gus and the kids, who'd heard the tolling on their way back from the island. But Sergeant Wenninger had gotten there first because, it turned out, he'd been suspicious of Nancy before I'd even talked to him about the doorstop, and had followed her to the church.

I probably should have made a public apology to the citizens of Newburyport for disturbing the peace. But anyone out in the street who thought the incessant clanging was unbearable should have been up in the belfry with Nancy. When Wenninger got to her, she was huddled on the floor, both arms wrapped around her head, sobbing, the awakened monster still swaying over her.

THIRTY

FOR THE SECOND TIME in as many weeks, Newburyport made *Boston Globe*'s North Shore section. Locally, Nancy's arrest was the talk of the town. We church members were more reticent; after all, she was a member of our family. Susan handled it beautifully, addressing the issue directly but with tact and empathy within the context of the following Sunday's service.

I did not see Nancy after that night. She was held in the local jail until her transfer to a state prison shortly afterwards. The following day I'd gone down to the station and given my statement to Sergeant Wenninger. I was told I'd have to testify at Nancy's trial sometime in the future, an event I didn't look forward to.

It seems callous to say, but the living go on living and however much the present affects us, it soon becomes the past. After a week, other things occupied our minds. After a month, we hardly thought about Nancy and Jason at all. By the end of May, when temperatures were averaging low-seventies, those events that had happened in the cold of early spring seemed to belong to a different era.

Funny thing, though, when I *did* think about that night it wasn't my close brush with death that haunted me, but Nancy's rational, matter-of-fact tone when she told how she bludgeoned Jason. I would never have pegged her for a cold-blooded killer. I continued to think about Peter Chambers and Hitty Prince and the Fire of 1811, too. But in the aftermath of Nancy's arrest for the murder of Jason Snoud, I took a hiatus on my research. I owed it to Gus, who was upset after the steeple incident, and to the kids, who knew enough about what had happened to want me close by for the time being. I knew I would eventually find out the truth behind Peter's death and the fire, but for now, after several uncomfortable weeks of having my family and myself thrust into the limelight, I was satisfied to let it lie.

OUR MANUSCRIPT MADE IT to Merrimack Press by deadline. Over the summer Ginger, Frank, and I got together several times to do page proofs and to go over the galleys. By the end of June, the completed project was back at the publisher, who promised to have two thousand copies ready for September's Tricentennial Celebration.

Summer passed uneventfully. Gus, the kids, and I spent a lot of time at Mayta's cottage out on the island, beach-combing, playing in the waves, and fishing. We got away for a long weekend of camping in the White Mountains, but that was all Gus could manage between summer school classes he'd taken on, private tutoring, and periodic demands of the negotiating committee.

The teachers' contract was settled by the first week of school, to the relief of all. An unsettled contract is not a great way to start a new year.

"Just goes to show," Mayta said, plunking a white bakery bag down on the counter. She'd stopped by to see the newly published *History of the Newbury Parish*.

"What do you mean?" I peeked in the bag, sniffing something cinnamony.

She lowered herself into a chair at the table. "Goes to show you can't count on a group of people acting in a certain way. And you can't underestimate the power of a person to change his mind and then influence others to his way of thinking."

"Are you talking about Ben Barrett and the school committee?"

She shrugged and grinned in that maddening way she has. "Maybe."

"So, what's in here?" My nose was in the bag again. "And can we eat it now?"

"Sticky buns from that new bakery on State Street and yes, we can eat them now. Providing you have coffee made."

I took down plates while she plucked out a book from the open carton on the floor. "I just picked them up today," I said. "Frank and Ginger haven't even seen them. They're coming over tonight."

"Looks nice," Mayta commented. She looked at the cover, a pen and ink drawing of the church, then thumbed through the book. "When do they go on sale?"

"After our presentation at the Tricentennial Program Sunday afternoon."

Gus came in then, kissed Mayta on the cheek, grabbed up a cinnamon bun, and launched into the story of the settled contract. "They came in with a different headset. We'd been miles apart on the language, then suddenly they were saying okay to this and okay to that. We compromised on a couple of issues and before you knew it, we had a contract."

"Your mother hinted that Barrett might have had a change of heart," I said to Gus as Mayta suddenly became engrossed in the book.

Gus pursed his lips. "Maybe he wanted things settled before the election."

"That's probably it," Mayta said hastily. She set the book down and clapped her hands together. "Hey! Let's celebrate the finished book and the contract! Actually, that's why I stopped by. I want to take you guys out tonight."

"Sounds good!" Gus looked at me. "Can we get a sitter?"

"Maybe, but I made plans with Ginger and Frank to go over our presentation," I said. "Tell you what, we'll be done early; I'll invite Ginger and Frank to come, too."

"It's settled then." Mayta pushed herself up from the table. "I've got some errands to run. How about we meet at the Grog. Is eight-ish okay?"

"She's up to something," I said when she was gone.

GINGER, FRANK, AND I were finished in less than an hour. Our part in the Tricentennial Celebration was simple: Frank would introduce our book and then each of us would read a selection. After settling the kids down with Molly's and Max's favorite babysitter who, miraculously, was free and able to come at short notice, the four of us walked downtown to meet Mayta.

The Grog, a popular bar and restaurant, is housed in one of the oldest brick buildings just off Market Square. Originally a tavern back in the 1700s catering to sailors, the building has had various other incarnations, including a stint as a Salvation Army store, before coming full circle to the modern equivalent of the tavern it once was. The interim years were managed without much loss of character and ambience; decor is exposed brick walls, lots of dark wood-paneling, floors, furniture—old lead-paned windows, and a couple of original fireplaces. Upstairs is more classy, with ferns and tablecloths and such. Downstairs, where we usually sit, is casual enough for workmen to stop by for a quick beer after a day's physical labor.

The first person I noticed when we were ushered to our table—a thick slab of highly varnished wood atop a barrel—was Ben Barrett. He was seated in a captain's chair, looking at ease in his navy pin-striped suit, though idiosyncratic because a few feet away on barstools sat a couple of the aforementioned workmen hunched over their beers. Next to Barrett was Mayta, looking suspiciously smug.

Barrett stood, greeted us, and then offered his hand to Gus. "Congratulations on your contract," he said heartily.

"Thank you, Ben." Gus accepted his handshake. "I think we

all came out well." As we shuffled extra chairs from surrounding tables to ours, I tried to catch Mayta's eye but she avoided me.

"The weather has been so lovely," Ginger commented, filling an awkward moment after we were settled.

"It has been," Barrett agreed, and we chatted about the weather until the waitress came for our drink orders. Then Barrett shifted his ample body deeper into his chair and rested his elbows on its arms. "This was my idea," he said. "When Mayta mentioned she was meeting you tonight, I invited myself. I hope you don't mind." We murmured polite reassurances and I wondered about Mayta's smugness. I'd have laid odds she'd set up this get-together with Barrett before inviting us.

"I found something in my genealogy research," Barrett continued, "and Mayta felt I ought to tell you directly, Andy." He glanced at the Van Amburgs.

"Ginger and Frank researched the history of the parish with me," I quickly assured him. Frank pushed his silver-rimmed glasses further up on his nose and leaned forward in his scholarly pose, and Ginger nodded curtly.

"Of course," Barrett said. "Before I begin, there's a small matter I should clear up. When you asked those questions about Merriman Tibbits in my office last spring, I was a bit defensive. I want you to understand that, while I have great respect for my ancestors and it would hurt me to find out any of them was a scoundrel, I would never hide the truth."

Our drinks arrived then. Barrett took a sip of his Manhattan and waited while the waitress took our food order. "Everything I told you about Merriman Tibbits was true, to the extent that I knew it," he continued. "But, after a lot of thought on the Embargo and smuggling, I went back and reread Tibbits' diary and papers." He cleared his throat. "It's true that he had a healthy smuggling operation going. I didn't deny it before and

I don't now. It wasn't unusual under the circumstances; with heavy investments in property, ship owners couldn't afford for their ships to sit in dry dock when the government made their livelihood illegal."

"It was a tough time for Newburyport," Gus acknowledged.

"For all seaports." This from Frank who was looking over the top of his glasses which had slipped back down his nose.

I nodded impatiently; we'd had this conversation before. "From what I've read, I'd say historians have been generous in their understanding of smugglers' motives during the Embargo."

"Besides making it possible to survive themselves," Barrett went on, "some believed that smuggling helped by stimulating the economy."

"Now that's interesting," said Mayta dryly. "I never heard that one before."

"It sounds misguided," he acceded, "but think about it: more goods brought in drives up the competition, brings down prices, and increases consumer spending."

"Yeah, but did it really work that way?" Gus said. "What was to keep smugglers from banding together and demanding whatever prices they wanted?"

"Nothing, and I'm sure sometimes that happened. I'm only saying that some believed it could work that way," said Barrett. The waitress brought our meals then and we turned our attention to eating.

"So Merriman Tibbits believed he was stimulating the economy," I prompted after a few minutes.

"Er, yes, among others. That's why he continued to smuggle after the Embargo was lifted. He wanted to rebuild Newburyport into the grand seaport it once was."

"Is this what you found in your research?" I asked. "That Tibbits had this philosophy he was helping out the city by smuggling?" Gus nudged my knee with his.

"Yes. I didn't put it all together until I read the papers again. But that's not all. The new information I have to tell you is something I recently found."

"Was this 'something' found in the family papers you took back from the Historical Society?" There was an immediate sharp retort on my ankle.

Barrett looked surprised. "Actually, no. It was in a book I had all along."

"So, tell us!" said Ginger, her enthusiasm injecting a different tone into the conversation. Bless her heart, I thought. Why couldn't I be more tactful?

Barrett smiled at Ginger. "Tibbits was a proud and powerful man. The Embargo took away his respectability and made him into a smuggler, however he justified it, and he became bitter and twisted in his thoughts. I found a letter he'd left for his brother, Davison. He must have written it close to his death because it doesn't appear to have been sent. It was stuck between the pages of a blank account book, one I hadn't given much attention to because it hadn't been written in. It's hard to tell if Tibbits himself put the letter there, or if it was found and put there."

"What does this letter say?" I asked.

"I made a copy for you." Barrett patted the left side of his suit jacket. He rose, extracted several sheets folded together in thirds, and handed them to me. "It's self-explanatory. I just wanted you to understand that Merriman Tibbits was a powerful man brought down by the Embargo. He became a different person afterwards. His emotional state deteriorated with age, and while he prospered financially to a certain degree, he never regained his prior economic status."

"You're not leaving," said Ginger as Barrett remained standing.

"I must. I have a late meeting back at the office."

"Aw, sit down, Ben." Mayta patted the arm of his chair. "You haven't finished your dinner."

"I'll give you a call, Mayta, and we'll do this again sometime," Ben said, and winked at her.

"Sure, Ben," she said offhandedly. "Talk about old times." She was grinning as she watched him leave. "Old coot," she muttered under her breath.

"I think I know who's been influencing Ben Barrett now," I teased.

"Shut up and open that letter."

THIRTY-ONE

THE OLD INK had copied clear and strong. There were three sheets of handwriting, the strokes bold and slanted as I'd seen them before in church records, their only weakness now in veering off line as they traveled across the paper. A strong man brought down—but not humbled—by infirmity, he had perhaps been lying in bed when he wrote it, forcing a recalcitrant arm to move across the page.

"It's dated September 3, 1812, a year after the fire. Shortly before his death," I said. "Okay, here goes: *My dear brother, Davison, When you find this I hope you will read it carefully, and understand the reasoning behind the course of my actions.*" I tilted the page to better catch what meager light came from the small glass oil lamp in the middle of the table.

"I wonder why it wasn't sent," interjected Gus.

Ginger peeked over the top of the page. "He used the word 'find,' not 'receive.' He meant for his brother to find the letter."

"Which he obviously didn't, because like Ben says, it was among Tibbits' papers, not Davison's," said Mayta, who waved impatiently for me to continue.

"I suppose," said Frank frowning, "that either Tibbits hid it too well—maybe in the very book where Barrett found it—or someone else, not realizing what it was, stuck it away before his brother could find it."

"Go on!" Mayta burst out, unable to contain herself any longer. "Read it!"

They leaned in close as I continued in a low voice, *"'As I grow weaker, I feel the need to answer your questions more fully than I have in the past: firstly, concerning the fire of one year ago, and secondly, concerning the girl, Mehetabah.'"*

"Ah ha!" exclaimed Mayta. "You were right, Andy. Tibbits set the fire."

I went on. *"'You know how strongly I feel about restoring Newburyport to its rightful place as mercantile center of New England. Continuing trade during the Embargo was the only way to keep wealth flowing into the city until such time as the city was restored to its previous station. We have discussed this many times, you and I and Eleazar and Thomas and the others who share our views on this matter. What I have to tell you now is that we were wrong. Newburyport will never be the great mercantile city it once was. Its decline began long before the Embargo; we have refused to see it. Our fair city's future lies down other paths I cannot and do not want to imagine. I will be glad to be released from this life shortly for I do not want to see what Newburyport will become without her ships and shipyards.*

"'But those are my feelings now. Back then, during and following the Embargo, I felt justified in my actions. As you well know, when those British blackguards captured my best vessel, the Brig Torrance, and its entire shipment in 1810, it became imperative that I make the most from each shipment the following year so as to make up for that loss. For that reason, and because of my belief in keeping as much wealth as possible in the city, I continued to bring in goods secretly even after the Embargo had been lifted.'" I had reached the end of the first page. Quickly, I shuffled it to the back and skimmed the second page.

"Go on!" Mayta urged.

"Here it is! Listen to this: *'What you did not know was that when the customs officials became more diligent in their investigations, I resorted to diversionary methods in order to bring in goods undetected. I hired a boy, an apprentice to the baker Stockwell, to set a small fire on a night I brought in a shipment.'"*

"This is it!" Ginger said excitedly.

"Shhh!" admonished Frank. "Let her finish."

I took a sip of wine, tilted the page closer to the lamp, and continued reading. "*'He was to set a fire somewhere in the city away from the waterfront, where we would be loading goods into the tunnel to take up to the house. I hired him to do this two times. As God is my witness, I only intended slight distractions. He was strictly instructed that they be inconsequential fires that could be easily put out.*

"*'However, unknown to me, this boy enjoyed setting fires. He began setting them at times when I hadn't arranged for him to. I had decided never to use him again, as he was not to be trusted, when a large shipment arrived ahead of schedule, on May 31. There were increased patrols downtown and along the waterfront that week due to the additional fires that this boy, Peter Chambers, had set on his own, and I was desperate to bring the shipment in.*

"*'I hired Chambers one more time, sternly admonishing him against deviating from my instructions, which were to set a small fire away from the waterfront. I told him that if he did exactly as I instructed he would be handsomely compensated and that I would arrange a new work situation for him in New Hampshire.'"*

"Are you folks all set?" The waitress appeared at our table, smiling benignly. For her solicitousness she received three frowns, a glare from Mayta, and a curt "Yes, fine!" from Gus. She hurried away and I bent my head to the paper again.

"*'I should never have made this final arrangement, I should*

*have realized by then that the boy was answering to a larger
call, the thrill of setting fires, a bigger, better one each time. I
was to leave money in my pew box for his job. Instead, when
the fire in town was well under way and I realized the magni-
tude of it, I went to meet him in person, hoping with all my heart
that the conflagration that had occurred was not of his doing.*

"'*When I got to the meeting house, he met me with a prideful
heart. The fool believed that I would be pleased with what he
had done. He bragged that he had chosen his spot well: an
empty stable, dry and filled with hay, amongst other wooden
buildings. He had not set a flame that would be found quickly
and put out; he had set one that would be well started before
it was detected, one that would succeed in doing serious
damage. I don't doubt that he even hoped it would result in destroying the city. With anguished heart, I realized that I had unwittingly ordered this devastation. I became so angry at the boy
that I beat him severely with my cane. Fully believing I'd killed
him, I left him lying there in the meeting house.*'"

"He did kill him!" exclaimed Mayta. The two workmen at
the bar looked our way again, but minus Benjamin Barrett, we
didn't hold their attention.

"Wait," I said, lowering my voice. "Let me finish. '*My blows
did not kill him, but this I did not know until later. When it
became obvious that a perpetrator had caused the fire, I confessed my misdeed to Thomas and Eleazar. I foolishly swore
them to secrecy in order to protect my family's good name, convincing them that their own good names would be besmirched
by their association to me.*

"'*I am ready now, however, to accept responsibility for my
actions. Upon my death, I ask that you speak with Thomas and
Eleazar and release them of their vows of secrecy. Enough time
has passed that the truth can be told and hatred can be justly
heaped upon myself, no longer of this earth, and not upon the*

innocent still living. As for Mehetabah Prince, whom we found hiding in the meeting house that night, it is true that this sorry little bound girl was living in an intolerable way at the baker's home and that it would have been cruel to send her back there. What I did not tell you was that she was a friend of the boy, Peter Chambers, and had been planning to run away with him on the night of the fire. Not only did Chambers recover from the beating I gave him, he stole the silver tankards despite Hitty's pleas not to, and took off for New Hampshire, leaving her behind. I fear for the residents of whatever town he ends up in for the scamp will be a menace to the end of his days. Hitty was quite distressed because she did not want to go back to the baker. For this reason, and also because she knew of my part in the fire and I wanted her away from here, I arranged a new life for her with you in the country. Her master, caring only for the money given in compensation, was easily persuaded to let her go.

"'I no longer care if Hitty tells what she knows as long as the blame does not come back to her. The girl has thrived in the company of your family, seeming a different child than was brought whimpering to you a year ago. I would prefer that her arrangement remain the same, if that is agreeable to you. Thomas and Eleazar have expressed interest in sharing her guardianship. She has come to symbolize to us how something can be helped to flourish in the aftermath of tragedy.' That's it." I said. I aligned the pages and handed them to Frank.

"Then Tibbits really was responsible for the Great Fire," said Gus softly.

"The ending seems a bit abrupt." Mayta craned her head sideways to look at the letter. "Maybe he meant to add more later and then died before he could."

"But he signed his name." Frank pointed out the signature with Tibbits' trademark flourish. The letter was passed around the table as each looked it over.

"If Chambers survived and went to New Hampshire," Ginger said thoughtfully, "who did we find in the steeple?"

"The body in the steeple was definitely Peter Chambers," I said. "The forensic report supports it; his age, description, the flour on his clothes, even the injury to the head fits. Besides, he had the silver tankard. The question is who killed him?"

Mayta spoke up. "Either Hitty lied about Peter going to New Hampshire or Tibbits lied about her saying that."

"Why would Tibbits lie?" Gus asked. "He confessed to hiring Chambers to set the fire and then bashing him. Why would he say Chambers survived if he didn't?"

"Bashing someone with a cane isn't as bad as killing someone with it," Frank said. "It's conceivable that he'd admit to the lesser crime."

"Maybe," I said. "But I tend to believe Tibbits. I feel that this letter was a full confession, a clearing of his conscience, knowing that he was going to die soon."

"Then you think Hitty lied about Peter going to New Hampshire," said Mayta.

"Not necessarily," I said. "Maybe he really did leave for New Hampshire—"

"And then was killed, brought back, and stuffed in the steeple?" said Gus.

I tried again. "It might make sense if he came back on his own without Hitty's knowledge and reentered the church and *then* was killed."

But Gus shook his head. "Too contrived. We're missing something simple."

"And what about the other silver tankard?" demanded Mayta. "The letter says Peter had both of them when he went to New Hampshire. Since we found one with Peter in the steeple, where's the other one?"

THIRTY-TWO

THAT NIGHT, unable to sleep, I went downstairs and made a cup of tea. I kept thinking about Gus's comment about missing something simple. Perched at the kitchen counter, I had the manila folder with all my notes and photocopies from research, Carl's forensic report, and Tibbits' letter. I drew a line down the middle of a piece of paper and wrote "Peter" on one side, "Hitty" on the other. Then I sorted the information, extracting all facts that mentioned either one, and jotted them down, whether or not I thought they were important, underlining commonalities.

Peter	**Hitty**
14 years old at time of fire	13 years old
<u>Malnourished</u>	<u>Malnourished</u>
Left-handed	?
<u>4'10"</u>	<u>"Small"</u>
Poor teeth	?
Apprentice to abusive baker he hated	Orphan bound to <u>abusive baker</u>—did she hate him?
<u>In church at time of Great Fire</u>	<u>In church at time of Great Fire</u>
Called "untrustworthy," "prideful"	Called "pitiful" before fire,
Liked to set fires	?

Stole one—maybe two—tankards	?
Hired by <u>Tibbits</u> to set fire	Supported by <u>Tibbits</u> after fire
Planned to <u>run away to New Hampshire</u>	<u>Planned on going to N.H.</u> with Peter
Died night of fire	"Thrived" after fire for three years
<u>Died young at 14</u>—bashed on head	<u>Died young</u> at 16 of influenza

Both had been small and malnourished and had died young—although under very different circumstances; both had suspicious ties to Tibbits; both had planned on running away and were in the church at the same time on the night of the fire (also the night of Peter's death). If these correlations added up to anything that would lead me to Peter's killer, I couldn't see it.

My thoughts turned again to Tibbits. He had admitted striking Peter and it was a fact that Peter's skull had been cracked shortly before death. But Tibbits had declared him alive afterwards and I tended to believe him. This was where my figuring got stuck in a circular track: it seemed most likely that Tibbits killed him, yet I believed him when he said that he hadn't.

Okay, I said to myself, throw out all assumptions about Peter Chambers' death and start from the beginning. Carl McBride said that Peter could have lived with the injury to his head; I decided to assume that he had. So, if Peter was struck by Tibbits but survived, the opium on the shirt might have been taken for pain, as Carl had suggested. Maybe he'd left the church to get medicine. And then came back. *But why?* And then had died. *How?* I was stuck again.

Leaving it for the moment, I turned over the paper and made two new columns. This time I compared Peter Chambers,

victim in the past, and Jason Snoud, present-day victim. I don't
know why I did this, other than Snoud's murder kept coming
to mind whenever I tried to figure out who killed Peter. I sorted
through my research again.

Peter's Murder	Jason's Murder
<u>Stole tankards to pay for new life</u>	<u>Wanted silver to sell for new life</u>
Age at death: 14	Age at death: 37 or 38 (?)
<u>Killed (presumably) at church</u>	<u>Killed at church</u>
<u>Death may have been caused by</u>	<u>Death by trauma to head or ??</u>
Weapon: rounded end of <u>heavy object</u>	Weapon: <u>granite doorstop</u>
Found in steeple 200 years later	Found in vestibule next morning
Killed by ????	Killed by angry girlfriend

Again, I underlined the similarities. They had been different ages, but had Peter Chambers lived and completed his apprenticeship, he might have been in the same social strata as
Jason Snoud, a steeplejack. Both wanted the silver for the
money it would bring; both were killed by trauma to head (not
definite in Peter's case) with a heavy object at the church. The
only other similarity was that both were untrustworthy.
Granted, Chambers was clearly the worst on this score; besides
not being a model employee, he was a thief and an arsonist,
whereas Snoud was respected in his work, his only dishon-
esty—that I knew about—being his extramarital relationships.

I looked back over both lists, feeling that I was missing that something simple that Gus had mentioned. I gave up and went back upstairs to bed.

It came to me as I was about to fall asleep. Instead of comparing friends (Hitty and Peter) or victims (Peter and Jason), I should compare *murderers*. The common thread was motive. The more I thought about it, the more I was sure I was right. But first, I had something to ask Carl McBride.

"YOU SAID THAT many medicines used to contain opium. Which ones would have been used in 1811?" I'd waited as long as I could stand it to call Carl the next morning but had still gotten him out of bed. After apologizing profusely, I blurted out my questions. "And what form were they in—powders, liquid?"

"Um, let me see." Other than responding a little slowly, Carl acted as if it were routine to be quizzed on medicinal practices of the nineteenth century first thing on a Saturday morning. "Codeine and paregoric were used then," he said. "Also laudanum—all had opium or derivatives of it. Often, they were prepared as alcohol solutions."

"Laudanum." I seized upon the name. "I read an article on microfilm about a woman who committed suicide by overdosing on it."

"Yes, it wasn't hard to obtain any of these medicines. A person could buy as much as he or she wanted at the apothecary."

"How deadly was an opium solution?" I asked. "I mean, how much would be needed to kill someone?"

"Not much. In a solution the alcohol speeds up the effects of the opium. Depending upon the size of the person, a teaspoon could be enough. Reaction time is twenty to forty minutes. Symptoms are sleepiness, loss of muscle power, respiratory difficulties, unconsciousness, and then death two to four hours after ingestion."

"There must have been a lot of accidental deaths back then, given the accessibility of the drug and the small amount needed to overdose," I commented.

"Actually, I don't think there were. People tended to be very careful."

"Thanks, Carl." I scratched down notes quickly. "Sorry again for waking you." I set down the receiver. A couple of niggling notions had formed into hypotheses in my mind. One of them—the location of the second silver tankard—could be proven right or wrong with a little investigation. The second hypothesis would be more difficult—maybe even impossible—to prove, but if I was correct about the first, then I could be pretty sure about the second, which had to do with the identity of Peter Chambers' killer.

THIRTY-THREE

"IT WAS SOMETHING you said, Susan, that kept coming back to me." I spoke from my kneeling position inside the broken corner support on the bell platform of the steeple. "You said that since the tankards were lost at the same time they should be found together. The more I thought about it, the more likely it seemed that they were never separated." I backed up slowly, careful where I placed a knee or a hand while two expectant faces watched me. Gus had agreed to accompany me on what might prove to be a ridiculous venture. Susan, who had unexpectedly been in her office this Saturday morning, wouldn't be put off with the simple explanation that I just wanted to prove something, and had followed us over to the church, and up into the steeple. Both were now crouched at the edge of the support.

"I wish you'd let me do that," Gus said impatiently.

"You wouldn't fit," I told him again. "I can barely squeeze in with these pieces of wood crisscrossing the area."

"Please be careful," Susan pleaded. "I shouldn't be letting you do this."

Work on the steeple had ceased upon Jason Snoud's death in the spring. The building committee had hired a steeplejack from Boston who'd put in a reasonable bid to complete the project; however, because of his busy schedule, he couldn't start work until October. Therefore, the support had been stabilized, but not yet repaired.

"When Jason brought me up here," I said, "I noticed that the floor had broken away around the back edges and was tilted downward." Carefully, I maneuvered back into the corner, bending my head to avoid a two by four that bisected the space. I drew my legs up at a forty-five degree angle and put the flashlight in my lap. "There, I'm where Peter Chambers was when we found him."

"So, what are you trying to prove sitting all cockeyed like that?" said Gus.

"Exactly that," I said smugly. "Sometime during his long rest up here the floor in this corner broke away, causing Peter's body to fall against the wall like this." My shoulder "fell" against the support. "Did you notice my flashlight?"

"It almost rolled off your lap," said Susan. "What are you getting at, Andy?"

"Right," I said, ignoring her question for the moment. "Now, let me ask you this: where would the flashlight have gone, if I hadn't caught it?"

"Onto the floor," Gus said, impatience beginning to show in his voice.

"And then," I said, "down through the crack between the floor and the wall."

"Then I'm glad you caught it because that's our only flashlight," Gus said.

I leaned over and examined the crack. "Yep. Just as I thought. It's plenty big enough for one of the tankards to have slid down into it."

"One of the tankards?" asked Susan, looking uncomfortable stooped over.

"She thinks that both tankards were here with Peter," Gus explained.

"It's my guess that Hitty left them in this secret place," I said.

"Whoa! Why Hitty? What about Peter?" Susan shifted the

weight on her feet, catching the hem of her skirt under the toe of her left black pump.

"He was already there—in the support. Think about it: Hitty couldn't have carried him up here. Nobody else—that we can figure out, anyway—was around so he had to have gotten himself into the hiding place. Remember, this was a boy who had been beaten, left for dead. He wasn't in any condition to be running away to New Hampshire, nor even to escape the church and even if he was, he'd be afraid that Tibbits would be outside waiting for him. His only recourse was to hide."

"You said Hitty left the silver…" Susan prodded.

"Okay. Let me back up a bit." Ideas were coming together in my head and I wanted their reactions. I moved onto a more comfortable spot on a level board. Susan remained in her crouched position but Gus, putting his impatience aside for the moment, sat down on the rough asphalt floor covering and crossed his legs.

"I don't think Hitty was involved in the fires," I began. "She probably didn't know that Peter was setting them—at first. She tagged along, hoping to escape her horrid situation by running away with him. Of course, he didn't take her—"

"Because he died," Susan finished.

"Because he refused," I corrected. "He never intended on taking her. My guess is that Peter normally had little to do with Hitty—she was younger and described as a 'pitiful' thing. He wouldn't have jeopardized his escape by taking her along."

"But that's all beside the point," Gus said, "because he didn't escape. He died."

"Not really beside the point," I said. "Hitty was with him when he died. I think she was dosing him up with medicine after he'd been beaten, hoping he'd get better so they could run away. Then something happened and he died."

"I'm confused. Did he die from the beating or not?" asked Susan.

"No. He died from poisoning." I rushed on before either could interrupt. "Do you remember that Carl found traces of opium on Peter's clothing? Opium was the base for a lot of painkilling medicines of the time which were easily gotten from drugstores—apothecaries. These medicines weren't regulated like they are today and could be lethal if you weren't careful with the dosage. Now, since Peter was too weak to go get medicine for himself, it had to have been Hitty."

"So she accidentally gave him too much medicine?" Susan asked.

"No. Carl said it was unusual for people to accidentally poison themselves; they tended to be very careful. I think Hitty poisoned Peter on purpose."

Gus stopped picking at loose pebbly pieces of roofing material that littered the floor and Susan was visibly formulating a response. I hurried on with my hypothesis. "Hitty didn't care about the silver; according to Tibbits she tried to talk Peter out of stealing it. All she wanted was a new life. That was what got me thinking. Nancy Freeman also didn't care about the silver. She helped Jason find out its worth on the Internet, but that was when she thought he was going to marry her.

"So, when did things go from awry to deadly in both situations? When these women were jilted. Peter was going to take the silver and run and so was Jason. Nancy felt justified in killing Jason for his infidelities and I think Hitty felt justified in killing Peter for setting fire to the town."

"You're saying the motive in both cases was anger over being rejected? I don't know, Andy," said Gus.

But Susan shook her head. "No, I see what she means. I've felt that these deaths were tied together in some way—like human nature—that transcends time."

"That's what I thought at first," I continued, "but it's not that simple. These were different women in different time periods.

Because she's my contemporary, Nancy is easier to understand: the anger caused by rejection motive works. Hitty is more complicated. Given the social mores of a time when death was an accepted consequence of criminal behavior, Hitty could have poisoned Peter because he committed a heinous crime or to prevent him from doing it again, or even to save him from a worse death if convicted. We can't ever know her motive for sure."

"Okay, so give us a scenario," said Gus. "How do you think it went?"

"My guess is that when Hitty found Peter hurt, she helped him get up into the steeple to hide and then went out to get medicine for him. I don't know the time sequence but at some point, while they were both hiding in the steeple, Peter let Hitty know about setting the fire. Setting a fire back then was tantamount to murder—mass murder. Because buildings were all made of wood any kind of fire endangered the entire community. Therefore, arson was considered the most serious of offenses and was punishable by death regardless of the size of the fire set and whether any lives were lost. Hitty, if she was the 'responsible' girl she was supposed to have been, would have viewed what Peter did as an abhorrent crime that was unforgivable. She would have felt it her responsibility to turn him in, and if she couldn't bear to do that, then to make sure that he would never set another fire. She might have believed it inevitable that Peter would be caught and therefore wanted to save him an awful execution.

"Whatever was going on in her mind, I think she purposely overdosed him, under the guise of giving him medicine for his pain. However, I think her sentiment was different from Nancy's. She took the time to wrap him in a blanket and place the silver with him, which indicates tenderness."

"Nancy killed out of vindictive jealousy and Hitty killed out of compassion," said Susan quietly.

"Something like that, yes."

"Perhaps there was some iron will and conniving beneath the poor little girl image," said Gus dryly. "Hitty lied about Peter going to New Hampshire because she was guilty of his death. Then, when she was conveniently found in the church by Tibbits, she probably told him she knew of his arrangement with Peter to set the fire—remember the letter Tibbits wrote to his brother about getting her out of town? So he offered her a nice situation for the rest of her life in exchange for her silence."

I shrugged. "Perhaps. We're looking at it from a distance of almost two hundred years. We can put together a few facts, try to interpret them in light of the times, but then we have to guess at the rest. She could have seized an opportunity to trade her miserable life for a better one, but I like to believe she was more compassionate than conniving."

"Then there's the silver. Why did she leave it with Peter?" asked Susan.

"I think she wanted him to have it, but that's the romantic in me. Most likely," I hurried on as Gus snorted, "it was too risky trying to get it back downstairs." I got back onto my hands and knees and began inching backwards. "Now, let's see if I'm right about that tankard."

When I reached the corner, I maneuvered into a position to explore, straddling the sloping floor, knees braced on the new two by fours that secured the broken sides. I flicked on the flashlight and pointed the beam down into the gap where the sloping floorboard had separated a good eight inches from the side wall. "I wonder what—" Something below twitched curiously and I bent down closer to the opening. A musty decaying odor rose from beneath the boards.

"What is it? What do you see?" Susan demanded.

There was squeaking and scratching as small furry bodies scurried into the recesses. I jerked backwards, bashing my head into a two by four and almost dropping the flashlight. "Yech! Mice!" Then, as I rubbed the sore spot, I moaned, "My head!"

"Be careful, Andy." Gus's irritated tone steeled me. I gripped the flashlight and advanced again, with trepidation this time. Positioned on all fours above the crack, I lowered the flashlight down into the crack, and fanned it, the beam making arcs that reached further into the corners. There, at the edge of my light, caught between two cross pieces, sat a very tarnished, but easily identifiable silver tankard.

THIRTY-FOUR

THE CHURCH SILVER, in its entirety for the first time since 1811, was on display at the front of the sanctuary, its polished gleam reflecting the purple and gold of the fall bouquet in the center of the table. Gus had extracted the tankard from its resting place and once again Ben Worthy at Silvercrafters had been called into service to inspect a long lost piece of silver for damage— only one small ding—and to polish it.

From my seat on the long horsehair couch behind the pulpit I looked out over the congregation. The pews were filled to capacity as was the gallery overhead. Other than at Christmas Candlelight Service, I'd never seen the church so teeming with humanity. It occurred to me that this must have been the way it was in the early eighteen hundreds when whole families crowded into their box pews every Sunday, sometimes perching young children on the window sills.

I squinted, blurring my vision slightly so that I could imagine long dresses and bonnets on the women, longer hair and high collars under suit jackets on the men. I imagined Merriman Tibbits, tri-corner hat atop his white queue, seated with his family in number seventy-seven, close to the front where the well-to-do owned their boxes. Adjacent pews would have held the Tooles, the Rands, the Browns. I looked up at the gallery and pictured James Stockwell, the baker, and his wife, both dressed in their Sunday clothes seated there; would they have brought Peter Chambers and Hitty Prince with them? The choral call to worship awoke me from my reverie and I refocused on the present.

The Tricentennial Celebration brought together young and old. First to address the congregation was a retired minister who was well-remembered and loved by the elderly members. He spoke eloquently about our liberal traditions, begun with the first minister, John Lovell, back in 1725, that continued down to the present. Mark Levenson was next. His hair, not in its usual pony tail, hung loose over the shoulders of his severely cut black suit jacket. Underneath, he wore a tie-less bright blue silk shirt, its top two buttons undone. Mark surveyed his audience stiffly before he commenced a dissertation on past illustrious members, including Merriman Tibbits, wealthy ship owner who gave leadership to the church and city at a difficult time in its history. I smiled to myself, thinking of the information missing from his talk—information that was likely to be missing for some time yet.

Ben Barrett had agreed with Ginger, Frank, Gus, Mayta, and me that the truth concerning Tibbits and the Great Fire of 1811 needed to be told and that the one to disclose it should be Barrett since Tibbits was his ancestor. However, with the sensation caused by the discovery of two bodies in the church, Barrett wanted to wait until a calmer time—by which we figured he meant after the election—to release the information to the Historical Society. That was okay with us; we didn't wish his campaign harm. Since the contract settlement, even Gus had softened towards Barrett.

At the close of the second hymn Frank introduced our book. His humorous remarks about the three of us working together made me think how much I'd miss his dry wit and Ginger's graciousness now that we wouldn't be meeting regularly. I vowed to invite them over for dinner soon—Mayta, too; maybe she'd offer to cook.

After Frank's introduction, Ginger read a selection from the book, and then it was my turn. I was a little nervous as I took the pulpit. This time, though, instead of summoning up figures from the past, I looked squarely into the faces of the present and the future. Up front sat Mayta and Gus with Max and Molly, both of whom were already fidgeting on the hard benches. Across the aisle, in one of the boxes equipped with amplifying headphones, sat Herb and Frieda Cole, Herb being the one who needed the headphones. Next to them sat Ben Barrett and his daughter. I wondered if Barrett was going to follow through with that dinner date with Mayta. Scanning the sea of pleasantly expectant faces, I picked out Miss Cardigan, Molly's teacher, and Joan Soffet, who owned the framing shop downtown, Ross Thayer and his wife, the Jensen family—all seven of them, the children like little tow-headed steps. I was surprised at how many of these people I knew: by services they provided in my daily life or committees we'd served on together, or through like interests or the common activities of our children.

It occurred to me that I liked these people—most of them, I amended, catching sight of Mark's blue shirt out of the corner of my eye—and that I looked forward to knowing them better in years to come. A warm swelling in my chest told me that I belonged, that at some moment I couldn't pinpoint, I'd crossed over the line from outsider to insider. And now, in retrospect, I wondered how much of the initial resistance had been my *perception* of Newburyport's guardedness toward me, how much had even been my own guardedness. Whatever the resistance had been, and even though part of me would always think of Detroit as home, I now knew that belonging here with these people was my choice.

The selection I had chosen to read was on the planning of

the new meeting house. It seemed fitting at that moment and I think I gave it extra emphasis because of my expansive mood. "'The land they bought was ledge,'" I began. "'The committee determined that it was appropriate to construct their new house of worship on rock like the biblical verse. It would be built from the sturdiest timbers so that hundreds of years later it would still stand strong. The most highly skilled ship's carpenters and finishers to be had in this seaport community would ply their crafts to this end. The style would be taken from the Greeks. It would be simple, beautiful, classic. Its only embellishment would be the spire, delicately constructed to be airy with many windows and openings…'"

As I read, I noticed here and there a head tilting or pivoting to examine some architectural detail: the arched ceiling, the Doric pillars supporting the gallery, or the raised pulpit. Like me before I'd begun this project, they hadn't thought about the careful consideration behind the architectural choices. My final sentence dissipated into silence and I sat down, knowing that our forefathers had accomplished their goal. Despite human errors, petty greed and hatreds, and righteous actions that had resulted in tragedy, this sturdy, beautiful building still stood to inspire us.

Susan mounted the pulpit. Clothed in her black robe, her diminutive stature took on more substance. She delivered a sermon on blending old and new traditions and what that meant for us and for future congregations. The past and the present, the old and the new. I thought about the people—Hitty, Peter, Nancy, Jason—and the events that were now tiny strands in the unique tapestry of the First Parish, and decided that, overall, I felt pretty good about having helped to weave them into its history. It was especially satisfying to think that my snooping into the past had helped restore a lost part of our inheritance: the silver tankards.

At the close of the sermon, the combined children's and adults' choirs began one of the lilting old hymns whose lyrics had been changed in recent times to reflect more politically correct attitudes. This time, however, I didn't find the words jarring. In fact, I kind of liked the mix of tradition and modernity.

June 1, 1811
2:39 a.m.

Despite the cacophony outside and the worry of flames igniting the meeting house in which she huddled, and especially despite her resolve to watch for Peter's departure, Hitty had fallen asleep. It was the clank of the door latch that jerked her awake. She barely had time to slide off the bench and duck under it before somebody entered the sanctuary.

Her cheek smarted where it had lain pressed against the edge of the window sill, and her throat was parched from breathing the caustic air. Pressing a fist to her mouth to stifle a cough, she wondered that the roar of flames, crashing of bricks, groaning of wood structures, and mutual agonized cries of humans and beasts had all receded. What miracle had kept the fire from devouring the meeting house and the two people it sheltered?

Peter! How long had she slept? Was Peter already on his way to New Hampshire? Rising despair was smothered quickly with resolve: she would go after him and when she caught up—too far away for him to send her back—he would have to let her stay with him. She would not return to the harsh life at the bakery without him. But first, she reminded herself with a small ray of hope, she had to find out if he was really gone.

Hitty crawled out from under the bench and peeked over the pew wall to see who had come into the sanctuary. Although she could see only shadows in a smoke-filled darkness, she determined that there were two men and that they were not any of the others who had come before. These men were quiet, their treads stealthy, and she sensed they'd come for a different purpose: to loot.

"You look up there," one said, "an' I'll see what's in that little room out back." He disappeared into the robing room while the other mounted the pulpit. A few moments later they met at the bottom of the pulpit steps.

"What'd ya find?" said one.

"Nothin'," the other said in a low growl. They proceeded almost noiselessly back out to the vestibule, and ascended to the gallery where, Hitty thought with satisfaction, they would find the clock safely removed. Then she remembered Peter; if he was still hiding up there somewhere, would they find him?

Crouched down in the corner of her pew, Hitty listened, her nostrils filled with the acrid stink of smoke mixed with the pungency of her own sweat. But there came no sound of discovery, no third voice. After a while—minutes? A quarter hour?—she heard the men descend the gallery stairs. From their ponderous, synchronized treads, she guessed they had found something weighty worth carting off—a piece of furniture, perhaps. Two more times they climbed the stairs and descended. Then the outside door, which creaked regardless of how careful one was, opened and there was shuffling back and forth before it was shut again with a tiny clink of the latch.

Hitty slipped out of the pew, leaving her shoes under the bench. Light on bare feet, she ran up and down checking pews, not expecting to find Peter in such easily accessible places, but wanting to be thorough in her search. Upstairs, she looked through the choir room wardrobes, and had started toward the organ and the staircase that led to the steeple, when she heard voices from below. She darted behind the organ, tripping over an object on the bottom step and sending it clattering to the floor. She dropped to her knees and, wildly flinging out her hands to locate and silence the offending sound, touched metal. She ran her fingers over the object and determined it to be a smooth cup with a lid: a tankard. Was it one of the two Peter had when he went to hide? She grabbed it up, and fumbled for its companion, finding it on the same step, among with other items not readily identifiable by touch. Peter must still be here! However, her relief was quickly replaced by concern: had the looters found him?

The voices got louder. Clutching the silver pieces to her breast, Hitty pressed herself to the wall behind the organ. One of the voices was accusatory in tone. Hitty caught the word "stealing" and guessed that the looters had been apprehended trying to reenter the meeting house, probably on their way back to get the silver and the other things in the pile that Hitty had just tripped over.

Still carrying the tankards, she flew up the narrow staircase, bumped open the door with her elbow, and entered the steeple. "Peter!" she whispered into the large attic over the sanctuary. A dim glow—the fire—shone through the window at the far end, allowing just enough light to see by. She tiptoed along the massive middle beam that ran the length of the attic, calling softly, and peering into the recesses. At its end she was drawn to the window. The fire was a distance away—in the southern part of town—and had lost its earlier menace but it was what lay between Hitty and the fire that was now alarming. She stood at the edge of a scorched wasteland; everything that could be seen in the smoky moonlight was blackened, broken, desolate. A sick feeling washed over her. How could Peter have done such a terrible thing?

Hitty turned away, ran back along the beam, and up the stairs in the steeple, stopping at each landing. As her eyes adjusted, she could see into most corners, and where she couldn't she felt around with a foot or an arm, all the time softly calling Peter's name. On the top landing she found him. Even though at any moment she had been expecting to touch his arm or bump against his leg, or hear him retort suddenly from a black corner, she shrieked when she fell over his crumpled body.

"Oh, Peter," she wailed, setting down the silver and leaning over him. His breathing was shallow and uneven and his forehead cold and damp. Gingerly, she touched the side of his head; the old wound had opened again. Or was it a new one? The looters had done this; they had found Peter and hurt him when they took the silver. Which brought a new worry: what if the looters told their captors about the boy in the steeple and the captors came after Peter?

Hitty tugged on his arm. "We have to hide! Hurry!" But Peter only rolled his head to the side and mumbled unintelligibly. "I have the silver," she tried. "We have to hide it upstairs, Peter, or they will take it and you can't go to New Hampshire." She alternately pulled and pushed him into a sitting position. Surely the looters would be arrested and taken away. But what if they talked themselves out of trouble and returned to get the things they left behind the organ? Finding the silver missing, they would know to look in the steeple. "Stand up!" Hitty shoved on his back. "Hurry, Peter! Or they will take the silver!"

Peter grunted and lurched forward. Hitty took hold of his hands and with great effort pulled him to a tottery standing position. He draped his arm over her shoulders and, leaning heavily on her, shuffled the few feet to the staircase. She put one of his hands on the side rail, and tugged on the other one.

Peter stumbled on the step and fell on his knees. Hitty reached down but he swiped her hand away. On all fours, he crawled upwards.

"Good, Peter. You do it that way." Hitty scuttled around behind him and followed closely, worrying all the while that somebody might bound upstairs and find them. When they came to the final ladder, Peter reached for the rail, missed, and fell into the rungs. Hitty sprang to help but he shoved her away again, and laboriously hauled himself up step by step.

At the top, when Peter paused to get his breath, Hitty scampered up alongside and pushed hard on the trapdoor. It swung lazily up into the air and fell to the side with a thunk. She crawled out onto the bell platform and then turned back to Peter. His body sagged against the rail, his face white in the smoke-hazed light of the moon. "Come on!" She took hold of his arm and this time he didn't resist. She pulled with all her strength until he got one leg over the edge and was able to drag himself onto the deck. Then, on all fours, she scurried over to the corner support and dislodged the panel, setting it on the floor.

"Get in!" she ordered. But his energy was spent and Peter lay prone, face to one side, mouth smashed into the floor. Hitty tugged on him, then leaned down to say in his ear, "I'm going to get the silver for you, Peter. But you have to go into the hidey hole. Please, Peter! They will find you!"

When there was no response, Hitty left him, and went back down into the steeple. She had just snatched up the tankards when she heard voices again, this time from inside the meeting house. She scampered back up the steps and onto the platform, letting the trapdoor down as quietly as she could. She placed the silver tankards in the hiding place, then went to Peter. Taking his arms, she dragged him to the opening, rolled him over onto his back, and shoved him to a sitting position. Then she thrust him sideways through the opening in the boards and pushed until his entire body was inside. Just as she was squeezing in beside him, she heard voices immediately below. Quickly, she reached out for the board and fit it into place.

"The s—" Peter began.

"Shhh!" Hitty covered his mouth with her hand. After some moments of quiet, she whispered, "I got the silver right here. When you're feeling better, Peter, you can take it and go." The words sounded false but wanting to comfort him, she continued, "And I won't follow you. It's all right, Peter, I won't go."

It's all right, Hitty thought with immediate acceptance, because she'd never really expected to go anyway. As a child she'd pictured beautiful things in her mind: a mother and father with whom she ate meals around a table or went on country walks. But the pictures had lessened over time until they stopped altogether, and now she no longer envisioned things that couldn't be. She guessed that imagining was like most things; when they didn't lead to anything after a while, you quit doing them. Which was probably why she didn't feel any particular disappointment over not going to New Hampshire; she couldn't imagine herself doing it.

Hitty did feel sorry about Peter, though, for she realized that even if he managed to escape a hanging, and run away to New Hampshire, he was doomed. He would never escape the demons inside that drove him to do worse and worse things. Setting the fire was not the same as staying out after curfew, or letting the oven go cold, or even stealing; it was a horrible crime. And worst of all, Hitty thought, recalling Peter's excitement when he showed her the fire, he would repeat this misdeed as he had those others. Given the opportunity, Peter would set another fire. Hitty shook her head sadly, thinking that she could no longer help him.

She put her thin arms around his shoulders and drew him

close. He made an attempt to pull away, then fell back against
her. For a long while, as Hitty listened to his soft groans and
shallow raspy breathing, her thoughts flitted around. Gradually
they came together in a single idea, but she scattered them
again. When they continued to come together in the same way,
she began to consider that maybe there was one last thing she
could do for Peter. One last thing to save him from the gallows,
and also from the demons he could not disperse on his own.

She felt under her dress for the hem of her underskirt where
it had been hoisted up into a knot. Her fingers trembled as she
untied the knot and extracted the medicine. Holding the bottle
by its neck, she swished its contents back and forth to determine the amount left while, once more, she considered her
decision.

He was sleeping and did not respond when Hitty whispered,
"I will take care of you." Propping his head into the crook of
her arm, she opened the bottle. She felt that his lips were
already parted so she tilted the bottle to let a few drops pass
over them. He shuddered and shook his head against the
cloying saccharine taste, but it was a weak effort. Hitty bent
her elbow more acutely, creating a firmer grip on his head, and
poured in more drops.

She could not see in the dark, but when she heard the liquid
bubble up in his mouth, she waited a few moments before continuing. It became a pattern: pour in a few drops, listen, feel
for his lips, tip the bottle again. With only a mumble now and
then, Peter accepted the drug without further resistance, and it
was easy for Hitty to think she was just giving him medicine
to stop his pain.

After what seemed a long time, Hitty set down the empty
bottle, and began to rock him back and forth. Suddenly, a
violent eruption of vomit—like a purging of those interior
demons—spewed from Peter, and he doubled over, emitting a

strangled sound, "Aaaa, aaa." Hitty locked her arms around him and rocked harder.

"It's all right, Peter," she cooed as tears streamed down her face. "I will take care of you." She repeated it over and over until he relaxed, eventually falling limp against her. She continued to rock him until her own sleep shut out the heat, the uncomfortable position, the sticky syrup on her hands, the reek of vomit.

Sometime later, Hitty opened her eyes. She felt for Peter's heartbeat, knowing as she did so, that he was gone. With a sob, she gently propped him against the wall in a sitting position. Then she opened the panel and crawled out. The early morning sun was hazy on a ragged and charred horizon void of life. Whatever hadn't been destroyed in the fire was stilled. Whoever survived now slept.

The pile that had been on the steps behind the organ was gone. Hitty paused for a moment, letting the silence reassure her that nobody was present, then tip-toed to where she'd left the bucket of water. She rinsed her hands, then splashed water onto her face and dress, brushing off dried flecks of vomit. She searched the pews until she found a lap blanket, then carried it and the bucket up to Peter.

With the last scrap she could rip from her underskirt, she washed him, carefully removing the blackened blood from the side of his head and the dirt from his hands. With the remainder of the water she wiped off his shirt. When he was as clean as she could make him, Hitty positioned Peter again, wrapped the blanket around him, and placed in his lap the two silver cups she had promised him. She would make this steeple his tomb: she could think of no better one, anyway.

As she sat back to regard him one last time, she noticed a small piece of paper on the floor next to his foot. She picked it up and saw it had only a number on it. Thinking that it must have belonged to Peter, she opened the lid to one of the silver cups and placed it inside.

"Goodbye, Peter," she whispered, her eyes filling with tears. She reached up to touch an unruly thatch of hair that stuck out from his head. With reluctance, she drew away then, backed out of the space, and fit the board back into its grooves.